W9-BNT-247

far from
burden dell

CHRIS COPPEL

Brown Barn Books
Weston, Connecticut

Brown Barn Books
A division of Pictures of Record, Inc.
119 Kettle Creek Road, Weston, CT 06883, U.S.A.
www.brownbarnbooks.com

Far From Burden Dell
Copyright © 2005, by Chris Coppel

Original paperback edition

The characters and events, other than historical ones, to be found in these pages are fictitious. Any resemblance to actual persons, living or dead, is purely coincidental. Many, although not all, of the places mentioned may be found in London.

Library of Congress Control Number 2004111712

ISBN: 0-974648167

Coppel, Chris
FAR FROM BURDEN DELL

All rights reserved. No part of this book may be reproduced in any form without permission from the Publisher, except by a reviewer, who may quote brief passages in a review. For permissions, please call Brown Barn Books, 203-227-3387.

Printed in the United States of America

I've seen a look in dogs' eyes, a quickly vanishing look of amazed contempt, and I am convinced that basically dogs think humans are nuts.

— *John Steinbeck*

Dogs have given us their absolute all. We are the center of their universe, we are the focus of their love and faith and trust. They serve us in return for scraps. It is without a doubt the best deal man has ever made.

—*Roger Caras*

LONDON

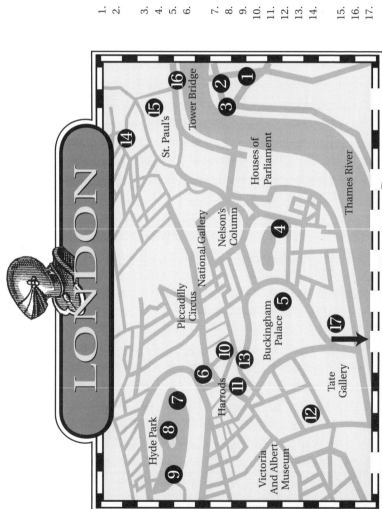

1. Bad Kennel
2. Anchor and First View of the Thames River
3. Westminster Bridge
4. St. James Park
5. Buckingham Palace
6. Rear Exit of Palace Grounds, Hyde Park Corner and Underpass
7. Hidden Cave and Restaurant
8. Shelter Island
9. Bridge Across Serpentine (Lake)
10. Harrods
11. Fast Food Restaurant
12. Police Station Behind Walton Street
13. Kinghtsbridge Tube Station
14. St. Paul's Station and Underground Parking Structure
15. Sewer Tunnel
16. Tower Bridge
17. Battersea Dog Home (Good Kennel)

dedication

To the animals that have been part of my life.

I would not be who I am today had it not been for
their companionship, forgiveness and unquestioning love.

one
· · · · · · · · · · ·

Amy couldn't have been happier.

She awoke from her early afternoon nap and blinked in the brightness of the spring sun. As she looked down at her shiny golden coat, she felt her chest swell with sheer pleasure and contentment with life.

She watched a mallard leading her four ducklings to the pond at the end of the garden. Amy smiled as she observed the mother duck watch as each child garnered sufficient courage to jump into the water to join her. Once in, they immediately regrouped into a single line and moved off, following their mother with great purpose and direction.

Amy was reminded of her own youth and the strict disciplines her mother had imposed on such trips into the wild.

Beyond the pond Amy could see the fields of the Grangers' farm. Two large chestnut mares were peacefully strolling up a gentle slope. Their heads were close together as they walked, probably discussing their strategies for the upcoming horse trials at Wembley Stadium. Their strides were fluid and supremely confident, and Amy had no doubt that one, if not both, of Granger's fine horses would return with a trophy. She could imagine the buzz as the entire village relived every second of every event from the easiest two-foot cross-pole to the fearsome heights of the wall.

Amy rolled over and stretched, sending a warm rush through her muscles and limbs. She then stood and looked down in fascination as each blade of grass on the lush lawn where she had been lying slowly straightened up.

Amy slowly wandered to the top of her hill and looked out over the sprawling vistas of the West Sussex Downs. Hill upon hill stretching out endlessly to... actually she really wasn't certain where they stretched to but that didn't matter. She wondered how some of her friends who lived in London could cope with their limited view of the world. And the smells! In the city, Amy could distinguish little over the constant reek of burning vapors coming from the thousands of manmade traveling machines. Here, however, Amy could even detect the scent of a particular thistle that she knew to grow some three fields away.

She turned and looked at her home. It was old—even Amy knew that. Someone had said it was medieval, and though not understanding what that meant, she knew it meant, well... old. The heavy white walls were dazzling, and the heavy thatch of the roofing was so perfectly set and cropped that it was hard to imagine it was mostly made up of pieces of the hay on which she'd spent many an afternoon napping contentedly.

Amy walked into the cool interior of the cottage. She loved the smell of her home—the mixture of old stone, polished wood, exquisite kitchen odors and her favorite, the tangy scent of the half burned logs in the hearth that permeated everything. She could feel the timeless cold that rose from the worn smooth stone floor.

Amy made her way into the kitchen to see what Cook was up to. It was a little soon after lunch for Cook to begin the next meal in the cottage, and Amy wasn't surprised to find the room empty.

She heard the gentle sound of Cook humming somewhere in the distance. Amy moved to the bay windows of the breakfast nook and put her front paws on the sill to look out the window.

This was not her favorite viewing window as the glass was set in tiny triangular sections with lead frames. Each piece of glass was uneven and gave the world a distorted, almost watery look. On a sunny day, each pane caught the light in a burst of multicolored specks, which would dance and dart about the kitchen walls. Amy vaguely remembered a time when she used to try to catch the luminous specks with a frustrating lack of success. Now, of course, she knew better. But after all, she was now almost three!

She squinted through the glass and could make out Cook kneeling at her small vegetable garden. Oh, the vegetable garden! Now that was a lesson well-learned! Amy could almost feel the surprising pain that had been dealt out that fateful day by Cook. Amy didn't hold a grudge; in fact Cook had quite correctly used the "bad voice" quite a few times in warning before having to resort to hurting Amy's nose. Despite Amy's short memory, she still vividly remembered that day.

Amy had been only eight months old and was in the garden enjoying her afternoon nap. During such naps, she would occasionally open one eye and watch the clouds form and reform high above her. She would imagine seeing a face that immediately would change to some other form. One second a rabbit, next a huge oak. For weeks, Amy had also watched Cook dig up some of the smooth green blanket of lawn. As if that hadn't been odd enough, Cook then proceeded to remove a large quantity of soil, only to replace it with yet more soil a few days later. The new soil had a musty, earthy scent that you could almost taste on your tongue. Amy had tried to join Cook to offer support or even help, but Cook had turned her away and pushed her off the plot each time. Amy had been surprised, having seen nothing of any great interest in Cook's project, but she had accepted her banishment with calm indifference. But the day of the hurt was quite different.

Amy was awakened from her nap by the sound of Cook tapping little lengths of wood all along the perimeter of the earthy patch she had dug up earlier, refusing Amy's help. As Amy looked on, Cook finished tapping and then proceeded to string heavy twine between the wood posts. Amy tried to step over the twine but immediately heard Cook using the unmistakable "bad voice." She stepped back and looked on as Cook began burying things in the earth. Different things. Some from thin little envelopes, others from paper bags. It was simply too unusual and tickled Amy's curiosity. She had to find out what was going on. She knew why she buried items but could not remember ever seeing a human doing the same. She tried to cross the barrier again, but once more was barraged with "bad voice" from Cook.

Amy walked away and eased herself down onto the green lawn, pretending to doze, all the while keeping her eyes on Cook and the mystery plot of land.

Cook eventually finished what she was doing and then stepped over her string perimeter and headed back to the house. She hesitated and then approached Amy. She wagged a finger at her, then pointed to the plot. Her voice did not contain the "bad" edge, but it was firm and definitely not the voice that signaled a hug or a tasty tidbit.

Amy understood the message clearly and for a few seconds decided to abide by it. But there was a far stronger force at work inside her. No sooner had she set her mind on giving Cook's land a wide berth than she found herself slowly approaching the garden. She knew she should stop but somehow just couldn't. She had to know what was buried in there. She just had to.

She tried to make her approach seem casual and only occasionally glanced fleetingly back at the cottage. Suddenly she was at the perimeter. She cautiously stepped over the barricade and felt the moist warmth of the turned soil as it spread between her toe pads. She sniffed at the earth to get a clue about the buried treasure beneath but picked up nothing except the twang of the rich earth itself. There was nothing else for it. She began to dig. The soil piled up rapidly behind her as she used all her strength in the effort. Suddenly, her nose picked up a new scent. She was close. She was going to solve the mystery. Her entire body was electric with excitement.

That's when she heard Cook.

She'd never imagined that Cook could sound like that. Her voice was so loud and so shrill it almost hurt her ears.

Amy turned and spotted the waddling form as Cook stormed toward her. She had one of the funny bundles of paper that her Man liked to sit and stare at every morning. Her Man would grab the bundle the moment it arrived and then sit staring at different parts of it for ages. What was odd was that, no matter how much attention he paid these bundles each day, her Man usually ended up setting fire to them inside the place where the logs were burned.

Humans can be strange.

Amy couldn't imagine what Cook was planning to use today's paper bundle for. As Amy watched, Cook rolled the bundle into a tight tube as she neared the plot of land. Amy cocked her head to make sure Cook understood her curiosity. Amy offered Cook a smile, but to her amazement and then horror, saw Cook bring the paper tube hard down onto her nose.

Oh, the pain!

It was as if for a brief moment her body became pain itself. And for a fraction of a second, Amy's world exploded in bright light. She shook her head to clear her vision and immediately saw that Cook was about to do it again. Amy responded by pure instinct and ran. She didn't even know she was running until she hit the twine fence. She didn't have time to think about jumping; she just went right through it… well almost through it. Somehow the string got tangled up in her legs and before she knew it, she was halfway across the garden towing the entire length of Cook's perimeter fence, posts and all. She could clearly hear Cook calling after her in a tone she had never heard from a human before. She remembered hiding under the stairs for what seemed like forever until her Man coaxed her out of her hiding place and back into the kitchen. He had tried to reconcile Amy and Cook, but Amy could sense Cook's hostility, not only for that night but for weeks after that. There were no pats, no tidbits, no sweet talk, nothing. The little plot of land was re-barricaded, strenuously guarded, and before long, produced an array of vegetables. Eventually Cook had forgiven her and things had returned to normal but the memory of the pain.........

Amy stretched to her full length and then sauntered out of the kitchen. She moved down the narrow hall to her Man's day room. As usual, the heavy door was shut as he worked inside. She tried pushing the door open with her nose, but it was securely shut. She considered a good bark to let him know that she was ready for a walk, should he be interested, but decided instead to wait him out. The rug in front of his door was one of Amy's favorites, so she settled herself down for a brief nap. She began trying to remember a thought she'd had only moments earlier then fell asleep. Almost immediately she started to dream.

Amy was chasing a rabbit through impossibly high grass when suddenly she found herself at the edge of an abyss. The surroundings were dark and menacing. With a sense of foreboding, Amy knew that something unspeakable was hunting her. Her only escape was to jump into the void. She began to tremble in fear.

She was awakened by her Man kneeling next to her, stroking her head and speaking gently to her. She could hear her Man's words clearly; she just couldn't fully understand them.

"Come on, Girl, it's all right," her Man gently said. "What a dream you were having!"

He patted her golden coat affectionately and eased himself to his feet.

"How about a walk?"

If there was one word that Amy always recognized, it was that one. Walk! She untangled her legs and jumped to her feet giving him two eager barks. Two barks were the exact and appropriate response needed to convey total interest without any appearance of desperation. Amy's mother had been very strict and specific when teaching the subtleties of barking to bipeds.

One bark was really just to let people know that you were around. Two was... well we covered two. Three was the first stage of more serious need or concern. The number of barks was then to progress in direct proportion to the given urgency of the situation. Her mother had been specific that the bark was never to be abused, as often happened with some of the smaller breeds.

Her Man opened the front door for her and waited as she scrambled out into the late afternoon sun. Knowing the routine well, Amy then stopped and sat as her Man slipped a leather ring over her head and then turned it so that the shiny metal disk was under her chin. Amy had no idea what this ritual achieved, but it was religiously carried out before each walk. When her Man had first started making her wear the... what was their word... ah yes, collar... she tried everything to get it off. She'd rolled on it. She got her paw under it. Once she even managed to get it stuck in her mouth and couldn't free it. Eventually, however, she realized that it didn't bother her all that much and since it seemed important to her Man, she decided to allow it to stay in place.

They walked out the front gate, and Amy held her breath in anticipation, hoping that her Man would choose the Taddlesham path. This was by far her favorite walk. Her Man hesitated. Amy thought it was a glorious day for a good walk toward Taddlesham, and she let out the briefest of whines and took a single step to the right, hoping that he would pick up the extreme subtlety of her move. His face brightened into a warm smile as he looked down at her.

"I suppose you'd like the Taddlesham walk, wouldn't you?"

Amy pretended to not understand him and cocked her head to one side.

"You can't fool me with that look," he said in mock serious-ness. "Come on, then."

Yes! He turned to the right, and they walked alongside the ancient Roman wall until they reached the tiny white sign at the beginning of the West Taddlesham path.

As always, she remained at her Man's side until they were off the road and on one of the many trails and paths that webbed out from their cottage. They had taken no more than a few steps when he gave the command.

"Go on then," he said.

That was all Amy needed to hear. With her ears pinned back and her golden tail outstretched, she charged full speed down the narrow path.

On either side of her, the farm animals turned and watched her tear by with mild interest. The herd of Jerseys moved to the fence to get a better look, but then, the mere fact that sun rose every day astonished them. They were kind and sweet but not very bright. Amy always gave them the single bark as she passed, just to make sure they didn't miss the moment.

As she rounded the corner down by Blakely's farm, she slowed down. This was her favorite part. She stopped and waited for her Man to reach her side; then together they contin-ued on. They came to another narrow path that led into a dense but startlingly beautiful patch of greenery. Within moments, they came to her favorite place in the whole world.

Burden Dell.

It was little more than a small grassy clearing within the trees and bramble. The grass was almost ten paws high, densely packed and emerald green with highlights of pure gold.

Amy was about to move into the Dell when she saw to her astonishment that it was already occupied. A fawn stood only a few feet away, calmly chewing a mouthful of the succulent grass as she looked back at her.

Her Man came up alongside Amy and whispered "Easy, Girl" which was unnecessary.

She carefully and calmly walked over to the fawn, and with slow and cautious moves stepped to within inches of her. The fawn was a beautiful animal. Her moist brown eyes were huge and fringed with the longest lashes Amy remembered ever having seen. Her tan coat was smooth and soft, touched in a few places by almost perfect white circular spots. She stopped her chewing and looked at Amy without any fear. Amy took a step closer and touched her nose to the fawn for just the briefest of moments. The fawn then playfully stepped back and teased Amy into a game of tag. Amy looked over at her Man to make sure this was acceptable and saw that he was smiling. Amy took this for approval and then proceeded to play a fabulous game of tag with her new friend.

Amy hadn't had much experience with the deer family and was pleasantly surprised at this one's skill and agility at the game. The fawn seemed able to balance perfectly both the subtlety of the stalk with the tenacity of the chase. Her final cornering leaps were spectacular. They played for some time, then without warning and with only the briefest pause, the fawn turned and ran off. Amy was surprised until she heard an incessant stream of barks. Not even the slightest attempt at proper barking courtesy was being made. Just a random flow of attention-seeking barks. There was little doubt to whom it could belong.

Jimmy, the Scottie, came charging out of the trees and into the tall grass. He leapt, he danced, he rolled, he barked. He had, it seemed, no self-control whatsoever. True he wasn't pure bred, but still, decorum! decorum!

The little dog was on form. He wouldn't stay still for a second. Amy tried to calm him down long enough to set up some ground rules for a game of tag, but he just couldn't seem to concentrate. Amy politely attempted to play with him for a while but soon tired of her small friend's frantic actions. She moved over to her Man and remained on her feet looking back toward the path. Her Man understood her, and the two left Jimmy to his antics within the sanctity of Burden Dell.

As they regained the path, they spotted Jimmy's Man trotting along looking concerned. "Have you seen…?"

Amy's Man didn't wait for him to finish. "He's in the Dell."

The other man shook his head and headed off to locate Jimmy. Amy and her Man shared a smile, then headed back to the cottage.

two

before Amy opened her eyes the next morning, she knew Cook was baking fresh bread. The smell had all but taken over the house. Freshly baked wheat loaf was one treat that Amy adored. She hurried down the hallway to the kitchen and stuck her head around the door so that Cook would know that she was awake and available should a piece of cooled wheat bread be in the offing.

"You'll be wanting a piece of new bread, I bet," Cook said. "Well, you'll have t'wait for it to cool, you know that."

Amy turned and moved through the cottage to the mudroom and out, glancing over at her bowls. She thought for a second that they were empty! A cold shiver ran the length of her spine. She dashed over to them and immediately saw she had been mistaken. Her food bowl was filled with the usual mix of both dry and moist food, a tasty combination by any account, and her water bowl had just been cleaned and refilled. As Amy looked at the clear water, a tiny moth landed right in it. Typical! It sent out a pattern of concentric waves to the edge of the bowl. Amy was fascinated by the ripples made by the wings of the struggling creature, but she realized she had to help before the poor thing wore itself out. Slowly and gently, Amy placed her nose in the bowl and brought it to within a hair's breadth of the baby moth.

It seemed to know what to do and managed to climb onto the offered muzzle. Amy carefully raised her head and with concentration, focused her eyes down her nose and saw the tiny survivor clinging on for dear life. She moved over to the nearest bush and placed her nose among its leaves. It took a while for the small aviator to dismount, as it was totally preoccupied with drying itself off. Amy was, however, in no rush and allowed her passenger the necessary time to pull itself together. Finally, satisfied that it was in one piece, the little crash survivor stepped onto a nearby leaf and opened its wings fully to assist in the drying operation. Amy backed away and thought that she must return later to check on its progress.

She went back to her bowl, feeling suddenly quite hungry and pleased with a job well done. As she reached her food and sank her muzzle into the well-deserved breakfast, something caught her eye. She turned to her water bowl and was stunned. It couldn't be! There were now four tiny moths, all desperately paddling for dear life. The water in the bowl was quite choppy as the moths struggled away. Amy realized that she was going to have a busy morning.

By midday Amy was exhausted. She had rescued the four moths, had a marvelous game of chase with a small rabbit who ran from her with such convincing enthusiasm and drama that it was almost as if he believed the pursuit had been serious. She had helped Cook pick some fresh tomatoes from the vegetable garden (Amy stayed outside the perimeter, of course) and had been rewarded with a piece of indescribably delicious wheat bread (cooled to perfection). Most recently, she had had an exceptionally good roll on the front lawn. All this and it wasn't even quite time for her Man's midday break.

Amy was in mid-ponder about what to do next when she heard Old Fergus, the mailman, pedaling up the gentle hill toward their cottage. Sometimes her Man would seem pleased at what Old Fergus left, sometimes a cloud would cross over his normally pleasant features. On one occasion he even tore up the paper that Old Fergus had left him.

Amy was awakened from a brief nap by some strange sounds coming from the cottage. She eased herself to her feet, stretching as she did so, and then made her way toward the odd noises emanating from her house.

Suddenly her Man and Cook came dancing out the front door. Dancing! They were spinning around on the front lawn while her Man laughed almost to the point of crying. Cook was trying to act as exuberant as he but was clearly focusing her full attention on staying upright as he swung her around.

Assuming it was expected of all parties, Amy stepped between the pair and began to bark joyously (this was one of the few times that random barking was permitted).

Suddenly her Man let go of Cook with near disastrous consequences and then ran into the house. Cook and Amy stopped dancing and composed themselves as they watched the front door, waiting for him to reappear.

They heard a loud pop and glanced at each other curiously until her Man came charging out of the cottage with a bottle in one hand and three glasses in the other. White foam was pouring out of the dark green bottle and leaving a trail behind him.

He messily poured a glass of the bubbling stuff for Cook, who looked aghast.

"Oh, Mr. Cotter, I don't think I should" she cried.

He held out the glass to her and grinned boyishly.

"Beth," he said, "this is probably the happiest moment of my life and if that isn't cause for celebration, I don't know what is!"

"In that case," Cook responded, "I'll try just a wee sip." She took the glass from him and downed it in one gulp.

He looked at her in amazement. "I was thinking of a toast!" he said.

"That one was for thirst," she purred. "This one'll be the one for toasting." She held her glass out to him.

He refilled her glass and then looked at Amy "This concerns you, too!"

He poured another glass and placed it on the ground in front of Amy. She approached it cautiously, circling it once to make absolutely sure it was safe.

He finally poured his own glass, then held it high in the air.

"To you, Beth Windle, and to you, Amy Cotter, I offer a toast," he announced grandly. "Without you this could never have happened. I would like to offer you both my deepest gratitude for all you've done."

As he was about to drink from his glass, Cook cleared her throat loudly.

"Yes?" he asked.

"I'm sorry to be interrupting your fine toast there, Mr. Cotter, but are you aware that we still haven't got the foggiest notion as to what you're prattling on about?"

Amy had finished inspecting her glass and finally decided to risk taking a small taste. She lowered her tongue into it and was immediately rewarded by a strange prickling sensation climbing her tongue and assaulting her nose. Before she could stop herself, she backed up a step and let out a volley of surprised barks. Oh, the embarrassment! She realized what she was doing almost as soon as she started and immediately ceased, but it was too late. What a faux pas! And in front of her Man and Cook! She looked up at them with guilty eyes, and to her surprise saw that they were not at all shocked by her disgraceful display, indeed they both began laughing joyously at her outbreak. Humans! Who could ever tell what they were thinking?

Amy decided that the least she could do was give the liquid another go. She again approached the glass, this time prepared for the gaseous assault. She closed her eyes and downed the entire contents in a matter of seconds. This seemed to please her Man and Cook, who laughed even harder.

Her Man tried to bring himself under control and looked at both of them. "I'm so sorry!" he said between laughs. "Of course you don't know! Today in the mail I received a letter from Hollywood…"

"Hollywood in America?" Cook asked in disbelief.

"None other," he responded, "and they tell me they intend to make a film from one of my books!"

Cook's jaw dropped open. "A film for the cinema," she stammered, "of your book?"

"Does that surprise you?" he said, feigning hurt.

"No," she replied as tears began to roll down her cheeks. "Not at all. It's just the best news I've ever heard in my life."

"There's more. I am being paid to go to Hollywood to write the movie myself." He also had a happy tear in his eye.

"No!" she screamed with delight. "Hollywood!"

Amy looked on with fascination. Not at their antics, but at the fact there were now four of them on the front lawn. Clearly anything that made them this happy had to be a good thing for her as well.

She hiccuped gently, then felt her eyelids closing. Oh, well. A nap might not be so bad. Amy lowered her head to her front paws and was asleep within seconds.

three
. . . .

"**S**ix months!" Cook exclaimed, "That's a fair bit of time to be away!"

"It is, isn't it," Amy's Man replied while pensively looking out the sitting room window. "I had no idea they'd need me for that long. I thought two to three weeks, maybe a month, but no. 'We'll need you here spittin' out pages right up to and through-out production,'" he said, mimicking an American accent. "You'll simply manage the cottage as you do now," he contin-ued. "Just cook less food!"

Cook tried to smile but found it difficult. "I'm not going to pretend that I like the thought of you being out there among those savages for that length of time," Cook said.

"If you're referring to all those gangs and hoodlums we hear about," he said, smiling, "I wouldn't worry. I'm sure they're kept a suitable distance from the film studios."

"Gangs and hoodlums indeed! I'm talking about the savages in the studios!" she said with conviction. "I read the magazines. I know what goes on out there!"

He couldn't help smiling at Cook's concern. "I'll try and keep to myself when I'm there."

Cook nodded just as Amy entered the room. She was still a little dizzy after the earlier goings-on outside but at least her vision had cleared. She felt the tension at once. Cook and her Man were sitting facing each other in the two huge chairs by the bay window. Amy didn't think she'd ever seen Cook sitting anywhere but in the kitchen before. They both watched Amy as she approached.

"What about Amy? She'll pine something terrible for you while you're gone," Cook said with a slight quaver to her voice. "Could you not take her with you?"

He looked over at Amy with affection, then turned back to Cook. "I can't. I mean I could, but what with the flights back and forth, my having to spend half my time on the set and then let's not forget quarantine when we come back... I just don't think it would be fair to her. She'd spend her time in a cage, a hotel room or a kennel."

"Oh my!" Cook exclaimed, wringing her hands. "Well, we can't have that. She'll simply stay here and have to put up with me for a while."

Amy stood between the two and allowed them both to stroke her.

Her Man smiled at Cook. "I somehow don't think that would be such a hardship for her. You'll probably end up spoiling her rotten and I'll come home to the only Golden Retriever in England too fat to even stand."

"You might at that," she chuckled. "Aye, you might at that."

Amy wandered into the kitchen and checked for tidbits. There were none, so she made her way down to the pond. A cloud passed in front of the sun, momentarily turning the vivid colors of the landscape into muted pastel shades. At the pond, Amy lowered herself to the ground and dipped her tongue into the still waters. The water had an earthy taste that quenched Amy's thirst. As she drank, she watched the ripples spread out from her tongue and traverse the entire length of the pond, rocking the small fleet of lily pads. She stopped drinking, and as the water stilled, Amy spent a moment looking down at her own image.

It didn't seem long ago when her Man had had to fish her out of the water more than once when she'd tried to chase what turned out to be her own reflection. It wasn't that she had been stupid, just that she didn't understand reflections. Her Man had finally, with a wonderful display of patience and caring, lifted her and carried her into the cottage and up to his room. He had opened his closet door and shown Amy the mirror. After her exhaustive examination of the mirror, her Man again picked her up and carried her back to the water's edge and her mirror image there. He repeated this three more times. Amy had understood after the second trip, but was so enjoying being carried in and out of the house that she didn't let on until she saw her Man tiring.

Amy adored her Man. She couldn't have picked a better one had she tried. He was still a man and therefore a human, but aside from his breed's usual shortcomings, he seemed to have a far greater insight into the thinking of most other creatures. He had never hit Amy even when she was young and seemingly bent on single-handedly laying waste to the entire cottage and surrounding property. When she had misguidedly chewed through his favorite footwear or shredded sheet after sheet of scribbled-on pieces of paper in his private room, he hadn't hit her. In fact, he had hardly even raised his voice. Instead he had sat her down and held in front of her the remains of her bad deeds and slowly explained why what she'd done was wrong. Even without being able to understand her Man's words, she had clearly understood the meaning. When he wasn't buried in his work, he would take her for long, sometimes magical walks into the small village, and would never forget to introduce Amy to acquaintances. He was indeed a good man to be paired with.

Even as she thought of her Man, his image suddenly appeared over hers in the pond's reflection. He was smiling down at her. "Where's Shoe?" he asked. "Come on, find Shoe!"

Amy scrambled to her feet. It was time for an unscheduled game of Shoe! Shoe was what remained of one chewing indiscretion that transpired long ago. Her Man had given her a talking-to while holding out the gnawed remains of one half a pair of penny loafers. The barely recognizable shoe had then become one of Amy's still-favorite playthings.

Amy charged across the lawn to the back of the cottage where in a small recess in one wall she stored her favorite possessions. A deflated soccer ball, a fuzzless and permanently damp tennis ball, the wooden handle to some gardening implement now long vanished, and of course... Shoe!

She grabbed the damp, almost unrecognizable piece of leather and dashed back to her Man who dropped to his knees, patted her affectionately and reached for Shoe. This was when the fun really began. She couldn't simply let him have it. No, part of the fun was to make him work for it. Amy took a good strong hold of Shoe, and even as her Man rose to his feet and pulled with all his weight, she held on tightly. He tried to turn it from her mouth but she clenched her teeth even harder. He tried to lift it but Amy simply rose with it. He stepped back, dragging Amy along the lawn.

There was no question that he had some good moves when it came to Shoe, but then again, so did she, and at just the right moment, she let go suddenly, causing her Man to topple over backward. Once on the ground, he made his biggest blunder and loosened his grip on the now moist strip of leather. Amy lunged and grabbed Shoe in her mouth before her Man knew what was happening. She kept running as he laughed after her. Completing her customary victory lap around the pond, she eased her pace to a gentle trot and approached her Man. She gently deposited Shoe next to him and waited for his next move. She made sure that she kept her gaze firmly on Shoe with only the briefest glances at her adversary. Expecting him to make a sudden move on Shoe, she was caught entirely off guard when he instead lunged at her! Before she knew it, he had her flipped over on her back and was tickling her stomach with abandon. Then as if that wasn't enough, just when she was almost delirious with love and adoration for him, her Man grabbed Shoe and was instantly on his feet. Brilliant maneuver! Amy got up and charged after him as the game continued.

Amy had no idea that this would be the last game of Shoe, or indeed of any sort, that she would have with her Man for a long time.

Later, after dinner, Amy settled herself by the unlit fireplace and gazed up at her Man as he worked on a pile of papers. She dozed and dreamt of Shoe and reflections in the pond. At one point Amy opened her eyes and saw that her Man was looking down at her with an expression of love and concern. Amy moved over to him and placed her head on his lap, looking into his eyes.

"What's up, girl?" he whispered. "Can't you sleep?"

She gave him the double tail floor tap so he'd know that she was fully receptive to whatever he wished to say or do.

"I'm going away for a while," he began explaining. "I'm going to a place called America. Ever heard of it?"

Amy provided another pair of tail taps.

"It's a huge place," he continued, "larger than anything you could imagine. I'm going to be gone quite a long time, do you understand?"

Again, double tail tap.

"I'll be leaving you in charge here, so you will have to promise me that you'll take care of everything, and especially Cook. She won't be able to walk as far with you as I can, so have patience with her." He held her head in his large hands, and in a voice filled with emotion said, "I've never been away from you for more than a few days. I'll miss you, Amy, more than you will ever know. Please try and realize when I'm gone that it's not forever though to you it may seem like it. I can't make you understand, I know, but please don't hurt too badly for me. I will be back."

That was all he said. They slowly readjusted their positions so that he could resume his work on the paper. Amy fell into a deep and contented sleep at his feet as he continued to work long into the night.

When she woke the next morning, her Man was gone.

four
. . . .

Amy was surprised to find her Man out of the house. It had happened before on a couple of occasions, and both times his absence had proved highly traumatic to her. She hoped this was not the case this time. She nosed her way to the dark little storage area under the stairs and found that the square thing he carried his clothes around in when he went away was indeed gone.

Even when he was totally preoccupied with his papers and didn't play Shoe or even take Amy for a walk, life was more complete just knowing he was huddled over his desk up in his private room.

Of course, as with most bad situations, there is always some good to be found, and in the case of her Man going away, Cook seemed to feel this warranted over-indulging Amy at every turn. Amy considered pointing out that this really wasn't necessary, but finally decided not to spoil Cook's fun. So with a brave face and rapidly enlarging belly, Amy would somberly accept tidbit after tidbit from her. All right, it didn't replace her Man but it helped... slightly.

The first day passed in relative ease. Amy spent the time catching up on naps and lower garden exploration. On the second day she even found time to mark out some unclaimed areas at the farthest reaches of the property. When she woke on the third day, she didn't feel quite right. She couldn't put her paw on it, but she definitely felt an unease somewhere deep within her. By the afternoon of that day, the feeling had grown to one of deep concern. Her Man had never been gone this long. Something had obviously happened. Amy began pacing the cottage, checking her Man's usual spots repeatedly and with growing frequency.

By early evening Amy was a wreck. She didn't know what to do. She kept rushing between the front door and the kitchen, where Cook would offer her something to eat, but Amy was beyond tidbits by this point. Finally in despair, she climbed into her Man's chair, and though this was normally frowned upon, she was left unhindered as she fitfully dozed without leaving that spot for the next three days.

Cook was at a loss. Amy wouldn't eat, she wouldn't go outside, she wouldn't even leave the chair. Cook's prayers were answered on the seventh day when the black thing in her Man's room began to ring. Cook placed it cautiously against her face, then suddenly bubbled over with excitement.

"Oh, Mr. Cotter you have no idea how glad I am to hear from you. Amy's pining away somethin' awful fer ya. She won't eat, she misses you so!"

Amy, hearing his voice respond on the black thing, came charging into the room. She began barking frantically at Cook and the black thing. She had heard her Man and was going to bark till she dropped.

Cook could hardly hear a word he was saying and finally turned to Amy and with a rigidly pointed finger, gestured to a spot on the floor inches from her.

"Amy!" she commanded "You come here this minute and SIT!"

Amy knew when an order needed to be obeyed and did as she was told. Then to Amy's amazement, Cook held the black thing to Amy's ear. Amy was about to protest when she heard his voice. Distant and mildly distorted, there he was, or wasn't. It was confusing. He obviously couldn't be in the black thing, but then where was he? Amy sniffed the air; he certainly wasn't near by.

"Hello, Girl!" her Man said from his mysterious location. "Sorry I'm not there to give you a big hug. Don't be sad, Amy. I'll be home before you know it." Amy's legs went weak at the sound of his voice. She wanted him so much that she let out a small whimper, but what was the point? He wasn't anywhere close. She knew that. She listened to his voice, knowing at least that he was all right and seemed in fact quite happy.

Cook finally held the black thing back to her ear and after a few brief words, put it back into its holder on the desk.

"Well, I hope you're feeling a wee bit better now that you've had a chat with him."

Amy looked up at her and sighed deeply. She felt empty and all of a sudden slightly hungry. Actually not just slightly, very hungry!

She realized to her amazement that she couldn't remember her last meal.

Cook stroked her head and asked "Would you like a wee spot of dins?"

Dins! Cook's word for food. What timing! Amy leapt to her feet, wagging her tail rapidly in agreement.

"Well, well, who's back with the living then!" Cook exclaimed.

Amy took the stairs two at a time to reach the kitchen and some dins.

The days passed slowly as Amy watched summer slip quietly away. She thought of her Man every day but began to realize that though she was able to frequently hear his voice on the black thing, he was obviously never coming back.

After a light lunch, Amy moved out to the garden to have a nap. She was dreaming of Burden Dell when a smell twitched her awake. She could smell meat. Fresh, raw meat! She opened her eyes and excitedly looked around.

To her amazement, she saw two men leaning over the front garden wall, one, holding a large, tempting steak in his hand waving it gently from side to side. Behind the men was a gray vehicle similar to her Man's but longer and windowless. She'd noticed it on their street for the past few days but thought nothing of it. Although she could only see the top halves of the men over the wall, they seemed different from the humans she was used to.

Seeing that Amy was now awake, the men began to coax her over to their meaty offering. She couldn't imagine what they could possibly want, but that meat did look good. Oh, why not, she decided and trotted toward the men. When she was within a few feet of the wall, the man tossed the steak onto the lawn next to her. She looked over at them to be sure there was no misunderstanding, and then seeing their eager gesturing, began chewing with delight for it was, as she suspected, delicious. As she ate, the two men watched her intently. Amy found this slightly odd, but if that was their only condition for sharing this... Amy suddenly felt dizzy. Just for a second then, it cleared. Strange! She lowered her head for another bite, then felt it again. She also felt sleepy. She decided that maybe a sip of water would help. She tried to get to her feet but couldn't. It was as if her legs were made of rubber and simply wouldn't support her. She now felt most peculiar. Her vision was blurred and distorted. She also felt a little queasy.

"Oh my," she thought. She felt herself spinning. She tried closing her eyes but that only made things worse. She looked over at the two men hoping that they could help and saw that they were climbing over the fence. She couldn't keep her eyes open any longer and was now feeling very warm. She felt hands on her and realized the men were lifting her. Thank goodness. They would take these nasty feelings away. She was being raised. She managed to open one eye and saw the cottage swimming in a gray haze. Cook was running out the front door screaming. Why was she screaming? Amy hadn't done anything wrong.

Her eyes closed, and as she felt herself being carried over the wall, she heard Cook's voice reach a higher and higher pitch. Amy sensed all light suddenly vanishing and then heard the sound like her Man's vehicle made before it moved. She could still hear Cook's voice, only now it was far away. Amy slipped into a dream of Burden Dell again, only now instead of being surrounded by fawns and other animal friends, there was no one there but herself; she began to feel afraid and alone. She wanted badly to wake from this dream but she couldn't. It went on and on. Amy began to cry in her dream and though unaware of it, in reality as well, as she lay in the back of the gray van as it sped out of West Sussex on its way to London.

five

· · · · · · · · · · ·

Amy didn't want to open her eyes. She was painfully tired and still frightened by the terrible dream she'd had. No, she'd just keep her eyes closed a while longer. She adjusted her position and realized how hard and cold the floor felt. She must have rolled off her rug during the night. Her other senses began relaying discomforting signals to her foggy and slightly achy head. The smells weren't right. There was no scent of fresh food being prepared or of polished woods or... there were no smells of home at all, only smells of dirt and stone and other odors that Amy simply refused to acknowledge.

The sounds weren't right either. She could feel a steady rumbling all about her almost like the noise vehicles made on the High Street, only a hundred times stronger. She could also hear other dogs, only they didn't sound like any she'd ever heard before. These voices all sounded pained and forlorn. Some were singing songs of misery, others of imprisonment and ill treatment. Then there were those who were simply crying. Not about anything in particular, just crying openly and with total abandon. Could she still be dreaming? Amy slowly opened her eyes.

She definitely was not at home. She was in an old worn brick enclosure not much wider than herself and only maybe twice as long. The floor was not stone as she had earlier thought but a smooth hard stone-like substance, which sloped gently to one corner where a small hole was located. Amy had no idea what the hole was for, but even from where she lay she could smell vile odors coming from it. The fourth side of the enclosure was heavy, rusted wire mesh. A reinforced gate was securely latched shut on one side of the mesh barrier. Amy could see an identical enclosure to her own across a narrow and dark passageway. It was empty.

She got to her feet with difficulty. Her legs felt like rubber. She shook her head, trying to clear the cobwebs that still lingered, and stiffly moved to the front of the enclosure. By resting her head on the rusty fencing, she was able to look down the passageway. She was shocked at what she saw. It seemed to go on forever, one enclosure after another. Most of the enclosures were occupied, their canine occupants either leaning against the wire fencing or standing at it. Some were barking, others crying, while still others simply stood there with blank, helpless expressions on their faces. There must have been close to a hundred dogs in the place.

Amy backed away from the gate and used all her willpower not to dissolve into tears. She was frightened and hungry, but she knew that she mustn't cry in this place. She didn't know why, just that she had to keep her emotions in check until she found out what was going on. She was obviously not meant to be here. There had been some silly mistake which would certainly be discovered shortly and she'd be returned immediately to her cottage and Cook and breakfast.

She felt a sudden tension run the length of the passageway, then heard a door opening. The other dogs began to howl and bark; some even threw themselves at the wire mesh.

Amy didn't understand what was going on. Then she began to pick up a word here and a word there. The mix of breeds and their diverse accents made them difficult to understand, but she soon realized that this was feeding time. Thank goodness. Maybe after a nice breakfast Amy could focus better on what to do about her situation. She wondered if there would be any fresh bread, though even the wet and dry mix would go down quite well this morning.

She continued to look down the passageway and could hear a strange high pitched squeaking that hurt her ears. She continued looking and finally saw the source of the din. A fat, shabbily dressed man was pushing a cart with squeaking wheels along the passageway. As Amy watched, the man opened one cell after another and tossed a dented metal bowl into each one. She found it odd that as he reached each cell and opened the gate; the occupant stepped far inside, not even attempting to offer the most perfunctory of good mornings.

After what seemed an eternity, the man reached Amy's cell and opened the gate. Amy stepped forward to introduce herself and was about to raise a paw when the man, without any warning whatsoever, raised what looked like a long cylindrical piece of wood and brought it down with amazing speed and force on her rump. Her back legs gave out suddenly, and she collapsed to the cold floor. She looked up at the man with pain in her eyes and complete bewilderment. She'd never been hurt like that before. This was not like Cook and the rolled up paper. This was different. This man had clearly intended to cause her pain, but why? She didn't recall ever having seen him before and certainly didn't remember having done him wrong in any way. As she looked up at him, he glared down at her for a moment and raised the piece of wood again. He didn't swing it, just held it up as a warning. Amy slid her sore backside away from the gate and moved as far back into the cell as possible.

The fat man lowered the wood thing slowly and then tossed a metal bowl onto the floor. He slammed the gate shut and moved on to the next cell. Amy tried to stand but found it too painful. Her eyes were brimming with tears but she still held them back, bravely determined not to show any emotion. She moved carefully across the cell toward the bowl. She knew she'd better eat something if only to keep up her strength. She approached the food and saw immediately that this was certainly not her usual dry and wet mix; in fact it was like no food she'd ever seen. It was gray! Light gray! The only parts that weren't light gray were areas where whatever it was had started to congeal. These were dark gray. And the smell! There was nothing meaty anywhere to be found in its scent. It smelled of metal and… and yes, mould, that was it. Amy had never smelled anything quite like it, especially something she was meant to eat. She took a small bite, hoping that it would at least taste of something recognizable. It didn't. In fact, it tasted of surprisingly little, which after the smell, was a bonus.

Amy realized she wasn't hungry anymore. Her backside was throbbing and the look of breakfast had diminished what appetite remained after the unexpected beating. She was, however, very thirsty and suddenly noticed that she had no water bowl. She thought about approaching the gate and advising Fat Man about it but decided against it. He might after all still be angry with her for whatever had set him off in the first place.

Amy lowered her head to her front paws and tried to recall the events leading up to this, her unjust and totally unforeseen imprisonment.

Her thoughts were interrupted by a loud "psst!" She looked toward the gate and saw a small Yorkshire Terrier standing in the passageway, anxiously checking both directions.

"Psst!" the tiny animal repeated.

"Are you speaking to me?" Amy asked in amazement.

"Shh! Don't say a word." The dog had a strong but pleasant Yorkshire accent. "I've only got a second. I heard you get the bat earlier. Don't get near the gate when they open it. Got that?"

"Well, I…" Amy began

"Quiet. I told you not to speak! Just move to the back of the cage when they open up. I'll tell you more in the courtyard later. Oh, by the way, you'd better eat that slop. I know it's vile, but it's all you'll get all day."

The Terrier scanned the passageway nervously. "I'll fill you in later." He vanished out of sight.

"But who are you?" Amy called out.

The small dog instantly reappeared. "Rodney, and for the sake of us all... shh!" and again he was gone.

Perplexed and yet relieved to know there were some friendly breeds incarcerated with her, she lowered her head again to the ground and fell asleep.

She dreamt of Cook and of a huge loaf of fresh bread that was just out of her reach. She turned to Cook and asked in her best and most well mannered way if it had cooled enough for her to have a piece when Cook's face distorted into a vicious leer. She brought her hands from behind her back; one hand held a dented metal bowl filled with gray food and the other, a long piece of wood. Amy woke up with a start to find her gate was open. She only had the briefest instant to ponder this when Fat Man appeared and stepped right into her cell. He walked around her and to the back of the enclosure. He raised his "club" and began shouting unintelligibly at her. She had no idea what he wanted. She suddenly realized that perhaps she had offended him by not eating her food. She rose painfully to her feet and took a step toward the bowl. The man yelled even louder and raised the piece of wood still higher. "Get out!" snapped a powerful-looking Boxer dog from the passageway. Amy hesitated. "Now!" the dog barked.

Amy looked up at the man and cringed for the first time in her life as she obeyed the Boxer's orders. As she moved toward the gate, the man lowered the club. She stepped into the passageway and saw that all the cells were open and that their occupants seemed to be heading to the far end of the hall toward an open door.

Amy tried to ask a few of her fellow prisoners what was going on but was told to shut up. So she followed the group as it neared the exit. For one brief moment she thought that this was perhaps the end of the nightmare and that the door would in fact lead back to her cottage and gardens. As she neared it, however, she saw immediately that this was not to be the case. The doorway led to a dark and dreary stone courtyard. As Amy stepped into the damp and surprisingly chilly air, she saw that the square concrete yard was flanked on all four sides by high old, stained brick walls, on the top of which were strands of vicious looking barbed wire. Amy realized she truly was imprisoned.

As she stepped into the yard she saw how the dogs immediately formed into groups and began talking in whispers among themselves. There were a few newcomers like her, but the others appeared either to prefer their own solitude, or in the case of one sobbing, pathetic-looking King Charles Spaniel, to be totally despondent.

Amy approached her, hoping to console the miserable creature, but every time she tried to get a word in, it would sob even louder. Amy soon gave up and with a gentle nod, backed away from the pitiful creature.

She walked slowly around the perimeter of the yard, feeling self-conscious and out of place as she encountered the various groups and felt their eyes on her as she passed.

Suddenly she saw Rodney, the Yorkshire Terrier, holding court before a group of much larger breeds, who appeared to be hanging on his every word. Amy stepped into the group and smiled over at the small Terrier. Rodney stopped talking instantly. The others all turned and glared menacingly at her.

"Hello," Amy stammered. "Sorry to intrude, I thought I'd just introduce myself. I'm…"

The group instantly disbanded, leaving Amy with her mouth open as she looked down at Rodney.

"Lesson number two," Rodney said in a patient and calm voice, "never step into a group uninvited in this place, especially until the dogs get to know you."

"But why…" Amy began.

"Just listen for now," Rodney said, interrupting her. "We don't have long outside. You probably haven't the vaguest idea where you are, have you?" Amy shook her head.

"That's usually the case," Rodney said knowingly. "You were, to put it in simple terms, dognapped!"

"What! But that's ridicul…" Amy began to exclaim.

"Hush! Let me finish," Rodney said sternly. "I don't know where they took you from, the south, I'd wager from the color of your coat, but you're now in London. The Docklands, to be exact. And these breeds are not, I'm certain, the sort you are used to dealing with. I've only been here a few weeks, but I gather that the bipeds are part of a much larger ring involved with smuggling and possibly even worse."

"But what's a biped and what do they want us for?" Amy asked incredulously.

"Bipeds are what we call humans, and they use dogs to smuggle when the load is small enough. There's a couple that you'll see… Anyway, so I told them it's steak or nothing for me." Rodney's voice and manner completely changed as he spoke the last sentence.

Amy looked at him with confusion and was about to say something when Rodney gestured with a brief flick of his head. She couldn't at first understand what he was referring to and then realized that it had something to do with the Boxer that was just passing them. He nodded to Amy, then to Rodney and continued on his way. Once out of earshot, Rodney stepped close to Amy.

"That was Champ," he began, "and don't let his demeanor fool you for a second. He'll turn you in to the bipeds as soon as look at you. He's a bad'un, that one. He's sold a few of us out already for no more than a few scraps of beef trimmings, I'll tell ya. Anyway, so where was I… Oh yes, I remember… there's this couple you'll see occasionally. Very posh and toffee-nosed the both of them. Apparently they put on this charade of traveling to some place with their dearly loved family pet in tow. Of course, the pet is one of us and we're dearly loved because we have something valuable and illegal hidden in or on our selves."

"In?" Amy asked with a look of revulsion on her face.

"We'll cover that later," he continued. "Once the delivery is made, they have no use for us anymore, and besides, they're then out of the country and couldn't bring us back if they wanted to with the quarantine and all. That's why they pick the sort they do. Good breeding, fine health and with a gentle disposition."

"What's quarantine? What could be so valuable as to need to steal dogs and what happens to the dogs after they are used?" Amy asked in a rush of words.

"Quarantine is the law here. They say it keeps us healthy. If you leave the country for even five minutes and you don't have the right papers to come back, then you get locked up for six months. As for the valuables, who knows? I hear sometimes it's these little shiny stones and other times some kind of powder. Whatever the stuff is, it's important to the bipeds."

"And after the dogs are used?" Amy asked hesitantly.

"We don't know. We know that they never come back. I suppose the best we can hope is that they're let go free wherever the journey ends."

"And the worst?" Amy asked with wide horrified eyes.

"Let's not think about the worst; that's not going to happen to us," he said encouragingly.

"But how..." Her words were cut off by a sudden piercing whistle being blown. They both looked over at the doorway and saw Fat Man as he raised the whistle again to his mouth.

"Just don't worry, Goldie," Rodney said in a whisper, his voice urgent as they began to move toward the door. "Just take my word for it! Things will only get better."

Amy was caught in a sea of dogs as they funneled back into the building and was soon separated from Rodney. She tried to see his tiny frame among the teaming mass of fur but couldn't. She realized suddenly how much better she'd felt talking to the tiny Terrier, and now he was gone as well. Amy kept up with the flow and found herself in front of her cell. She wasn't certain how she knew it was hers, but she did. She also found out why the dogs were given the break outside. All the cells, hers included, had apparently been thoroughly hosed down. The entire enclosure was wet from the ceiling to the floor. A diminished but still sizeable stream of water ran along one wall and down the black hole in the corner. Amy suddenly felt incredibly tired and desperately wanted to sleep but couldn't even contemplate doing so until the cell had dried off at least partially.

"Psst!" Rodney signaled.

Amy turned and saw her new friend just outside her cell trying to not be swept away by the flow of dogs returning to their enclosures.

"I was trying to tell you before we were separated," he said in an excited whisper, "don't get depressed at this place. You won't be here that long."

Amy's entire frame sagged "You mean they're going to use me to smuggle?" she began tearfully, "and then leave me in some foreign country or even... even something worse. How can I..."

"Will you shut up, you silly girl!" he snapped. "There'll be no more smuggling or anything out of this place." He smiled smugly as he let his words sink in. Amy looked over at Rodney and tried to read something, anything, from his expression.

"Get in your cages, ya bloody mutts!" Fat Man yelled from the far end of the passageway, sending dogs slipping and sliding chaotically down the hallway as they tried to carry out his order. Rodney, however, remained calm as he leaned against her cell.

"Tomorrow, my golden beauty," he whispered in a serious, determined voice "We're going to stop taking this nonsense."

Amy tilted her head in curiosity.

The Yorkie gave her a huge smile "We're going to break out!"

SIX

"Oops!" Rodney exclaimed, noticing too late that the untrustworthy Boxer was behind him and within earshot.

"Do you think he heard?" Amy asked anxiously.

"Hard to say. Fact is, he was going to be taken care of prior to the big event anyway, so don't worry about it. I'm not going to." With that, Rodney briefly winked at Amy and sauntered back to his cell.

Amy spent the rest of the day, as did the other inmates, shut in her enclosure attempting to grab fitful naps. Amy had made a few attempts at conversation with an Afghan hound in the cell adjacent to hers but found the other animal to be almost staggeringly vain and not very intelligent. The Afghan was far more concerned about the condition of her coat than of her own skin. "Different needs for different breeds," as Amy's mother used to say.

The one constant during the day was the endless crying from the Spaniel she'd seen earlier in the yard. She'd heard her called Angel, which pretty much indicated her previous pampered existence. Apparently her entrapment had been totally unpremeditated. The dognappers had their eye on her housemate, a fine, even-tempered Labrador.

As in Amy's case, the piece of steak laced with a sleeping powder had been used, but as the gentle Labrador made his way with slow dignity toward the offered piece of meat, Angel had appeared, and before the men could dissuade her, she had grabbed the steak and devoured almost half of it. She keeled over right in the middle of the front lawn just as her owner was pulling into the drive. The men, not wishing to leave any trace, had waited until the owner was in the garage and then grabbed Angel, who still had the remains of the meat clenched in her jaws. Apparently the whole cellblock had heard the row when the dognappers were refused any payment for Angel's capture.

Now the poor creature simply cried constantly. Amy had at first felt sympathy for her, but by mid-afternoon, she'd had enough of Angel's bawling. Occasionally other dogs would yell threats down the passageway, but these seemed to have no effect on the distraught creature. Fat Man had even given her a dose of "the bat" but this seemed to only change the intensity of her crying, not stop it. Amy knew that if she didn't shut up, it was only a matter of time before some great harm would befall her, but she also knew that there was little she could do. Besides, she had her own future to worry about.

By late afternoon Amy was very hungry. She hadn't touched any of the gray slop they'd given her for breakfast and upon returning from the yard, she found the metal bowl gone. Earlier in the afternoon each dog had been given a small plastic bowl of water which shortly after was also taken away.

Sometime in the evening Amy heard the passageway door open and a group of human voices coming slowly toward her cell. There were three of them. A female biped that Amy felt was, even for humans, exceptionally unattractive, accompanied Fat Man. She was short and squat with a face that seemed to be permanently pinched into a sneer. She was holding a white cylindrical tube in her hand and occasionally placing it in her mouth and sucking on it. Amy could see that it appeared to be burning and that after sucking on it, the woman would breathe out a large cloud of smoke. The third human was equally frightening. It was a tall, thin male. The skin on his face was pulled far too tightly over his bones, giving his head a skull-like appearance. His black hair was long and greasy and pulled into a ponytail at the back. He was dressed in black and was also sucking on a burning tube, only his was brown and longer. The three stopped at each cell and gave the occupant a long look before Squat Lady and Skull Face gave Fat Man an instruction that he would note on a piece of paper he was carrying.

After what seemed an eternity, the group arrived at Amy's enclosure. As was her well-mannered way, she got to her feet and acknowledged their presence. This seemed for some reason to please the skull man whose lips pulled back across his long, yellow teeth in what Amy had to assume was some horrific parody of a smile.

"This is a fine bitch," the ghoul stated. "Put her down for the Geneva run."

Fat Man nodded and made some squiggles on the paper. The males moved on, but the female stayed back for a moment and squatted down close to Amy's fence. Amy decided to risk it and moved over to her. The woman stared back at Amy through the wire mesh, then suddenly expelled a plume of pungent smoke directly in her face. Amy recoiled, almost tripping over her own feet as the woman shrieked with high horse-like laughter and then rose to her full height and rejoined the others.

Amy felt something inside her, a tightness and raging heat that she'd never felt before. As she lowered herself to the cold floor she could only think of the ugly woman and her sour, smoky breath. She could not seem to take her eyes off the fencing or let her body relax in any way.

Though she didn't realize it, Amy was, for the first time in her life, feeling real anger.

When much later she finally fell asleep, she dreamt of stalking something through a dark and dismal countryside. She didn't know what she was hunting, only that she was driven body and soul to seek it out and destroy it.

seven

· · · · · · · · · · · · · · · ·

Amy woke the following morning to distinct electricity in the air. She could almost see the tension.

When Fat Man appeared with the gray slop, Amy was certain that the big moment had arrived. But as she listened to him toss each bowl into a cell, then retrace his steps along the passageway with the squeaky cart in tow, she realized that the breakout Rodney had told her about was not at hand after all.

She decided that she should try to eat something as she was bound to need her strength for whatever lay ahead. She took a mouthful of the slop and almost gagged. She finally managed to eat half the bowl, but instead of the rush of energy she'd hoped for, she simply felt heavy and a little queasy.

She tried to settle down and relax until the morning exercise in the yard but couldn't stop herself from pacing in her narrow cell. Finally, after two eternities, Fat Man reappeared and opened their enclosures. The inmates were all clearly anxious to get into the open air on this special day. Amy could feel the excitement as she stepped into the throng of other dogs who almost tripped over each other in their effort to reach the door.

Amy was one of the last into the yard and could immediately tell something was wrong. The sense of excitement that she'd felt only moments before had vanished. She looked into the crowd for Rodney to find out what was going on but couldn't see him. He was small, so this didn't particularly faze her. She began a more thorough search and soon realized that he wasn't there. Rodney wasn't in the yard at all.

Amy was shocked. She stood rooted in place as her mind swam with possibilities. He was sick. He'd left without them. He'd... He'd... She couldn't stand not knowing where her new trusted little friend had gone.

She was suddenly nudged quite roughly. Turning, she saw she was facing three large, tough-looking male dogs. Two Dobermans and a Rottweiler. One of the Dobermans stepped forward and looked her coldly in the eye.

"Rod said you was alright,." he said in a surprisingly rich tone, with an East End accent. "We noticed you was looking for something."

"Yes. Yes, I was," Amy said, trying to keep the trepidation out of her voice. "Where is Rodney... Rod? I thought today was..."

"Shh!" the Doberman whispered forcefully. "It was, but something happened. They came for him during the night. They've taken him on a bloody run, haven't they?"

Amy couldn't believe what she was hearing. "You mean he's gone? Just like that?"

The Doberman tried to look understanding. "That's how it works around here, luv."

"Oh, my." Amy tried not to let her emotions get the better of her. "Does that mean the... well you know... is off?"

"Has to be," he said in a voice heavy with disappointment. "He was the only one who could pull off the plan."

The Rottweiler suddenly cleared his throat loudly. They followed his glance and saw that the Boxer was approaching.

"Filthy snitch," the Doberman growled.

The Boxer looked their way and with a distinct lack of concern walked right up to and through their little group. The other Doberman at first blocked his path, but then with a brief growl let him go.

"I was looking forward to dealing with him," the Doberman said in a frighteningly cold voice.

"Is he really that bad?" Amy asked.

"Ha! There have been two attempts to get out since I've been here and on both occasions, guess who alerted the humans?"

"Oh," Amy said in a shocked voice.

"And what's more," the Doberman continued, "on both nights following his squealing and after the escapees were dealt with, very brutally by the way, who do you think got a nice big steak for dinner while the rest of us bloody starved?"

Amy simply shook her head as she watched the retreating form of the Boxer as he paraded around the yard. "So what happens now?" she asked. "With Rodney gone?"

"Not much! He was the key to the whole plan."

"Can't I help?" she offered. "I'm certain I could do something to…"

"You're too bloody big," the Rottweiler interrupted.

Offended, she stepped up to the dog. "That's hardly called for! I'll have you know that I take good care of myself. I eat sensibly and…"

"Not your figure." he said with exasperation. "You! You're simply too big. We all are! Look, without drawing any attention, have a gander over at the wall on your right. You'll see a small hatch. Got it?"

Amy nodded.

"Well, we've been working at that for weeks and it's now to the point where with one really good shove it'll give way but only one of us could ever fit through."

"Rodney!" Amy said finally understanding the Doberman's point.

"Right!" He continued " Rod was gonna do a bunk through the hatch and then nip round to the outer wall on the left where there's a door. A door without a latch on this side. Well, according to our little missing friend, his master had the same type of door at the bottom of their garden. Rod had, so he said, become quite the little expert at jumping up and smacking the handle down as he dropped. He guaranteed he could do the same with that one."

"Isn't there anyone else who could get through the hatch?" Amy asked hopefully.

"There's no one here close to Rod's size. The only other small-ish breed in the whole place is... well forget it."

"What do you mean forget it?" she said urgently. "Who is it? Come on, if there's any chance at all, we have to take it. Now tell me, who is it?"

All three males turned their heads and together looked over to a far corner where a lone dog sat in the shadows. Even from the distance Amy could see that the animal was in a terrible state as it whined pathetically to no one in particular.

"Angel?" she asked.

"You asked!" retorted the Doberman.

"Has anyone spoken to her?" Amy asked.

"What's the point in that?" the Rottweiler said, stepping closer to the group. "Look at her, she's a mess. You can't even get a word in between her sniffling and whining. Typical female!"

The Doberman cleared his throat loudly.

"Present company excepted, of course, miss," the Rottweiler hastened to add, nodding at Amy.

"Do you mind if I give it a try?" Amy asked hesitantly "After all, maybe female to female...?"

The three males looked at each other and shrugged.

"Why not?" the Doberman said.

Amy gave them an encouraging smile and then moved casually across the yard to the shadowed corner and the pathetic Angel.

"Hello," Amy began. "I couldn't help but notice how upset you seem to be. I thought that perhaps a nice chat would help."

Amy was stunned when the Spaniel, instead of calming under her gentle words, broke into an even louder and more intense outbreak of tears.

"Now, there's no need for that," Amy chided gently. "I only want to help."

Angel was clearly nearing a state of hysteria. Her sobbing and wailing was beginning to attract the attention of others in the yard, including, to Amy's horror, that of the Boxer who was now facing them.

"Please lower your voice. We don't want to attract any attention," Amy whispered urgently, with no effect on the other animal whatever. Amy turned to the yard and gave the onlookers a calm and unconcerned smile, and then while pretending to sniff at the base of the wall, gave Angel a brief but sharp nip at her backside. The Spaniel leapt to her feet with a yelp of surprise and looked into Amy's face for the first time.

"What was that for?" Angel said tearfully. "Why'd you bite me?"

"I'll bite you again harder if you don't stop carrying on," Amy retorted.

"Leave me alone, I don't want to talk to anyone."

"That's just too bad," Amy responded with a sharp edge to her voice. "I happen to wish to speak with you, which I most certainly cannot do with you making noise enough for six dogs."

"Well, I'm miserable," Angel whined pathetically.

"We all are, you silly girl. Look around you. Do you think any of us wants to be here? Do you think we wouldn't all prefer to be home with our masters right this minute?"

"I guess," Angel pouted.

"Then stop behaving like a spoiled puppy," Amy continued. "And maybe, just maybe, we can all work together and find a way out of here."

"How?" Angel asked.

"That's better" Amy whispered reassuringly. "You see the little latch over on your right? Well…"

"You mean the one Rodney and his cronies have been working on for the past two weeks?"

"Keep your voice down!" Amy hissed. "What do you know about that?"

"I know they've been wasting their time," Angel said with certainty. "This yard is below street level and that hatch is the bottom of an old coal drop."

"A what?" Amy asked as she felt a knot in her stomach.

"A coal drop. This yard was the storage area for some sort of factory, and that hatch is the lower end of a chute that leads to the street."

"That sounds promising," Amy tried hopefully.

"No, it doesn't," Angel corrected. "It's probably a four-foot drop to the hatch, and at street level there will be a set of double doors which will almost certainly be locked even if we could climb up the chute which, by the way, we most certainly could not. Oh, another thing, the door that Rod thought he could simply open with a quick leap and a tap..."

"Yes?" Amy asked suspiciously.

"Check out the hinges," Angel gestured with her head. "They are rusted solid. That door hasn't been opened in years and certainly couldn't be opened by anyone from this group."

"What makes you so knowledgeable?" Amy asked in a troubled voice, dreading having to pass on Angel's information to the others.

"Just am, that's all," she said confidently.

"But this escape is important to them. Were you just going to stand back and watch them fail?" Amy asked as she stared into the Spaniel's face.

Angel didn't speak for a long moment, then calmly said, "No, I was in fact going to take full advantage of the situation."

"How's that?" Amy queried.

"Look," she said, scanning the yard for anyone listening in. "You've heard my crying and carrying on, haven't you?"

"Who hasn't?"

"Exactly," Angel said proudly. "But that's all you've heard, isn't it? You haven't heard the work I've been doing in my cell, for instance, have you?"

Puzzled, Amy shook her head.

"Because I'm the pathetic, harmless little one, they thought nothing of leaving me in a cell with a window."

"What!" Amy exclaimed.

"Shhh" Angel snapped. "Have I got to tell *you* to keep quiet?"

"Sorry," Amy whispered.

"It's high up, and at first I didn't know how to reach it, but after a while I found that with a good run up, I can push off the side wall and get up on the ledge."

"But surely it must be closed."

"Of course it is," she said smiling, "which is why I've been chewing off the window putty for the past two weeks. That's why I've been making such a din with the crying and such. To cover my work."

"Haven't they noticed the bits of putty in your cell when they hose it out?" Amy asked incredulously.

"Why do you think I'm over here every day?" Angel asked as she gestured toward a well concealed small drain tucked in the corner at the base of the wall.

Amy glanced down at the drain without moving her head and saw to her astonishment a sizeable wad of putty jammed down into it. Amy tried to stay expressionless.

"How much longer do you need?" she asked as her mind swam with this new possibility for freedom.

"I could probably force that glass out in a couple of days, but I was hoping for a good diversion to cover the noise."

A thought suddenly hit Amy. "You were going to break out alone, weren't you?"

"Absolutely! It's safer that way," Angel replied calmly.

Amy studied the other animal. "You realize I'll now have to tell the others."

"I guessed as much. Only do me one favor," Angel asked.

"Let me finish up first. I don't want someone to tip the humans off before I'm ready."

"But you were going to give it a go today if Rodney had been here and tried his plan," Amy reminded her.

"Yes, but I really need two more days. Please give me that," she pleaded.

"You won't go off without us?" Amy asked suspiciously.

"Not likely now that you know, is it?" Angel replied.

Amy shrugged.

"Just two days, then you can tell the others," Angel assured her.

"All right, you've got your two days."

"Thanks," the Spaniel said with conviction. "Now if you don't mind, I feel a cry coming on."

Amy nodded as the other dog began instantly to wail miserably. Amy grinned as she walked back to the others.

She certainly would not have felt so pleased had she the slightest inkling of what the next day would bring.

eight

Amy slept surprisingly well and woke feeling that things would somehow turn out all right. She even ate a good quantity of her gray slop, hardly gagging at all.

Her sense of well-being continued right up until midmorning, when an elegantly dressed man and woman appeared at her cell with Skull Face and Squat Lady. The four stood chattering for a moment, then Squat Lady opened the gate and stepped into the enclosure. She spoke in friendly tones, but after the smoke incident, Amy didn't trust her at all.

The woman placed a heavy collar over Amy's head. For the first time, Amy thought of her Man and of their wonderful walks. She could almost smell the deep grass that grew alongside…

She shook off the memory as Squat Lady attached a lead to the collar and then pulled her roughly out into the passageway. All the inmates seemed to be gathered at their fencing as she was led by. A few gave her a nod of encouragement, but most simply looked sadly back at her.

They passed by Angel's cell and Amy saw that she too was at her gate trying to force a smile for Amy's sake. They arrived at the door at the far end of the passageway, and as Skull Face reached for the handle, the door flew open and Fat Man almost ran into him.

"Oh, there you are," he said breathlessly. "I thought you might have left."

"Well, clearly we didn't, did we," said Skull Face nastily.

"Yes… I see that," Fat Man stammered on. "I just checked with the coast, and apparently there's a gale blowing in the channel. All ferry crossings have been cancelled."

The other bipeds looked upset at his words, though Amy hadn't a clue why.

"How long do they think it'll go on for?" Squat Lady asked while setting fire to a white tube in her mouth.

"Couple of days, apparently," he replied.

"Blast it," said the elegant man. "Well, let's put the dog back."

Fat Man reached down and roughly removed Amy's collar. "I'll put this back in the safe." He turned and opened the door.

Amy, misunderstanding what was expected of her, started to follow when suddenly Squat Lady grabbed her by the neck and literally threw her back into the passageway. She landed hard but froze in place so as not to upset the human any further. Squat Lady moved toward her looking very ill-tempered. Amy got shakily to her feet and backed away from the woman. She was not good at walking backward and kept stumbling. Finally she realized that she'd reached her own enclosure and practically dove into her cell. The woman appeared at the gate and with a nasty sneer, slammed it shut. She glared at Amy for a moment, then strode off.

Amy couldn't stop trembling. Even after Squat Lady left, she just couldn't relax. Finally with the help of some deep breathing (recommended by the Afghan) she began to calm down. By the time Fat Man appeared to release them for the yard, she felt almost canine again. She was surprised at the warmth of the greeting she received.

"That was close," the Doberman whistled.

"What was?" Amy asked.

The second Doberman, who had not yet said a word, said with a mild Welsh accent, "Young lady, do you not know how close you came this morning to being taken away?"

"No," she replied clearly surprised. "You don't mean—?"

"Yes, I do. That couple was here to escort you out of the country and just possibly out of your life, too."

Amy sat back heavily on her haunches. She suddenly felt quite dizzy.

"Now there, young lady," said the Welsh Doberman, "they didn't in fact take you away, did they? We will simply have to find a way to ensure that they don't, that's all."

"Maybe Angel's window will be ready soon," Amy said hopefully.

"Looks like she may have other concerns," the Rottweiler, exclaimed gesturing to Angel's corner.

Rain was pouring down in a steady and unrelenting stream. As Amy and the others looked on they saw that the water was not draining on Angel's side of the yard.

"The putty!" Amy exclaimed. "It's blocked the drain!"

Sure enough, Angel was frantically trying to dig out the mound of putty but with little success. They couldn't run over to help, as the Boxer would be curious. Amy and the Rottweiler casually strolled across the yard and through the rising waters. It was more than an inch high at Angel's end.

As soon as they reached the corner, they could see that there was nothing to be done. Angel had jammed the gray material tightly down into the narrow drain, and her attempts to dislodge it had failed. Now the drain was completely blocked.

They looked into Angel's face and were utterly surprised at the calm they read in her eyes. The water was now above their paws and it was only a matter of time before someone noticed. Amy glanced into the yard to check the whereabouts of the Boxer but couldn't spot him anywhere.

Angel got to her feet slowly and said, "I don't know about

you, but I can't think of a good reason why we shouldn't make a break for it today."

"You may have a point," Amy replied with a calm she didn't feel.

The Rottweiler nodded his agreement, and said, "I'll prepare the others. Can you two finish off the window?"

"We'll manage" Angel replied confidently.

Angel and Amy then slipped inside the passage door and eased it shut behind then. Once out of the rain and with all the other animals in the yard, the passageway was strangely silent. The two dogs moved silently past the empty enclosures, glad not to encounter Fat Man hosing down the cells. They didn't know where he was and didn't care so long as he wasn't near them.

They reached Angel's cell with relief, and froze in their tracks. Fat Man stood on his toes, examining the loosened glass in the window frame. At his feet was the Boxer contentedly chewing a slab of meat.

The man and the dog sensed the other two at exactly the same moment and swung their heads around. Amy just had time to notice how similar the two heads looked as they glared across the cell at her.

"Out!" Angel shouted.

Amy didn't have to be told twice. As she spun out of the cell, Angel turned around and with a hard flick of her muzzle managed to swing the gate closed, shutting Fat Man and the Boxer in her own cell.

The two dogs charged back down the passage and into the yard only to run smack into a veritable sea of dogs. They were being led by the Doberman and the Rottweiler toward the planned escape route.

"Sorry," Angel yelled to be heard over the rain, "spot of bother back there. Escape's off!"

There was a distinct murmur of disappointment from the crowd.

"What do you mean, off?" the lead Doberman asked.

"I mean our friend the Boxer's done it again," Amy replied, fighting to hold back tears of pure anger. "And, uh... we may also have upset Fat Man," Angel added.

"Oh, great," said the Rottweiler. "Now we're all in for it. If only there was some other way out."

"Well, unless you believe in miracles," Angel said forcibly, "I suggest we all... what is that awful noise?"

Sure enough, the air was filled with a terrible squeaking sound that was piercing even over the din of the downpour.

They all looked around but couldn't locate the source.

"Anyway, as I was saying we'd better just..." Angel continued, "set our minds to the fact..."

"When the blazes did you stop crying?" asked a voice from the crowd.

The mass of dogs parted to reveal a wet and even smaller-looking Rodney. "I hate to break up your little prayer meeting, but I've been pushing at that bloomin' door for hours, and now that it's open, I think the least you all could do is have the courtesy of using it to escape." Because of the rising water in the yard, only half of the Yorkie was visible above the water.

There was a moment of stunned silence, and then one by one, they began to move toward the door. Slowly at first, then progressing to a mad dash.

Amy, Angel, Rodney and the three males were suddenly alone in the yard. They all looked at Angel with expressions of contempt.

"So much for the rusted hinge theory," the Rottweiler said sarcastically.

"Well excuse me!" Angel retorted, "I only thought that—."

"May I suggest," Rodney interrupted, "that you continue this fascinating little discussion once we're on the other side of these walls?"

Angel and the Rottweiler gave each other a brief look, then both began to laugh.

"Come on, then, let's check out the city, shall we?" the lead Doberman said excitedly.

"On the double, if you don't mind," the Rottweiler said anxiously as they could now clearly hear the yelling and barking of Fat Man and the Boxer coming from inside what only moments before was the dogs' prison.

"Right!" said Rodney. "Follow me!"

With that, the six dogs marched across the sodden yard, out the partially open door and into the unknown city and what they hoped was freedom.

nine

·　·　·　·　·　·　·　·　·

Amy climbed the short flight of stone steps and walked out onto the cracked and filthy pavement. She thought they were still inside the prison. They seemed to be completely surrounded on all sides by tall, scarred, brick walls. It was dark and gloomy and smelled musty with age. She was feeling an anxious gnawing in her stomach when Rodney nudged her with his tiny sodden head.

"So what do you think of the big city so far?" he asked.

Amy glanced down at him worriedly.

"Don't worry, Goldie," he said, suddenly grinning. "It's not all like this."

"Yes," added the Rottweiler. "Some of it's worse!"

The others all laughed at the horror on Amy's face.

"They're just having you on," Angel said, glaring reproachfully at the others. "It's not that bad a place, really. We're currently in what's called the Docklands. It's a bit smelly and run-down, I'll grant you, but some parts have been done up and are actually quite nice."

"How do you always know so much about everything?" Amy asked.

"I think it has something to do with the size of my ears. I just hear more, that's all!"

The others all laughed until Rodney pointed out that they should put some distance between themselves and their recent jail. They all agreed and decided to make Rodney their temporary leader. Angel was clearly far more learned than the Terrier, but Rodney had recently not only escaped from his captors, but also single-handedly made his way across the city to free the entire canine population of the prison. He'd definitely earned the honor.

Rodney suggested that they first get out of the Docklands, and then, when they were safe, decide on a more formal plan of action.

The other escapees had clearly formed into their own groups and left. Only the Dobermans, the Rottweiler, Amy, Angel and Rodney remained. Amy imagined the others were probably all still running and quite probably were even out of the city by now. She had little idea of the actual size of London and thought that around just a few corners would be the rolling hills and sheltering woods of "her" countryside. She would soon learn otherwise.

Rodney arranged the six in single file, thinking they would be less conspicuous. They walked along one brick wall, then stopped at the first corner. Rodney stepped out, and then almost instantly jumped back.

"Blast it!" he whispered.

The others all carefully edged up to the corner and peered around it. Skull Man and Squat Lady were roughly manhandling a pair of dogs back into the front entrance to the prison. Fat Man and the Boxer stood by the door smiling as the escapees were forced back inside.

"They're simply going to restock the place and carry on as before," the lead Doberman said.

"And probably pup-nap more animals to replace those they can't recapture," the Rottweiler said angrily.

"They've got to be stopped," Rodney hissed through clenched teeth.

"Maybe," Angel interjected, "but not now and not by us. We just got out, and speaking for myself, I don't wish to go back just yet!"

The others all murmured their agreement, even Rodney.

"Oh no!" Amy exclaimed, "Look!" She gestured across the street from their concealed corner to a rundown entryway of what once was a large office block. In the doorway, sheltered from the rain and totally preoccupied with her reflection in a piece of glass was her cell neighbor, the Afghan.

"Brilliant!" snapped Angel sarcastically. "There stands probably the vainest and clearly most stupid animal I have ever met!"

"Psst!" Rodney hissed at the Afghan to no avail as the rain was drowning out most sounds.

Amy glanced over at the prison entrance and watched in horror as Skull Head and Squat Woman stepped back outside and began to scan the street for more escapees. The Afghan was still out of their view because of her position in the recessed entry, but as the dogs all looked on in astonishment, the Afghan began backing into the street to afford herself a better reflection from a larger piece of glass.

"Stay here," Rodney snapped. He suddenly broke into a fast sprint heading back along the wall and away from the group.

"Now what the...?" Angel began

"Hold on a sec," the Rottweiler said, grinning broadly.

They all stood stock-still and held their breath as the Afghan reversed her backside closer and closer into the biped's line of sight. Suddenly a loud yapping could be heard from the other end of the street. The two bipeds stopped and turned the other way. Even through the torrential rain, they could still make out the tiny shape of Rodney as he hollered furiously.

Skull Face and Squat Lady broke into a run of sorts and headed toward the drenched Yorkie. Rodney waited just long enough for them to take the bait and then dashed around the far corner and out of sight.

"Now! Quick!" the Doberman barked.

The three males dashed across the street, and to the total surprise of the Afghan, surrounded her on all sides and marched her double-time back across the street. They regained their corner just as Rodney reached them, breathless but clearly exhilarated.

"I've left a good distance between us," he panted, "but I think we should get a move on anyway."

There was no need for a vote on this and the group of seven moved off, their newest member bemoaning her now drenched coat and soaking wet paws. She was quite clueless as to just how close she'd come to being recaptured.

Rodney led them along some dark alleyways and back streets until they rounded a corner and entered a square. Smack in the center was a huge black, metal... actually Amy wasn't sure what it was. She stopped and turned to Angel questioningly.

"I think that's called an anchor," Angel said hesitantly, "but I don't know what it's for."

They were interrupted by the sound of Rodney noisily clearing his throat as he stood patiently with the others.

"We'd better keep moving," Amy said.

They rejoined the others, setting off again past the huge anchor thing and dark and abandoned warehouses.

They soon heard a new sound. It was hard to place. Amy sensed that it was a mix of sounds she knew, yet couldn't put the pieces together. There was a dash of the noise her pond made when the wind whipped the water into a frenzy and tossed it against the banks. Then there was a hint of the runoff as the rainwater rushed down their narrow street and vanished out of sight around the corner at the base of their hill. Whatever this new sound was, it was getting closer and louder. She glanced to the other but saw little concern on their five excited faces. Only five?

"Where's the Afghan?" Amy cried.

They all stopped suddenly and looked about frantically for the other dog.

"Great!" exclaimed Rodney "If she can't stay with us we'll have to..."

He didn't finish his sentence as the missing hound suddenly reappeared, rounding a corner a good distance behind them. She was humming contentedly to herself as she stared up at the patches of blue sky that were starting to peek out from behind the dark rain clouds.

"Yo there miss," the Rottweiler called. "Would you mind staying with the group?"

"Mmmm?" she replied distantly. "Have you ever noticed how blue the sky can be after a good rain? I often wondered how I'd look with blue eyes. What do you think?"

"I think you're a few puppies short of a litter!" Rodney mumbled under his breath.

"Shh," Amy said trying to keep a straight face. "Why don't you walk with Angel and me for a while so we can have a nice chat?"

Amy could feel the incredulous glare she was receiving from Angel without even looking at her.

"All right," the Afghan said cheerfully. "That would be nice."

The hound walked right past the group and clearly expected Amy and Angel to catch up. They gave each other a look of mild dismay, then shrugged and trotted after her. They heard her chatting away, oblivious to the fact that no one was in fact walking with her.

"…at the Suffolk County fair I took a second place," the Afghan rattled on, "which was quite unfair as I felt the winning animal was of questionable lineage at best. I mean, really, an English sheepdog with a French accent? I don't think so. Sometimes the humans seem quite unaware of what they're judging. I remember last winter at Crufts when I was up against a really quite impressive Irish Wolf Hound and as I…"

Amy allowed her thoughts to drift away as the Afghan's voice droned on in the background.

Amy was back at the cottage lying in a patch of warm sun as it streamed in through the kitchen windows. Her Man was kneeling next to her scratching her ears as they both watched Cook remove a fresh loaf from the oven. She could hear someone calling her name and wondered who it could be, and then suddenly felt a sharp pain in her rump. She spun around. Rodney was looking anxiously at her; it was clear that he had just bitten her.

"Ouch!" Amy exclaimed. "What was that for?"

"Step toward me carefully," Rodney said with forced calm.

"What are you…?"

"Now, Goldie! Don't ask any questions. Just do it," Rodney urged.

"Oh, very well" Amy said as she turned and moved toward Rodney and the others. They all suddenly looked relieved. "What's wrong with you?"

Suddenly she was deafened by a loud deep horn sound from almost directly behind her. She spun around and felt her knees go weak.

She was mere inches from where the pavement they'd been walking on simply vanished. Amy looked over the edge and saw a sight like nothing she'd ever seen before. There was water. More water than she thought possible. It was a huge band of water that seemed to be moving slowly, carrying on it strange vehicles with humans seated contentedly on them. There were little ones dashing in all directions honking horns at each other, and there were big ones like the ones directly under Amy's nose at the base of the drop. It was massive. Longer than many cottages put together. In its center was a tall cylinder out of which trickled a thin plume of smoke. As Amy watched, a sudden jet of steam appeared out of it accompanied by the loud horn that had startled her before. She realized she had almost fallen into the vehicle or into the moving waters of the… the…

"Never seen the Thames before, I take it?" Angel asked with a mix of relief and exasperation.

"The what?" Amy stammered.

"The Thames River! The big wet thing you almost fell into," Angel said with sarcasm.

"Oh, that" Amy replied, nodding her head knowingly.

"You've never heard of it, have you?" Rodney asked in a gentle tone.

"Actually, no," Amy said.

"Well, neither had I until yesterday," Rodney reassured her. "How about you?" he asked turning to the others.

The three males shook their heads in unison, then looked at the Afghan who was again staring up at the sky.

"How about you, miss?" Rodney asked in a somewhat louder voice.

"Mmm?"

"Never mind," Rodney mumbled as he turned back to face Amy again. "You must have been daydreaming or something. We turned a corner, and then lucky for you, Angel here noticed you'd strayed off."

Amy gave Angel a nod of thanks.

"Well, if that little scare is done with, can we keep going?" Rodney snapped.

"Sorry," Amy offered shyly.

Rodney was clearly embarrassed by her apology and stretched his tiny frame before forming the group back into a single line and moving them away from the river's edge and toward Central London.

ten
· · · · · · · · ·

they marched for hours, eventually coming to a road that spanned the river. Angel identified the oddity as the Westminster Bridge. On the other side of the water was a spectacular structure larger than Amy had ever seen. The entire building appeared to be made of gold. On one end was a tall tower with huge circles cut into it. On these there were long, pointed, arrow-like things. As Amy watched, one of the arrow things moved and pointed straight upward. The air was suddenly filled with the sound of bells, followed by a louder and far deeper toned bell that rang four times.

"That's Big…" Angel began. "Big… Bill. No! Bob, Burt… oh dash it! It's Big somebody or other."

"Well, I'll grant you" said the Rottweiler. "It *is* big!"

They all nodded in agreement as they looked across the Thames to Big Burt or Bill or whomever. They moved on and crossed the bridge in single file, trying to ignore the pointing and laughing from the many humans who were either walking by or sitting in their noisy, smelly vehicles.

Halfway across, Rodney stopped and looked back from where they'd come. He appeared pleased with their progress. Even the Afghan had kept up.

During the long morning's march, Amy had struck up a conversation with her and learned that her name was Prunella or Pru, as she preferred to be called. Pru was a city dog, it turned out. She had been on a two-week holiday with her mistress when she'd been napped. She was actually surprisingly bright if one could get her to talk about something other than herself. She was four years old, a show champion many times over and a devoted fan of the tellie, as she called it. This was that odd contraption that Amy's Man also occasionally sat in front of and stared into. A large box, which put out a bright light on which images danced and moved almost like real life. Pru told of how she'd sit with her Woman and stare at the thing for days on end sometimes. She would become quite entranced with the screen and find herself unable to break away from it. Her Woman on occasion would do the same, only, according to Pru, would also consume amazing amounts of salty little snack things. She would then take in a lot of liquid and then follow that with a lot of sweet foods.

During the week, Pru would be left alone in the home she shared with her Woman, but at the weekend would be powdered and brushed, and the two of them would get into their vehicle and seek out a beauty show. Pru had been doing this for so long that she was surprised when Amy told her that she had not only never been to such a show, she hadn't even heard of such a thing.

Amy asked Pru what she would do when she was too old to compete in the shows any longer and was amazed at the look of bewilderment that appeared on the Afghan's face. She had clearly never considered this eventuality. She became quiet after that, and at one point, Amy was certain Pru was actually crying but thought it best not to mention it.

Rodney started the group in motion again, but after a couple of steps, he froze in place. At first, the others weren't sure why. Then they spotted what he'd seen. Walking toward them were Fat Man and the Boxer. Rodney turned the other way and immediately spotted Skull Man and Squat Lady making their way along the bridge.

Rodney's reaction was astounding. He seemed to act on pure instinct and without any thought whatsoever.

"Follow me!" he yelled and then dashed into the line of vehicles that had slowed for a group of bipeds walking on the bridge.

The seven dogs weaved between the smelly things to the sounds of raised voices and angry horns. They crossed the center of the road, and if the second Doberman hadn't stopped Pru from moving any farther, a speeding van that tore by them in opposite direction would certainly have struck her.

"Thank you," she said in a startled voice and gave him a warm smile. Their eyes locked for a second and something magical passed for just an instant between them.

Rodney gave the all-clear, and they dashed the rest of the way across. They glanced back and saw their pursuers as they waited for the now fast-moving traffic to subside. Rodney led them at a fast pace to a set of old stone steps that dropped down one side of the bridge. They followed him down and found themselves on the bank of the Thames. Amy was startled by the majesty of the great river and would have liked to stay where she was and take in all that she was seeing, but Rodney clearly had other ideas.

"Come on, don't slow down," he commanded.

They followed him under the stone arch of the bridge and then up another set of steps. As they neared the top, Rodney signaled for the others to stay behind him. As he poked his nose around the corner of a wall and ensured that their trackers weren't in sight, he gave them an all-clear and they trotted up and onto the top of the bridge again.

"Where are they?" Angel asked in amazement.

"If it worked, they should be…" he said confidently, "right about… there!"

He gestured for the others to look through the stone pillars that ran along the side of the bridge. Far below and rushing away from them were all four of their pursuers. The Boxer was sniffing urgently along the riverbank trying to pick up a scent. Suddenly to their surprise, the Rottweiler let out a single loud bark. The Boxer stopped and looked right up at them and was about to alert the bipeds when Fat Man yanked viciously at his lead, dragging him after them. The Rottweiler apologized profusely for his outburst, explaining that the excitement had simply gotten the better of him.

The seven then all broke into laughter and sauntered the rest of the way across the bridge.

Pru came into her own as they reached a busy street that had to be crossed. She understood the odd red light-green light contraption and how one was to use it to know when it was safe to cross roads. At first the other six were highly skeptical of Pru's knowledge until she crossed the street with the odd light system three times without incident. Finally, the others followed her and made it across unscathed. Rodney was especially pleased, as he'd had to battle each street once he'd escaped from the fancy couple, without knowing about the crossing trick.

Food became the next issue. None of them had eaten properly that morning. Rodney in fact had had nothing since the night before.

The three males told them to hold on for a moment and they would remedy the situation. Amy had finally learned their names while waiting to brave the street crossing.

The second Doberman was called Lester, and he was from the picturesque (so he said) village of Denham, not far outside London. He had been grabbed as he'd been strolling down the village high street. His master knew he had good sense and maturity so allowed him to walk by himself. He loved to stop at this wonderful Italian restaurant on the High Street, where the owner's Whippet was teaching him to speak Italian. He'd in fact just had a lesson and was heading back to his home when the nappers had grabbed him.

The Rottweiler's name was Hans. He had never stepped foot in Germany, couldn't speak a word of the language, in fact had no contact with anyone or thing German, yet his Man called him Hans!

He came from a horse farm just outside Cambridge, where he had the task of keeping an eye not only on the humans and their home, but also on the horses themselves. According to him, his life was as near perfect as could be. He loved his bipeds and they him. Yes, the work was hard at times, especially in the winter months, but to watch and help turn stumbling foals into the cream of the horse-racing circuit made it all worthwhile. He told of times when his humans would let him travel with them to a race meeting and actually watch as one of his charges nosed across the finish ahead of the pack, destined to become a champion.

The lead Doberman was Rex. Unlike the others, he did not regale the group with tales of a contented home life and of special humans left behind. Rex was in fact a guard dog who had been taken from his home when he was young and trained to attack, restrain, and generally distrust any humans other than those who knew the special command words. His life was spent going from one assignment to another, usually outside in dark and terrifying yards, where he was made to stand guard alone through long nights. He'd demonstrated to the others his frightening ability to suddenly bare his teeth in a ferocious snarl while producing a deep guttural growl that caused the fur on Amy's back to stand on end.

When Amy had asked him where he'd go once they were free of the city, he'd thought long and hard and then turned to her. In a voice laden with sadness, he told her that he had no idea. Seeing the concern on Amy's face, he'd given her a huge smile and told her that she wasn't to be sad for him as he was in fact the lucky one. She and the others all had to go back to the same old predictable lives they'd had before. Amy would have Cook and the cottage, Lester his Italian lessons, Hans his horses, Pru her beauty shows, Angel her constant rivalry with her Labrador house mate, even Rodney, who had surprised them all when he'd owned up to having a male master whose job it was to cut people's hair into all sorts of funny shapes. Rodney had even confessed to being forced to wear bright ribbons on his head sometimes as his Man flitted around the heavily perfumed establishment where he worked. They would all go back to the same lives they'd left, but Rex would not. He saw his freedom as a second chance. An opportunity to live his life in some as yet uncertain pursuit that would allow him to finally trust others and let him roam free when and where he wished. No, he explained, he was the lucky one.

Rex, Hans and Lester strolled casually down the street, casing the store-fronts for a source of food. They stopped outside a shop in whose windows were hung slabs of fresh, red meat. The three paused at the entrance, and as the others watched in fascination, they devised a plan for getting some of it.

Suddenly, without warning, led by Rex, the three dashed into the shop. There was yelling and screaming and the sound of items being thrown. There was even the sound of one human laughing in a deep baritone voice.

Finally, after what felt like an eternity to the others, the three reappeared with their booty. Rex, still leading the group, had an entire leg of lamb in his mouth. He was closely followed by Hans, who had a standing rib roast clenched in his jaw. Lester, bringing up the rear, was indeed a sight. He had grabbed a string of delicious-looking sausages and was clearly unaware that he was trailing a substantial length of links behind him. As they came barreling out the door, a large angry man in a bloody apron chased after them with a sharp-looking cleaver held high over his head. A pair of elderly women began to scream at the sight of him. This din attracted the attention of a patrolling police constable, who thinking the elderly matrons to be in danger, tackled the butcher to the ground.

Through fits of adrenaline-spurred laughter, the animals all dashed round the nearest corner and kept going as the trail of sausage links whipped after them.

Rodney led them to the safety of a small square. Here they concealed themselves under some heavy shrubbery and tucked in to their fine feast. As they ate, Pru told them of a huge park with a giant pond in its center, only a few hours from where they were. Rodney felt he had a good idea where it was, and they all voted to try to find it the next day. According to Pru, it was large enough for them to stay in undetected while they came up with a more formal plan.

After dinner, Angel tried to get each animal to tell a bedtime story, but everyone else was too sleepy. As she began, she herself was overtaken by sleep before her story was finished. It was the first night spent in the open air for many of the group, but any anxiety they might have felt was soon dispelled by the realization that they were free from their captors and among friends.

eleven

Amy woke before the others when a small but surprisingly inquisitive gray squirrel began making angry noises in her direction. She opened one eye and saw that the little creature was only inches away from her nose, chattering away in what was clearly a display of pique. Amy cocked her head to one side to let the squirrel know that she didn't understand. Once her muzzle was off the ground, the squirrel darted under Amy's chin and began digging in the soft dark earth. Within moments it had uncovered a small cache of acorns, which it gathered in its cheeks. Once loaded, the squirrel angrily flicked his tail at Amy and then dashed out of the shelter of the bushes.

Amy sat for a moment listening to the morning sounds of the big city. Some were familiar, like the birdsong and the slight breeze as it rustled the leaves overhead. For the most part, however, the sensations were quite different. In the country there were spaces between sounds when, even with Amy's keen ears, there was nothing to be heard. At those moments when wind hesitated, birds sat silent, cows pondered and even the humans put down their tools, Amy could recall a feeling of total peace that seemed to blanket the world.

Not so in the city. There was a steady rumble that Amy knew to be omnipresent in this place. Too many people lived too close together doing noisy things. She was thinking how sad it must be not to have peace when she heard Pru stirring close to her. Amy looked over and watched as the Afghan raised her head and listened.

"What a beautiful morning!" Pru said joyously. "And listen. Isn't it peaceful?"

Amy knew she'd just learnt a valuable lesson. How one dog perceives a situation is not necessarily how the whole kennel will see it.

"Yes," Amy responded. "It is a fine day. You look stunning today, if I may say so."

"Do you think so?" Pru replied. "So often when one sleeps heavily one can't do a thing with one's coat in the morning."

"Well, I think your coat really does look smashing today, Pru," Lester said as he slowly rose and stretched out his long lean body. "I really do."

Pru looked at the Doberman, and again their eyes met, this time staying locked for a longer period.

"Thank you, Lester," Pru said breathlessly.

Rodney rolled onto his side and looked over at the pair. "Will you two please leave that until I've at least had breakfast?"

Everyone turned and smiled at the Terrier who at first looked serious, and then suddenly winked. They all laughed.

After some brief route planning, the seven eased their way out of the bushes and down a back alley. Pru gave Rodney some general directions as to the park's location, but for all of them, finding it was going to depend on keen instinct and even keener luck.

By midmorning, they could still detect no signs of the park. They hadn't eaten yet, and they began to feel stabbing pangs of hunger. The bigger animals like Rex and Hans and even Amy could cope with the problem, but Rodney and Angel were clearly starting to drag.

Rex had suggested that they check out the contents of rubbish bins as he'd heard these could be a good source of leftovers. The others were, however, none too eager and decided to hold that possibility as a last resort.

Rodney then demonstrated a wonderful trick. He located a suitable residence, then loudly whined outside until the front door was opened. He then swooned pathetically, allowing his tiny body to drop in a sad heap at the concerned human's feet. A human's reaction, Rodney had explained, was always the same, and as the others watched from hidden locations, he seemed to be correct. A frantic female biped scooped up the small Terrier and carefully carried him into the house. Less than ten minutes later, Rodney came flying out an open window, sending freshly laundered net curtains billowing out after him. In his mouth was a small, tasty looking piece of chicken. Rodney offered to share his prize with the others, but they all agreed that he'd earned it and besides there was really only enough for one. Displaying superior tact, Rodney took his breakfast a decent distance from the others so as not to offend anyone as he ate.

The others were so impressed by Rodney's display that after he consumed the chicken they inundated him with questions as to the finer points of his method. The most important part, he stressed, was to ensure that a good exit was available before even attempting the ruse. Look for an open window or door. If none exist, go to plan B. This is where you continue your dying swan routine on the doorstep but flatly refuse to go into the house. This can have two effects. The human will still take pity and bring the food out to you or sometimes take offense at your distrust of their home and shut the door in your face. Rodney then went on to explain Plan C.

"If you can't see any exits," he began, "and you don't want to risk plan B, then this one usually does the trick. First you get their attention, as with the other plans, but then, and this is where you'll need to bone up on your acting skills, you act in pain when they try to pick you up. This will keep you on the ground and under your own power. Then you act as if you're about to enter the house, but as you near the door, you cringe and back away as if there is something terrifying inside. Now when I say cringe, I mean cringe! You've got to make the human believe that you desperately want to go into their house but are simply too nervous to do so. They rarely take offense at this. If you're not getting your point across satisfactorily, go for the side-glance up at them and the mid-air paw wave. If you wish to try a light whimper at this point, go ahead, but don't overdo it. You mustn't let it appear over-rehearsed. If all goes well, the human will leave the door open, even once you're inside. They'll do this to make you feel comfortable."

The others listened with awe to Rodney's lecture.

"How do you know so much about this line of work?" Rex asked suspiciously.

Rodney stared back at the other dog with a slightly defensive look. "I get around," he replied, "That's all."

Rex nodded his head but was clearly not completely satisfied with the answer.

Angel stepped forward from the group and asked if Rodney thought she could give the scam a try!

"I don't see why not," he responded. "You've certainly got the looks for it."

Angel hung her head in mild embarrassment, then gave Rodney a brief lick on the forehead. Rodney pretended to ignore this and continued on, but he couldn't hide his smile.

"Come on then," he said. "Let's find you a good house to try it out on."

The group walked along the street and saw what most of them considered perfect sites for the trick, but Rodney simply shook his head and found something wrong with each one. Front windows shuttered, too big a drop from the windows, house not kept up well, even one where the brass letter slot and door handle were tarnished. He explained that though seemingly minor, such traits showed a home without pride and therefore a human who was probably lacking in true devotion to animals.

Finally, after a good half hour, he led the group down a narrow cobblestone lane, that dead-ended a mere hundred yards further on. On each side were little attached houses, all with bay windows and window boxes exploding with colorful displays of flowers.

Rodney chose one particular house halfway down the mews. It was painted a cheerful yellow with immaculate white wood trim. The bay windows were open and faced onto the lane with only a drop of a mere foot or two to the cobblestones.

"This'll do nicely" he exclaimed, "You know what to do? If you're not ready, I could go over it again or even give another demonstration. I don't want to rush you. I..."

"Rodney, stop!" Amy chided gently. "Let the poor girl speak."

"It's okay, Rodney," Angel said grinning. "I'll be perfectly fine."

Rodney looked uncertain.

"I promise," she added softly and with that, moved toward the front door.

The others all scattered to various hiding places to watch her performance. It was spectacular. She could easily have turned professional had she wished.

She began with the merest whimper accented with an occasional yelp of discomfort. She progressed effortlessly into an outstanding jag of howling while still maintaining an overall sense of hurt and anguish. The others were most impressed by the display.

Before long, the door opened, and an elderly woman poked her head outside. She looked to the left and the right before she realized the pitiful sounds were coming from under her nose. She reached down and stroked Angel's back. Angel let out a slight moan and looked up into the old woman's face with wide wet eyes that clearly captivated the poor unsuspecting human.

The woman suddenly scooped the poor creature into her frail arms and vanished into the house, shutting the door behind her.

Rodney looked over to the others with an expression of great pride as a teacher would for an excelling student. He was still grinning when he heard the distant sound of windows being closed behind him.

He spun around and saw that the woman had already closed one half of the bay window and was reaching for the other.

"We don't want you sitting in a draft now, do we, you poor little thing," the woman said as she shut and latched the other window.

Rodney ran to the house and verified what he already dreaded. There was no way for Angel to get out!

He turned and faced the others who had moved from their places of concealment and were now looking at him anxiously.

"Anything like this ever happened before?" Rex asked in a concerned tone.

"To be honest, no! It's always been a straightforward get-in-and-get-out proposition."

"Well she's certainly in!" Pru said.

Rodney studied each face in the group, knowing that they needed his leadership more than ever at a time like this. "Ladies, if you'll excuse us for a second," he said looking at Amy and Pru. "The boys and I need a moment to come up with a plan."

Amy looked to Pru with disbelief at the Terrier's inference that planning was the male's domain. She was about to speak up when Pru caught her eye and gestured her over to the side.

"Don't even think about it. They're as stubborn as humans," Pru warned her. "Let them have their little boy talk. It makes them feel superior. Don't take it personally. It's nothing against you or me. Males simply believe they're better, that's all."

Pru could tell by the look of astonishment on Amy's face that all this was new to her.

"Trust me, Goldie, this is how it is in the real world, and it's far easier to let them believe they're right."

"Not for me it isn't!" Amy walked defiantly across the mews and up to the brightly painted door. Only Pru was watching her. The others were in deep conversation. Pru wanted to say something to stop her but judged that Amy was upset and therefore best left to do what she felt needed to be done.

Amy reached the door and began scratching it roughly with her front paws. She saw that she was gouging the paint with her nails, and though knowing that such vandalism was normally an abhorrent act, she continued anyway, such was her anger and determination.

After a few moments and a good deal of paint, the door opened. The kindly woman spotted Amy.

"Oh my! Will you look at this! Another one! Well, I never. And I suppose you're also a hungry puppy? Well, I'm just going to…"

Amy didn't let her finish. She wasn't in the mood for human cuddle talk. She did something then she'd never done before but felt no remorse, only a great fury that was still churning in the pit of her stomach. She growled! Not only that, she barked! Not a single or a double bark, but repeatedly in a rough, completely unrefined manner!

The effect was highly rewarding. The color drained from the woman's face. She backed away from Amy, leaving the door wide open. Without a moment's hesitation, Amy stepped into the hallway and immediately spotted Angel. The Spaniel was lounging on a bed of fluffed-up pillows, nibbling on a plate of chopped meat right next to her.

"Goldie!" she said in a calm, almost sleepy voice, "come in, come in! Have some lunch. It's quite tasty."

"Come on, Angel, we're leaving!"

"No, I don't think so, this is just perfect for me. It's cozy, it's warm, and the old lady can't seem to do enough for me."

Amy walked over to the Spaniel, grabbed hold of the pillows in her teeth and pulled them forcibly out from under the other dog. Angel and the plate of meat went flying.

"What was that for?" Angel asked pathetically as she righted herself on the floor.

"That was for being a spoiled and selfish little... little... mongrel! Now come with me immediately or I'll really get cross!"

"I'm not a mongrel!" Angel whined as she stumbled to the door. "I'm not! I'm a purebred. I am! Really I am!"

Amy followed the subdued little creature out the door and then felt a strong pang of guilt. She turned back into the house. The elderly woman was still trembling as she leaned her fragile frame against the wall halfway along the hallway.

Amy walked over to her and with great courtesy and gentleness took her frail hand in her mouth and led her to the sitting room and a large overstuffed flowery chair.

The woman sat down as instructed but still looked at Amy with great fear. Amy did not want to leave the human with a bad memory of dogs. She placed her front paws on the arms of the chair and lifted herself up putting her golden head only inches from the woman's face.

The woman was scared, that was clear. There was only one thing for it. She leant over and licked the human's face three times with a slow and gentle stroke. That always worked. Some smaller breeds believed that quantity was the ticket and usually only succeeded in half drowning their victims in saliva. No, three gentle passes was the way Amy had been taught, and by the woman's reaction, this was obviously exactly the right approach.

The woman instantly began to get color back into her face and even formed her wrinkled features into a smile. She reached out and though still nervous, patted Amy tenderly on the head. Amy gave her hand a lick of thanks (standard protocol), then dropped to the floor and calmly walked out of the cottage, trying to ignore the powder from the woman's face which still clung to her tongue.

She strode over to the group who were standing around the subdued form of Angel and sat herself defiantly onto her haunches.

"So, you boys come up with a plan yet?"

twelve

Once they had left that neighborhood behind, the problem of food again dominated their thinking. All except Angel, who was not only far from being hungry after her gluttony at the hands of the old lady, but also was unable to refrain from belching quietly to herself as they made their way down a quiet side street. Amy had given her a couple of severe glances which had no effect except to make Angel cringe and keep as far from her as possible. Their salvation came in the form of a dairy van and its romantically inclined driver.

Rodney spotted it first. It was a strange-looking vehicle with an open back filled with every imaginable dairy product. The master of the vehicle was about half a block further down the street, chatting to a female biped who stood on the top of some basement steps. Much to the group's delight, the female must have said something funny as the milkman laughed boisterously and then after a quick glance up and down the road, followed her into the basement.

Rodney wasted no time and covered the distance to the dairy van in a flash. He sprang up onto the back of the vehicle and gingerly made his way to the top shelf and the prize products. He began handing down containers of things like yogurt and cottage cheese, calling out the name of each prior to unloading it.

Although they were not familiar to Amy, she was hungry enough to try anything. The group opened the containers and wolfishly gobbled down the contents of each one.

Just as Rodney was about to devour a loaf of brown bread, there was a loud screeching of brakes inches away from them. As they turned to face the source of the din, they spotted Skull Face as he jumped out of the passenger side of a gray van. The rear door suddenly flew open and Fat Man and the Boxer emerged. The dogs all gathered, cowering behind the milk van. Nobody moved until Squat Lady stepped out from behind the wheel of the van with an evil-looking gadget in her hand.

"A dart gun!" Angel shrieked "She's got a dart gun!"

Amy had no idea what this meant, but it didn't sound good.

No one will ever know if Rodney was brilliant that day or just exceedingly lucky. He began to back away from the humans as he crouched in the open milk van and somehow managed to tip a crate of milk bottles onto the road. As the crate hit, bottles flew everywhere. Some broke, sending plumes of milk into the air while others remained intact, rolling in every direction. The Terrier started to tip all the crates off the van, then screamed for the others to make a dash for it.

Even as he was giving them these instructions, he was himself in mid-air, having leapt off the van just as Skull Face was about to reach for him.

The seven broke into a furious gallop, not daring to look back as they ran. Finally Amy cast a brief glance behind and had to stop as laugher overtook her.

Their pursuers had not gotten far. As Amy and the others looked on, they giggled openly. Between the sea of milk and the rolling bottles, the humans were finding it nearly impossible to stay upright. Even the Boxer was having trouble, and he had four legs! The coup de grace came when Squat Lady got shakily to her feet and aimed the dart gun toward the group, then lost her footing. As she fell backward, the gun went off. The Boxer suddenly yelped in pain, then began to stumble around with a dreamy expression on his face until he toppled over, fast asleep. It was at this moment that the milkman came dashing up the stairs with his shirt un-tucked, yelling hysterically at the milk-covered humans at his van.

The seven decided that though all this was highly amusing, they'd better keep moving and trotted off around the corner, knowing that their ex-captors were unlikely to disentangle themselves for quite some time.

They headed down a wide tree-lined boulevard until, as they rounded a bend, they stopped to stare at the amazing sight in front of them.

"The park!" Angel cried. "Look, the park!"

"A park," Pru responded. "Not *the* park. The one we're after is still a ways on."

"What's wrong with this one?" Hans asked excitedly. "I mean it's big, it's green, it's full of trees and bushes. Look there! I just saw a squirrel. What's wrong with this one?"

"It's not that big, and it has policemen in it all the time," Pru replied.

The others all felt that perhaps Pru was being a little picky, obliging them to seek out one particular park when this one seemed to fit the bill.

"Trust me," she pleaded. "This is nothing! Where we're going is a real park! If I'm wrong, I'll get food for all of you for a week."

"How do you know this other park so well?" Rex queried with mild suspicion.

"It's where my biped took me every day for my walk when she got home. Even if it was dark, she'd walk me as far as the lake and then back to the apartment."

The others all felt her sense of loss and homesickness and silently decided to let her at least show them "her" park.

They continued on until they came upon an incredible sight—a magnificent human building surrounded by tall black and gold railings and immaculately dressed men in red and black uniforms.

Angel explained that this was Buckingham Palace and that it was the home of the Monarch. When asked to explain exactly what that meant, Angel hung her head.

"Hey," Amy said, nudging her, "just say I don't know. Nobody is going to think badly of you for that."

Angel raised her head and said weakly, "I'm sorry. I don't know."

True to Amy's words, the others didn't seem to care one way or the other. In fact, they were so riveted at the sight of the grand structure beyond the railings that they didn't react at all.

"Oh, oh!" Rex suddenly shouted as he pointed his long muzzle off to the side.

The gray van was emerging from around a corner, driving slowly as its occupants peered out looking for them.

"Come on!" Rodney cried. "Follow me."

"No! You can't do that!" Pru shouted as Rodney walked through the palace railings and onto the forecourt.

She watched as the others followed the Terrier's lead and then fearfully eased herself through the ornate fencing and followed after them.

They could hear peals of laughter coming from the crowd of human onlookers standing on the other side of the front gates of the palace. Amy glanced over and saw a sea of wide-eyed, amazed expressions as she ran by. She heard hundreds of camera shutters click as she passed in front of the tourists.

It looked as though they were actually going to make it across the palace forecourt and through the railings on the other side, when a line of uniformed humans appeared from within the building and cut off their line of escape.

The seven dogs came to an abrupt halt as they looked for another route. They turned back the way they'd come and saw that more uniformed humans had blocked off that route as well.

They began to panic. It couldn't end now! Not because of a silly shortcut.

"Psst," a voice said. "You lot. Over here!"

They turned and faced the palace. There, under an elaborate portico, were two Corgis signaling to them.

"Through here, quickly!" one of them commanded with a well-bred accent.

The seven didn't even have to think about this, as the humans were closing in fast. They dashed toward the two sturdy little animals and followed them through a side door and into the palace itself.

"I'm William," said one of their benefactors, "and she's Mary."

Mary nodded back at the others as they ran. They charged through a small hall, then into a far grander marble floored entrance. The highly polished floor caused them all to slip and slide as they tried to follow the Corgis down another passageway. This one had walls covered with deep red material on which were hung dozens of portraits of serious-looking bipeds.

Just before they reached the end of the hallway, the Corgis gestured for the others to slow down.

"We have to walk here," Mary stated.

"Rules of the house, you know," William added.

They led the seven down a couple of steps and into an attractive room decorated in rich blues and floral prints. As they passed through the room, they saw a female biped sitting in a large comfortable wing chair drinking a cup of what Mary announced was tea. The woman looked over the top of the two circular glass things that she wore on the bridge of her nose, and though clearly surprised, smiled at the passing canine troop.

The two Corgis gave her a slight bow, then proceeded on. The others all followed with the exception of Angel, who stood stock still staring at the woman.

"Angel!" Rodney snapped. "Yo! Angel, come on."

Angel turned and looked to the others with a dazed expression. "But that's.........that's...."

"*Now,* Angel!" Rex commanded.

Angel turned back to the woman and dropped her head to the floor in a grand bow and then backed the entire way out of the room.

The Corgis led them out of the floral room and into what was the most beautiful garden any of them had ever imagined.

"Do you know who that was?" Angel asked in a whisper as she nudged Amy.

"No, and we haven't got time for your trivia just now, Angel," Rex stated flatly.

"But that was the Queen!" Angel said in an awed tone.

"What's a queen?" Amy asked.

The entire troop came to an abrupt halt as William and Mary turned and stared at Amy in astonishment.

"Did I hear you correctly?" William asked incredulously.

"What's a queen!" Mary also sounded shocked.

Even Rodney was amazed "Amy! "

"Sorry," she said with a slight edge to her voice. "All right, so tell me. Who is the Queen and what's all the fuss?"

"The Queen, or, Elizabeth the Second, is the sole ruler of Great Britain, the Commonwealth, and all her kingdoms and subjects around the world," William stated proudly.

"She's the crowned Monarch," Mary added also with great pride.

"She looked a little familiar," Amy said trying to recall where she'd seen the face.

"I would think so." William tried to keep the exasperation from his voice. "Her Royal Highness is..."

"I know," Amy said excitedly. "It was on those funny little sticky things that humans put on papers before giving them to the mailman."

"What?" William exclaimed.

"I think she means stamps!" Angel volunteered. "I think Amy's referring to the picture of the Queen on postage stamps."

"Ah!" said William.

"I see!" said Mary.

There was a slight pause then as both William and Mary turned to Angel and asked, "What's a postage stamp?"

"I hate to break up this delightful and highly entertaining conversation," Rodney said, "but can we get a move on?"

He gestured back to the Palace and to the scores of uniformed humans flowing out of it.

"You may have a point," William said. "Come on then, let's make for the wall."

Mary and William broke into a fast run which surprised the others, considering the Corgis had exceptionally short legs.

They dashed through hedges, under thickets, over a stream and finally, out of breath, came to a halt at the base of an enormous wall. It was so high that Amy wasn't even certain where it ended.

"You're not expecting us to get over this are you?" Rodney asked nervously.

"Hardly, old boy," William responded matter-of-factly. "Actually, I'm going to show you a little trick of ours if you will permit my indulgence."

"Please!" Rodney replied, "Be our guest."

"Good! You see that door just behind those bushes?"

They did see a secure-looking metal doorway set into the formidable wall.

"Yes," Rodney said cautiously.

"Mary and I have been working on a little something that we've been dying to try out. What we hope will happen is that the guards will actually open the door for us, allowing you lot to make a dash for it while we keep their attention."

"Why would they do that?" Rex asked.

"Watch and see. Here they come," William whispered excitedly.

Sure enough, the guards were approaching the wall with long purposeful strides.

"Stay hidden till we give the word." Mary's voice was full of enthusiasm.

William and Mary edged along the wall and made their way to a small open drain located under a particularly thick bush. As the others looked on, William stuck his muzzle down the drain and began barking. Mary moved to the metal door and started whining and scratching at it in a believable and pitiful way.

The seven were definitely impressed. William was giving the impression that he'd somehow become shut out of the palace gardens. His voice, directed into the drain, did indeed sound muffled and distant. Mary's antics at the door completed the ruse, giving the bipeds reason to believe she knew her brother's location to be just the other side of the wall.

"Oh, blimey!" One of the guards exclaimed, "One of Her Majesty's Corgis has gotten out! Quick, open the gate!"

Another guard stepped forward and located the appropriate key on a large ring. He inserted it into the metal door and opened it wide. The guards stepped out onto the pavement. William chose this moment to dash out from under the bush, and together with Mary sprinted through the doorway and between the legs of the puzzled guards.

"Good luck," William cried to the others as he and Mary charged down the road, closely followed by the breathless humans.

Rodney led the group through the wall and in the opposite direction from the Corgis, who were doing an excellent job of keeping ahead of their pursuers. He kept the others running at a fast pace because, as he pointed out, the gray van probably wasn't far behind.

They came to a large road running into an even larger circular one. There were no red-green things to control the vehicles. Pru suggested calmly that they follow her.

She led them to a flight of steps into a large tunnel. They were slightly apprehensive, but Pru insisted that she'd traveled within these passages hundreds of times and although they smelled a bit rank, they were perfectly safe. They followed the Afghan down the steps and proceeded along the long tunnel, with amazed glances from passing humans.

As they neared the halfway mark and could clearly see the steps on the far end, they suddenly spotted two unmistakable shapes descending into the tunnel. Skull Face and Squat Lady. Both of them grinned menacingly as they approached the dogs. Amy looked over her shoulder, not in the least surprised to see Fat Man with club at the ready as he too descended the steps while eyeing the group.

"Quick! They haven't got us yet!" Pru cried and turned suddenly down an adjoining tunnel that the others hadn't even noticed.

They were instantly surrounded by a horde of bipeds, all oblivious to their presence as they dashed every which way.

"We're in a tube station!" Pru yelled, trying to be heard over the noisy crowd. "Keep going!"

They passed through the human obstacle course, the objects of more than one irritated shout. They came to another set of steps that delighted Pru enormously.

"You ready?" she asked excitedly.

"For what?" Rodney snapped impatiently.

"For heaven!" Pru cried over her shoulder as she bounded up the steps.

The others all followed as her excitement began to infect them. They reached the top of the steps expecting to see a different world but instead only saw a busy street filled with an astonishing quantity of loud, smelly vehicles. They could taste the odor of the street on their tongues and turned to Pru in anger for making them think that some form of utopia had been near.

Pru ignored their fierce glances and signaled them to keep moving. They were about to refuse when they heard a commotion at the base of the steps and saw Skull Face and the others break free of the tube station crowd and start up toward them.

They followed Pru, who after only a few yards turned sharp left and then waited for the others to catch up. As they reached her, they couldn't believe what they were seeing. Only one seemingly traffic-free road separated them from the biggest park in London. All they could see were trees and grass for miles in almost every direction.

"It's beautiful!" Angel cried.

"It is that!" Rex agreed.

"And it's all ours," Pru cheered. "Let's go get it!"

As they started across the street, they looked back and saw that their pursuers weren't following them into the park. It was simply too big a challenge to catch them there.

"We'll get ya, you little beasts!" Squat Lady yelled after them.

The seven kept running until their paws were solidly planted on the soft sweet-smelling grass of the huge city park.

"We should be able to stay hidden in here for weeks," Rodney said confidently.

"That must be how they named it," Pru said smugly.

"Named what?" Rodney asked as he lowered his muzzle to a little bunch of wildflowers at his feet.

"The park! It's the perfect place to hide. That's its name. Hyde Park"

"Nice going, Pru," Rex said sincerely. "Very nice going indeed."

thirteen

the park was as wondrous as Pru had promised. Even for a country dog like Amy, who was used to almost limitless expanses of green, Hyde Park had a great deal to offer.

As she looked about, she began to realize just how narrow her own view of life had been before she was captured. She had become comfortably content, believing that what surrounded her at the cottage was all that existed. It had never dawned on her that the world continued out beyond her line of sight. That was an entirely new concept for her. Amy began to realize that there was much more to life than she would possibly ever see. At least on that day. Maybe tomorrow she'd see it all.

Once they were in the park, the males' behavior astonished her. Prior to entering the green oasis they had been responsible, even if somewhat pig-headed, animals whose goal was to seek out shelter and food for them all. Amy considered these to be good sensible challenges and was therefore caught completely unaware by their startling actions once in the park.

Rodney was the first. His downfall was a lone pigeon that was attempting to sun itself on a small patch of dense lawn well off the pathway. One moment Amy had been having a thoughtful conversation with him, and the next, he was charging at breakneck speed toward the poor bird. Added to this was the fact that Rodney also began barking. Not in an adult manner, but in a rapid-fire, maniacal way. He began to drool, to pant, to yell and to chase his flying adversary in every direction. Needless to say, he never came close to his prey and only served to bring the group to the attention of any human within a two-mile radius. The pigeon finally gave up any hope of a restful moment in the sun and flew off toward the city for some peace. Rodney returned to Amy's side, breathless, and by that point, embarrassed by his slip in decorum. Amy was about to ask him what had made him go from a serious and mature leader to a ranting, dribbling beast in a matter of seconds when Rex suddenly yelled at the top of his lungs "Squirrel!"

Well, that was it. The four males practically tripped over each other to pursue one tiny gray creature whose only sin was to have descended from his tree to recover a dropped acorn. Amy could hear, even from where she stood, the poor animal's screech of surprise as the four barking lunatics charged toward it.

The squirrel made it to the next tree and scaled it in seconds, leaving the dogs barking like crazy animals at its base.

Unfortunately, this was just the beginning. The males chased every pigeon, every squirrel, even other male dogs for most of the rest of the day. At one point, Pru, Amy and Angel actually walked the other way, praying that no one would think them associated with the four wild animals that were clearly suffering from some sort of mental breakdown.

The last straw came when they first saw the lake in the center of the park. Amy was just thinking how serene and picturesque it looked when her four ex-friends came charging by her, yapping away like puppies and proceeded to chase a family of geese into the water. As if that weren't bad enough, they followed the poor waterfowl and, paddling as best they could with their non-aquatic bodies, tried to keep up with the geese.

When the males eventually wore themselves out, Rodney shook his soaking coat over them all, sneezed, then asked in a child-like tone, "So what's to eat around here?"

Amy looked at the wet Yorkie and then at the other three equally soaked and exhausted males and smiled. Her annoyance ebbed, and though realizing that she could not allow herself to let go to the extent they had, there was something clearly restorative to their actions. The four dogs looked young and alive as they stood panting and dripping before her. Their eyes held a new sparkle that had not been there that morning. There was a distinct glow emanating from them that Amy tried to accept as being the result of a day of sun and fresh air, but she knew better. This wasn't simply sheen on their coats. This aura was coming from inside. Their mad carefree chases had somehow released the spirit of their wild, unrestrained ancestors. Amy felt a pang of jealousy. She wanted to experience that total release of energy. She wanted for just a brief moment to relinquish all shackles of her heritage and training and behave like a wanton beast of prey. She didn't have a clue how to do this, just that she wanted it.

Lester must have read her mind because he suddenly stepped forward and spoke gently into her ear.

"No one will think badly of you, Goldie," he said in a peaceful almost dreamlike voice "Go on—give it a try."

Amy stepped back in shock with the realization that Lester had somehow picked up her thoughts. She tried to compose herself and ignore both him and her own inner urge. As she tried to fight down these intrusions into her usually sensible and correct thinking, she spotted a flock of pigeons landing less than fifty feet from them.

Even exhausted, Rodney and Rex looked about ready to charge this latest target when Lester stopped them and calmly told them to just hold on. They'd had their fun. It was time for someone else to try it.

Pru and Angel looked around wondering whom Lester could be referring to. Then with the beginnings of a smile, Amy moved away from the group and took a step toward the birds. She took another and felt no difference inside at all. She looked back to

Lester who simply gave her an encouraging nod while the others looked at her with puzzled expressions.

Amy realized that if she was going to do it she was simply going to have to let go. She took a deep breath, closed her eyes and charged.

For the first few yards she felt nothing special but then something happened. Maybe it was the wind blowing her coat out behind her. Whatever it was, Amy felt a rush of energy surge through her body. Joy and euphoria cascaded over her every nerve and cell. She ran faster and without realizing it, began to bark. Openly and with total abandon, Amy barked like she'd never barked before.

The pigeons could now see and hear her as she lunged toward them. They began to lift off into the safety of the uncrowded air space, but this didn't faze Amy in the least. She was no longer simply chasing after birds in a park. There was something older and more primeval swirling through her. She could almost sense the urgency and instinctual need to chase and consume rising from memories buried in her senses for thousands of years. These emotions did not evoke any real bloodlust in Amy. She simply felt more alive than she'd ever felt in her life as she charged through the rising cloud of birds. Her body tingled; her senses were ready to explode with delight. Oh what a feeling, she thought, as she gave up on the birds and rolled over and over and over on the soft, slightly damp carpet of green sweet-smelling grass.

She glanced over at the others and saw that the males were all beaming at her, fully understanding her experience. Pru and Angel, however, were looking at her with distaste. Amy was convinced they felt that she'd somehow let down their side. So what! Maybe for once she had, but she'd savor this experience for the rest of her life, of that she was certain.

She gave them a joyous bark, which the boys immediately acknowledged and returned. Pru and Angel, however, turned away, clearly embarrassed, and pretended to be in deep conversation.

"It's wonderful to be alive!" Amy suddenly cried out to the delight of the males and even greater embarrassment of the females.

She smiled to herself, knowing that on that day she was definitely one up on life.

fourteen

· ·

food! That was still the big issue. By early evening they were all exhausted after a long and arduous day. Most of all, though, they were hungry. They knew they'd eaten at some point in recent history. They could even vaguely recall snippets of images involving exploding milk bottles, but that was about all. The point was, when were they going to eat next?

They located a secluded spot at one end of the small lake. Just off a biped path, and within earshot of a strange modern glass structure in which humans had been dining all through the day, they stumbled onto a fenced-in area that encircled a small pictur-esque waterfall. Behind this waterfall was a cave. Not a real cave, mind you, it was more like a carved out area for storage of some kind. Anyway, it was perfect for the seven of them. They could look out but no one could see in.

Rodney crept out of their new home to check out the local food prospects and as they waited for him to return, they began discussing what they would do next. One thing was evident; they all wanted to go home. All except Rex, who of course didn't have one. The strange thing was that as he'd never had a proper home, the concept of a cozy family life was foreign to him.

It became a challenge to see who could think up the best examples of what home life meant to get the point across to the Doberman.

Pru felt that home was where almost constant grooming took place. Where one was brushed, teased, powdered, clipped and bathed on an almost continual basis and in addition, taken to the groomer's once a month. If you weren't in the midst of making yourself look beautiful, you were planning how next to tackle the challenge.

Hans felt that home was the feeling of warmth when he was let in after a hard day with the horses and allowed to stretch out in the midst of the family in front of a roaring fire.

Angel felt that home was the constant struggle of wills between herself and the family's other dog, the black Lab. After some prompting from Amy, however, she did admit that there was a certain feeling of security to her life when she took her place at the foot of her mistress's bed and molded herself to the warm contours of the young human sleeping beneath the covers.

Amy started to tell of how to her, home was where she was allowed into her Man's room upstairs and to lie at his feet as he worked, feeling his gentle hand caress her coat, when she noticed Rex turn away, his head drooping. She moved over to him and tried to speak to him but he simply pushed her aside and ran out into the fresh air, now cooling as the sun set. Amy followed him out.

Rex was standing alone under the gray silhouette of a large tree staring up at a single cloud as it passed across the night sky. Amy moved to his side and gave his neck a gentle nuzzle of greeting.

"I'm sorry, Goldie, I don't know what came over me. Those stories you were telling… they hurt me somehow. I felt an ache in my chest and… Oh, never mind. I've not had such a bad life really. I've been fed well and given shelter and… and…"

"Rex, it's me. Let it out. Maybe I can help."

"There's nothing to let out," he said, trying to bury his emotions. "I just got a little sad for a moment back there, but I'm fine now… Honest."

"You're sure?" she asked gently

"Absolutely!" he replied forcefully.

"Then you won't mind my finishing the story."

Rex simply stared back at her in silence. Amy couldn't clearly make out his expression in the darkness but she knew she had to get through to him while his emotions were near the surface. She had no idea what made her feel this sudden need to help this dog that she'd only known for a matter of days. She only knew that she had to.

"Late at night when the people were in bed, I'd walk slowly through the house and make certain that all was well, that the doors were securely shut, that the embers in the fireplace were dying out safely within the hearth and that Cook and my Man were sleeping soundly in their beds. There's a feeling at such moments, when they are entirely in your care, of pride at the responsibility you've been entrusted with. Maybe it's similar to how you feel when you stand guard on one of your assignments."

Amy's timing was obviously spot on. Rex looked into her eyes, and she could clearly see the tears as they welled up and held the reflection of the starlight from overhead.

"Oh Goldie, you have no idea what my life is like. I've never felt comfortable anywhere. I don't feel pride at guarding a fenced in yard filled with junk or an empty factory building. These are just objects. There's no emotion there. I was taught to attack people, not love them. I always thought that was normal and that all dogs were taught the same. Then I met you lot. Now I don't know what to think. I thought I was perfectly content to live alone and do my job every day and simply… simply…"

"Exist?" Amy offered.

"Yes, that's it! Exist. But now I feel this aching inside. I want to know what it's like to have a human brush me or hold me out of affection rather than a sense of duty… Goldie?"

"Yes, Rex?"

"What's it really like? You know, being stroked and petted and… all those things?"

She looked into his yearning face and couldn't help but smile. "It's wonderful, Rex. It truly is."

"I don't know why, but I thought it must be," Rex whispered dreamily.

"I'll tell you one thing that's for certain," Amy said with conviction.

"What's that?"

"You will know what it's like before long. I promise you."

"How?" he asked. "How's that going to happen?"

"I just feel it, that's all. I think that any dog that's as ready to love as you now are will find a way to make it happen."

"Do you really believe that?"

"Dog's honor!"

Rex looked up at the night sky deep in thought as Amy smiled to herself.

"Yo!" Rodney shouted from the direction of the cave "They told me you were out here. So tell me, just how hungry are you?"

Amy and Rex glanced apprehensively at each other as Rodney trotted over to them.

"Why?" Amy asked suspiciously.

"Well it's like this," he began timidly, "I've located food, lots of it, but there's a slight drawback."

"Such as?" Rex inquired as he looked down upon their fidgety leader.

"Such as," Rodney swallowed deeply, "it's in trash bins."

"No! I won't even listen." Pru had come out of the cave to hear this. She turned away and pretended to sniff at the base of the tree.

"It's not like it sounds, it's the bins out back of that restaurant place by the lake. For some reason, they dump masses of pretty good-looking stuff before going home. I had a good sniff and it wasn't half bad!"

"But Rodney!" Amy said, turning to face him. "Trash bins?"

"Look, I know it's not proper and all that, but I think we've all got to bend a little. Hopefully this ordeal will be over soon, but in the meantime, I think we'd better settle for just about any food and shelter we find."

"He has a point, Goldie," Rex added.

She looked at the two dark silhouettes, imagining the hopeful expressions that were hidden from her in the darkness.

"I suppose you're right," she said with resignation. "Let's go have a look."

"I think you'll be pleased." Rodney's voice was filled with pride.

"We'll see. We'll see," Amy said, pretending to be coldly critical. In fact, she was hungry herself.

As it turned out, the meal wasn't bad at all. The seven crept up to the deserted restaurant and then made their way to the back where the trash bins were kept, well out of sight of the occasional passing human.

The initial problem was that the upper part of the bins were filled with an astonishing amount of paper and cardboard, making scavenging beneath them complicated.

Rex had the solution. He placed his front paws on the metal lip of one of them and backed up, pulling the bin over and sending its contents cascading onto the hard ground. After Rex had pulled over a few more bins and Rodney had scouted out and retrieved the good bits, the seven retired to the grass for dinner—numerous whole or partially eaten sausages, two intact meat pies, four rashers of bacon, two chicken legs, one entire chicken breast and an unlimited supply of rolls.

Satisfied and suddenly sleepy, the seven strolled back toward their cave, marveling at their own shadows cast by the tall lamps that bordered the path. As they reached the waterfall, Angel stepped behind it and out of sight. Just as Pru was about to follow her, there was a loud hiss, followed by a volley of furious fowl language. Angel came yelping out straight through the waterfall and into the pond.

"Back!" Rex commanded sharply. "Get back, all of you."

He waited till they were a safe distance from the cave and then stormed in. Again there was a moment's silence before another even louder hiss and even greater torrent of enraged bird expletives. Then another noise filled the air. It was deep and guttural. A sound that made the hair on Amy's back rise. She knew exactly what it was, but still could not believe the intense ferocity that it contained.

Rex was growling. The bird abuse stopped suddenly. Moments later, an angry goose waddled out of the cave. He gave the group a filthy glare, and with an angry honk, rose into the night sky and was gone.

Rex stuck his head out and grinned at the others. "We talked. He gave me his opinion, I gave him mine, and we reached an agreement. It's ours for as long as we need it."

Angel rushed past him, mumbling to herself about how wild birds shouldn't be allowed out at night. She then gave her coat a good shake prior to entering the cave. The others tried to suppress their grins as they followed her inside the cozy sleeping place. The steady sound of the waterfall was almost hypnotic.

Amy awoke to a bright shaft of sunlight that cut through the waterfall and blanketed the sleeping forms of her friends. She watched as the light sparkled off the water, creating the illusion of thousands of diamonds.

She lowered her head back onto her front legs and tried to recall the events of the past few days. She felt on one paw that she'd been away from the cottage for a long time but also knew that it had in fact only been a matter of days. It was hard for Amy to keep time in any logical order. She could vaguely remember Cook screaming and the sensation of movement. She had a hazy recollection of her cell and the yard. She had a vivid memory, however, of Fat Man hitting her and of Squat Lady taunting her, but even these memories had begun to fade like some old piece of fabric.

One thing that Amy found surprising was that she no longer felt the fear she had only days earlier. Fear she could remember. It was not an emotion she'd been used to or enjoyed at all.

She looked around the cave at the others and realized just how important they had become to her. Through their company and camaraderie she had learned the importance of friendship and how, even when faced with fear or doubt, the burden could be greatly lessened when shared with others. As she looked at her sleeping friends, she realized for the first time how much she'd been craving the company of others of her kind. There were neighbors, of course, at the cottage, but these were mainly local breeds or farm dogs whose idea of a stimulating afternoon was to challenge each other to see how many trees they could stake out on one bowl of water.

Her thoughts were interrupted by a loud honking sound coming from outside the cave. She attempted to ignore it, but it was then joined by another and then another. Amy thought this odd. She poked her head outside the cave and stared with total disbelief. On the grassy knoll at the base of the falls, were well over thirty geese, all honking angrily at Amy. In front was the goose that Rex had ousted the previous evening, clearly in charge of the assembled flock.

Amy didn't speak much goose at all. Her mallard wasn't bad but goose… well she'd simply never had the opportunity to learn. She could only make out every other word or so.

"…come… you… my home… friends to help… out… You… now… or we… come… get you," the goose honked threateningly.

Amy understood the meaning clearly, even with the missing words.

Rodney appeared by her side, and after a brief glance outside, started leaping in place excitedly.

"Rumble! We're going to have a rumble!"

"A what?" Amy inquired.

The tiny Terrier dashed back into the cave and began waking the others.

Rex sleepily moved to Amy's side and with bleary eyes, stuck his head right through the waterfall. After a moment he withdrew it and faced Amy.

"Well, looks like the Yorkie's right. Those geese are asking for a rumble."

"What in heaven's name is a rumble? "Amy asked, exasperated.

"It's a fight, Goldie," he replied seriously. "They've challenged us to a fight for this cave."

fifteen

And so the rumble began. At first the geese stood back and simply honked abuse at the dogs who, coming out of the cave and around the waterfall, barked at them in response. The lead goose, who was called Vo, was by far the fiercest, urging the others on to greater and greater heights of ire.

The barking and honking diminished as each side began circling the other, evaluating the opponent. By instinct, battle adversaries were chosen, and the dogs and geese focused on those individuals they knew they were going to fight. Amy was amazed at her own calm assessment of three particular wild fowl who were in turn eyeing her with curiosity and apprehension. She was not scared, which surprised her. In fact, she felt exhilarated and was finding it increasingly difficult to hold back from charging the birds. She had no idea what she was supposed to do once the attack was sounded. She only knew that she wanted to get on with it.

Finally, Vo gave the signal and the geese lunged forward, all seeking out their chosen canine targets. It was like nothing Amy had ever imagined. She'd assumed it would be relatively well organized, and like all games of its sort, would be halted before any great pain or damage was done.

Amy learned almost immediately that a rumble was not that sort of game. In fact, it wasn't a game at all.

Vo was the first to attack. With a goose on either side of him, he went straight for Rex. Amy couldn't believe the ferocity of their attack and was transfixed watching it until her own opponents began their assault.

"Keep them away from your back!" Rodney yelled to her as he battled birds.

The first goose began a painful nipping at her ankle, as its surprisingly strong beak clamped down against her bone. She tried to shake it off, but a second bird took the other side, and began to assault another leg. Just as she thought things couldn't get worse, a third goose landed on her back and started in on her neck.

At this point, instinct took over. Amy spun herself in the air, shaking off one goose. She then dropped to the ground and rolled to the side, freeing her limbs from the other two. Without thinking, she lunged out with her back legs and connected with one surprised bird, who was thrown backward right into the pond.

"Nice one!" Rex shouted from his own battle area.

Amy didn't have time to enjoy her success as the other two leapt into the air and descended on her exposed stomach. Amy twisted away from them and with a ferocity that surprised her; she brought her jaws together on the rear of one bird who was trying to grab hold of her tail. It honked loudly in pain and pulled itself free, leaving Amy with a mouthful of feathers.

The battle raged on and on with neither side giving in at all. There wasn't one animal that wasn't hurt in some way, and in some cases quite seriously. Pru had a painful-looking lump over her right eye, while Angel was actually bleeding from a nasty wound on her hindquarters. The geese, however, had definitely fared the worst. There was an assortment of torn wings, bleeding legs, and even one dislocated bill.

Finally Vo honked to signal the end of the fight. He walked up to Rex, who appeared completely unscathed, and looked Rex straight in the eye.

"You fought well," Vo began formally. "I wish I could claim a draw, but I fear that you lot definitely took the match."

"I can't agree," Rex responded with perfect decorum. "It's too close to call. You and your flock fought bravely and I would like to say on behalf of all of us that it was an honor rumbling with you."

Vo bowed proudly, then turned to the other geese and raised his wings high into the air.

"The rumble is finished," he announced majestically. "The result is a draw."

The geese began honking, and those that could, flapped their wings.

Vo turned back to Rex and nodded his head. "A good rumble! A very good rumble!"

"Thank you," Rex replied graciously.

"I would like to invite you and your friends to a small post-rumble supper tonight," Vo offered.

"I would need to ask our leader and the others."

"Of course, I understand."

Rex turned and looked to Rodney, who simply smiled back at him. Rex tilted his head, puzzled by the Terrier's expression.

"Rodney?" Rex asked, "what's going on?"

"I agreed to be your leader while we searched for the park." The Terrier spoke in a calm controlled tone "But now that we're here, I think it's time this group had a real leader. Someone who can not only think but also show some power when needed."

"But…" Rex tried to say.

"No buts! I'm more of a rear-guard kind of dog anyway."

"What are you two rattling on about?" Amy asked as she approached the pair.

"I would like to announce that we have a new leader," Rodney said smiling broadly. "Rex, we are in your paws."

Rex glanced over at the others. They clearly agreed, and with a nod of thanks, Rex turned to Vo and accepted his invitation.

The supper was to take place on the bird sanctuary island just across from the lake's old dilapidated boathouse. Vo explained that it was only a few yards offshore where they would be undisturbed and able to enjoy what he described as the joint victory feast.

The geese gathered themselves up, collecting some of their more vital lost feathers and waddled off toward the lake. After tending to their wounds, the dogs returned to the cave and slept for a while to recover some of their strength after the morning's activities.

Sanctuary Island wasn't far. The dogs passed the restaurant whose trash they'd raided the previous night and then walked along the side of the lake until they spotted the tiny island only a few yards off shore. Vo saw them and waved them to paddle across. There was a moment's hesitation, then Rodney, impatient for dinner, dove in and paddled fiercely across the narrow stretch of water. At his lead, the others followed him in. Even Pru, who had spent the entire day ridding her coat of any signs of battle, slipped into the lake and gracefully swam across.

As they reached the island, the geese stood back politely as the seven soaked dogs shook themselves, sending plumes of water in every direction. The birds tried to keep a straight face, but the sight of the seven canines all shaking themselves in unison was just too hilarious.

Once dry, the dogs were led to a clearing in the center of the island out of sight of the shore. Amy was stunned at the turnout, having expected to see only the geese they'd battled that morning and perhaps a few family members, but nothing like the number she saw before her.

Many other geese were there, as well as swans, ducks, herons and some varieties that Amy didn't recognize. The geese had made arrangements with a team of pelicans that specialized in parties to deliver fresh fish from the lake continuously throughout the night. The ducks had brought tasty little pastries made from breadcrumbs, lake flowers and sunflower seeds, the swans had brought decorative baskets made of water reeds which they'd filled with wild mushrooms and fennel stalks, and the herons brought nothing, claiming they were unaware that it was a "bring something" kind of party. Vo whispered to Amy that they always said that and that if there was a more tight-fisted flock of birds anywhere, he'd certainly like to meet them.

The greatest surprise of the evening was the special drink that was being served in their honor. It was made from dandelion stems, cherry tree bark and orange rind. This latter ingredient was thoughtfully though unconsciously provided by the humans who left a seemingly endless supply of it behind in the park every day. The geese had used a hollowed-out log to hold the ingredients which had been mixed with fountain water (transported by the pelicans). The dogs learned that the beverage had been sitting for over two weeks and that the birds were delighted to have finally found a suitable excuse to dip into it. It tasted delicious, and after a couple of good gulps Amy also realized that it made her feel quite jolly.

After the supper, Vo honked loudly for silence. He hopped onto a raised mound of earth and looked down at the assembled multitude.

"My friends," he began, "those old and those new, I welcome you all to our little gathering. Today my gaggle and I went in search of vengeance for what I'd felt was an injustice carried out against me and mine. I felt that by forcing me out of my waterfall habitat, these animals were questioning my position within the community. I have been your leader for some time now, and I have always tried to make the right decisions for us all. When I called for a rumble this morning, I was wrong. These canines meant no harm to the community or me. They were simply seeking shelter for the night. I allowed my own pride to influence my thoughts and as I now stand here before you, I ask the forgiveness of all of you. Please join me in a toast to our continued well-being here within our park and of course to our new friends, Rex, Pru, Lester, Angel, Rodney, Hans and Amy. You are fine warriors and true friends. Welcome!"

The other birds all rose to their feet and began flapping their wings together joyously. The pelicans performed a dazzling fly-by overhead, which brought tears to Amy's eyes as she watched them gracefully pass before the muted illumination of the mist covered moon.

"Hey, look at me!" Rodney shouted from the clearing.

They turned and saw the Terrier dancing on his hind legs while hopping into the air.

"My biped taught me this," he stammered excitedly.

"I'm sure he did," Rex whispered to Amy. "I really am."

Amy tried not to laugh as they watched Rodney dance with abandon as the moon spotlighted him. His tiny eyes looked like luminous jewels as they twinkled beneath a wild bang of hair.

A silence descended over the party as everyone watched Rodney, letting their thoughts drift into the night toward their own particular dreams and fantasies.

sixteen

The next morning Rex led them on a brisk run.

After a few minutes, they came upon a large bridge that traversed the lake, bisecting it roughly in its center. They watched from below as bipeds sped across above them, some in smelly four wheeled vehicles, some on two wheeled ones that though smaller, made even more noise that the four-wheeled contraptions. There were even some bipeds on two wheeled things that they themselves had to peddle. Humans seemed to go out of their way to devise any means possible to not use their limbs for walking. They were a strange lot!

Back at the lake, the dogs stopped for a rest. Suddenly Pru loudly drew in her breath. As Amy turned to see what had caused this reaction, she saw the look of shock on her friend's face.

"Pru? You O.K.?"

Pru continued to stare at something farther along the shore without saying a word.

Amy tried to see what Pru was looking at, but aside from a small flock of pigeons and a lone human sitting on a bench, there was nothing out of the ordinary.

Pru began to walk down the shore as if in a trance. The others turned from the island and watched her, wondering what she was up to.

The flock of pigeons rose into the air, and Pru kept going, oblivious to their flight.

The lone human turned at the sound of the birds' departure, and Amy could see that it was a female who had recently been crying. She spotted Pru and suddenly stiffened. She looked squarely at the approaching Afghan as her expression turned to one of stunned amazement similar to Pru's.

The biped got slowly to her feet and faced Pru, who stopped in her tracks about twenty yards from her. They stared at each other for a moment. The female's face began to light up in a blaze of joy.

"Pru?" she called out with slight hesitation. "Baby? Is that you?"

Pru moved toward her, slowly at first and then as the biped took a step forward, she broke into a mad fur-whipped run. Suddenly they were in each other's arms, and even from where she stood, Amy could see that both of them were crying openly.

"Think they know each other?" Rex said trying to cover his own emotions.

As she continued to watch the pair hug and caress each other, Amy felt a sharp stab of longing to feel her own Man's caress. She was suddenly homesick and turned away from her friends. After a moment, Pru broke away briefly from her mistress's embrace and ran over to the others.

"I'm going home now," she said between tearful gasps. "Thank you! Thank you all for everything. Maybe I'll see you in the park when we walk."

With that, she trotted back to her mistress, and as the other six dogs looked on, the two walked off, both with their red hair billowing out behind them, and vanished into the city. As they walked away, it became clear to Amy that their relationship was not one of dog and mistress, but of best friends as they chatted and laughed comfortably with each other.

Once they were out of sight, the remaining six looked at each other with expressions of mild confusion until Rex stretched and then turned to face them.

"I hope you lot don't think that gets you out of finishing our little run?"

They all laughed as Rex again set a pace and the six dogs resumed their morning jog, though now with slightly heavier hearts at the loss of one of their own.

seventeen

they spent the rest of the day close to their new home.

During one nap, Amy dreamt that she was back in Burden Dell. At first it appeared as it always had to her, a gentle clearing of long sweet grass nestled between the aged and sheltering trees of the woods. In her dream, though, something was different. She turned and looked in every direction, unable to sense what exactly was wrong. Finally she realized that where normally there were gentle background sounds of birdsong and wind, now there was a steady hum of city noise. Amy looked at the line of trees to find the origin of the unwelcome sound and saw that the trees themselves were not what they appeared to be. They were in fact buildings. She spun around to check the other side of the dell only to find the same thing, only now the trees or whatever they were, were clearly closer than they'd been only moments before. She looked all about her and realized that the strange structures were slowly moving toward her.

She awoke with a start, causing Angel who was dozing next to her to jump as well.

"Sorry," Amy whispered with embarrassment.

"Bad dream?" the Spaniel inquired.

Amy nodded, then shook her head to rid her mind of the dream.

"Oh my," Amy said," that was most unpleasant!"

Angel grinned at her. "I was dreaming about a huge steak all to myself. I had just started to eat it when you woke me."

"Well," Amy responded, "serves you right for not sharing, doesn't it!"

She noticed a missing face.

"Where's Rodney?"

"He went out to check on dinner prospects," Lester replied, stretching.

"You know," Rex said with a look of concern, "the little chap's been gone quite a while. We may have to send out a search party if he's not back…"

"If who's not back?" Rodney asked cheekily as he stepped into the cave.

"About time!"

"Well, I've got good news and I've got bad news," the Terrier began. "First of all, the bins at the restaurant are out. For some silly reason they've put up a fence around them. There's no way in… I checked. I did a quick scout of the park, and I've got to tell you unless you're ready for a diet of nuts and berries there's no food here."

"But that's terrible!" Angel interrupted." What will we do? We have to eat. I mean how will we…"

"Will you let me finish, please?" he chided.

"Sorry!" Angel said as she lowered her head back onto her front paws.

"If you don't mind a slight risk and are ready for a small adventure, I may have the solution." Rodney's eyes sparkled.

"We're listening," Rex said cautiously.

"O.K. I'll need volunteers," he began. "What we'll do is…"

He laid out the plan in surprising detail. It was definitely a risk, but Rodney was convinced it could be carried out.

Fully briefed, Rodney, Rex, Lester and Amy left the safety of the cave, and under cover of darkness made their way diagonally across the park toward the lights of the city.

Hans stayed to guard the cave. Angel had desperately wanted to join the group, but as Rex had explained as gently as he could, she was too small to be effective in the operation and lacking in the necessary speed and maneuverability should a rapid escape be needed. She had clearly been disappointed but had taken it surprisingly well.

The team followed Rodney out of the park and soon came to a strange bridge that was actually a large building with a square taken out of it to fit a road through. As Amy passed under it, she looked up and could plainly see a group of humans talking behind panes of glass directly above her. Most peculiar!

Once past the bridge or tunnel, or whatever it was, they came to a terrifying intersection. The four of them saw vehicles of every conceivable shape and size converge from five different directions, avoiding certain destruction only by observing the little red-, green-, red-light things before them.

"Don't worry!" Rodney shouted above the din. "We don't have to deal with that!"

Rodney led them off to the right and to a tunnel that passed under one of the streets. They all stared at him uncertainly.

"Come on, you've done it before," he coaxed. "It's just like the one that got us to the park the other day!"

"Yes, and the bad bipeds were waiting for us, weren't they?" Amy said with conviction.

"They won't be down here, I promise, Goldie. I checked earlier. We're safe."

The other three stood for a moment summoning their courage, and then, with slow, cautious steps began to descend the steps.

Once at the bottom, they were relieved to find the tunnel empty of people. They took a few hesitant steps and then burst into a fast run, reaching the far end of the tunnel and the stair-way in record time. They laughed at their own nervousness as they climbed up onto another section of road. Rodney led them at a brisk pace around a corner shop, then urged the others down yet another set of steps and through yet another tunnel until finally they emerged at the base of a huge building that was decorated with what to Amy looked like millions of little stars.

"Wow!" Amy exclaimed.

"Not bad, is it," Rodney exclaimed as he continued pushing the team along the front of the immense building to pass win-dow after window of merchandise designed for bipeds to wear or sit on, or just look at.

"What is this place?" Rex asked in a voice filled with awe.

"I haven't the faintest, but it's quite something isn't it" Rod-ney replied.

"Ha...Har...Harro...Harrods...that's it, Harrods!" Lester announced with pride.

The others came to a stunned halt and turned to face him. He had stopped long enough to read the name of the store from the gilded lettering on a set of brass-framed doors.

"You can read?" Amy asked, astonished.

"Don't be ridiculous," Rex said sternly. "Dogs can't read."

"I can, actually," Lester replied meekly. "Not very well, but I can usually put the words together."

"You're not suggesting that you understand biped talk, are you?" Rex demanded.

"No, of course not... well, actually I can sometimes pick out a word here and there."

"Come off it!" Amy exclaimed. "No dog understands biped talk."

"Sure they do. I bet you understand when they say your name, right?"

"Well..." she responded hesitantly.

"Of course you do!" Lester said." We all do! That's the start, then you just concentrate on what they're saying all the time and you begin to pick out patterns. The trick is to look them right in the eye when they're speaking. It's amazing what you can tell from the words that way."

"Can we talk about this later?" Rodney said impatiently. "We have a mission to complete."

The others all nodded and followed him past even more of Harrods' beautifully arranged windows. No more was said about Lester's accomplishment as they focused on the task at paw. They reached the end of the block and waited as Rodney checked their route.

"Okay. We're almost there," he whispered. "You know what to do?"

They all nodded. Rodney gave himself a good stretch and then signaled for the others to stay close. They moved along the next block, carefully staying tight against the building, seeking out the shadows with every step.

"There it is," Rodney pointed with his muzzle toward the end of the next building to a brightly lit doorway. "Can you smell it?"

The others all raised their noses, and after briefly filtering out the other city odors, locked onto a tasty scent indeed.

"You ready?" Rodney asked excitedly.

They nodded as their noses twitched in joyous anticipation of the goodies to come.

"Right then, let's do it!" Rodney yelled as he dashed toward the light.

He reached the entrance and took his position by the open doors as team lookout. The other three followed him in, and as prearranged, split up to carry out their specific assignments.

The place was a small biped feeding stop specializing, if the displays were to be believed, in hamburgers, fried potatoes and other odd shaped items all breaded and forced between two tasty looking buns. There were about ten customers milling about, whom Lester immediately herded into a corner by baring his teeth and growling menacingly. The startled staff watched in horror as Rex and Amy vaulted the counter, and with the aid of a couple of fierce barks, forced them against one wall.

They were in luck. The staff had been packing a couple of large orders before being interrupted. Amy could see that there were two plastic carrier bags loaded with square plastic containers filled with food. She gestured for Rex to grab one as she grabbed the other. They were heavy but just manageable. They dragged them off the counter and across the white tile floor which was decorated with huge golden arches.

As they neared the door, one of the patrons, a large, unhappy-looking man, ran out of the place and bravely swung the doors shut, then leant his entire body weight against them from the outside.

They were trapped! Lester tried to push the doors open, but the male biped's weight was simply too much.

As Amy looked back into the restaurant, she saw that the patrons were beginning to overcome their earlier fear and were slowly edging toward the trapped animals. She turned and looked frantically toward Rodney, who was leaping in place yelping to no avail whatsoever.

Suddenly the man holding the doors let out a blood curdling scream and as everyone looked outside, they saw a proud King Charles Spaniel with a large piece of pant leg dangling from her mouth. The man ran off, limping and cursing as he went.

Lester held the door open for the others as they charged out into the night.

As they ran toward the tunnels and the park beyond, each one praised Angel from the bottom of their still anxiously beating heart. All she could say to each of them was "Too small, too slow?"

They made it back to the park, and despite one of bags rupturing so that they lost a good number of plastic boxes, their haul was substantial.

Once they reached the cave, they divided up the containers prior to opening them to make it fair. Nobody knew what they were getting until each container was opened, when they were startled to find that inside the buns and under the breaded batter was real food! Amy found chicken and Rex actually found some fish. Most of the containers, however, contained thin circles of well-done ground beef that weren't that bad once you'd shaken off the strange red stuff centered on each morsel.

They ate to their hearts' content. They finished off the meat, the buns, the fried potatoes, and even the strange pastry-like tubes filled with something like fruit.

As they ate, they regaled Hans with stories of their expedition. With each new telling, the details became more elastic as they expanded to quite astonishing dimensions. The team became warriors, the bipeds the feared and undefeatable foe, and the captured food... it may as well have been the Holy Grail itself, such were the embellishments.

Finally, sated and exhausted from their story-telling and feasting, the six dogs didn't even have the energy to clear away the debris from the meal and simply collapsed on top of the mass of wrappers and containers. They slept the sleep of the victorious.

eighteen

Even in her sleep Amy heard the sound of human voices. There were a few of them calling out in gentle coaxing tones. She opened one eye and saw Rodney and Rex standing at the cave entrance peering nervously outside.

"What is it?" Amy asked sleepily.

"We're not sure," Rex answered. "It doesn't sound good, though."

Amy jumped to her feet and joined them at the entrance. Through the wall of water they could make out a large number of humans encircling the cave. Suddenly the water stopped flowing and the fall simply ceased to exist. The three dogs were now standing in the unsheltered entry to the cave, visible to the humans. Without the sheen of liquid Amy could clearly see that there were at least a dozen humans, all male and all wearing dark blue uniforms. Each one wore a tall domed blue hat with decorative silverwork on the front.

Amy vaguely recalled seeing bipeds like that before. One had come to the cottage to talk to her Man after another human had tried to climb through the kitchen window one night. As far as she could remember, the uniformed biped had been pleasant, even taking the time to have a brief chat and a tummy rub with her.

The group outside didn't look particularly menacing. In fact, a few of them seemed to be quite enjoying the goings on, whatever the goings on were!

Then something else caught her eye. In front of the uniformed males was a pile of wrappers and containers identical to the ones strewn about the cave. How could that be? She gestured to the others, who upon seeing the colorful pile of debris, turned to each other with deep distress.

"Those are from the bag that broke last night," Rex said.

"Oh blast," Rodney sighed. "We must have left a trail the entire way."

"I'm afraid you're right," Rex agreed.

"So what do we do?" Amy asked, trying to keep the nervous edge from her voice.

"I rather think," Rex began, "that's up to our guests out there."

Amy turned and looked toward the humans who, though not appearing particularly menacing, were staring with amused determination right back at them.

As they wondered what to do, Amy woke up the others and explained their predicament. She was just getting to the part about the wrapper trail when Rex called for her to return to the entrance.

She saw immediately that the uniformed bipeds had been joined by six new gray-clad humans who were not only dressed differently, but were taking the situation far more seriously than the other ones. There were no smiles from the newcomers. As they stood in a line in front of a pair of grey vans, they coldly evaluated the cave and the three visible animals. One of the newcomers broke away from the others and climbed into the rear of one vehicle. He reappeared moments later with a strange canister clutched in one hand. He said something to the other bipeds and then walked toward the cave. Once he was about halfway between the dogs and the humans, he pulled something from the canister, then deftly tossed it over the heads of the three canines at the cave entrance.

Rex, Rodney and Amy watched as the thing bounced into their shelter and rolled into a corner. The others frantically danced out of its way, all staring at it nervously. Almost immediately the thing began emitting white smoke, which instantly started to irritate all the dogs' eyes.

"What's going on?" Amy gasped as tears rolled down her cheeks.

"I don't know," Rodney coughed. "But we can't stay here!"

"He's right," Rex gasped between his own bouts of tear-filled coughs. "Everybody out, now!"

They didn't have to be told twice. Whatever the humans were after couldn't be worse than the pain they were now feeling in their eyes and noses.

They dashed out of the cave and saw that the humans had moved close to the entrance and were holding a cordon of netting between them, cutting off the dogs' escape routes.

The six animals were scared and having trouble seeing clearly out of their tear-filled eyes. There were no ways around the humans. Angel was the first to be taken. She charged the center of the line, hoping to startle the humans, but they simply dropped the net before she reached them. She was swiftly grabbed and carried to one of the vans. Rex and Lester were next. They stood their ground and growled with full fury, only to find themselves netted and then bundled off to the other vehicle. Hans made a brave attempt at climbing up the dry waterfall gully but lost his footing near the top and fell into the pond where with a great deal of barking and splashing, he was captured.

Rodney gave Amy a brave smile and an encouraging nod and then made his move. He almost managed it. He pretended to charge one particular human, focusing on the man's ankles, then at the last moment leapt high into the air and actually made it over the net, only to be caught like a soccer ball in one of the blue-uniformed biped's hands.

That left Amy. She could see that she was well and truly trapped. The line of net-holding humans was closing in fast. She backed against the waterfall rocks and, out of pure fear and hopelessness, closed her eyes as she waited to be grabbed. At first she only heard one honk. She thought she recognized the voice but was too scared to open her eyes. Then she heard others and had to look. She opened her eyes just as at least fifty low-flying geese began dive-bombing the human net line.

The gray-clad humans were taken by surprise and realizing that they were greatly outnumbered, dove to the ground, covering their heads as the huge birds flew at them with great precision. The blue-uniformed bipeds, though having to protect themselves like the others, found humor in the attack. They were lying flat on the ground with their hands over their heads laughing themselves silly. Finally one human shouted a command and the others made a break for their vehicles. This made the blue-uniformed ones laugh even harder as they rolled across the grass trying to keep their blue domed hats in place.

Amy would have laughed herself if Vo hadn't landed in front of her at that moment.

"Sorry we didn't get here sooner," the goose said breathlessly. "You'd better follow me!"

"What about the others?" Amy asked anxiously.

"It's too late, Goldie! They've been taken."

"But I can't just…" Amy began.

"Yes you can, unless you want to just wait until they come back for you. Now move it, girl!"

With that, the goose took to the air and with Amy running along earth-bound, led her up past the restaurant, along the bank of the lake and to the dilapidated old boathouse. Vo landed on the roof and scanned the area.

"OK, Goldie, it's all clear. Ready for a swim?"

"Swim?" she replied confused.

"Yes, swim! You can't stay over here, can you? We'll just have to put you up on the island for a while until we work out what to do next."

"It won't be too much of an imposition?" Amy inquired politely.

Vo laughed at the dog's sense of propriety at such a time.

"I think we'll manage," he responded with amusement. "Now get in the water."

Amy did as she was told and dove into the lake. She paddled across the narrow stretch and was met by a couple of anxious ganders who led her through the bushes and out of sight of the shore.

"You poor thing!" one of them cried.

"What an awful situation," the other added.

Amy gave them both a brave smile and was about to shake off her coat when she stopped and asked them to step back. Once they had moved a respectful distance from her, she shook herself and moved into the clearing just as Vo landed next to her.

"Why don't you rest for a while? You're safe here," Vo said.

"Oh, I couldn't!" Amy exclaimed, "My friends, they've been captured. I have to…"

"You have to what?" Vo interrupted. "There's nothing you can do. They're gone, Goldie. What you need is rest. You'll be able to clear your mind, and then when you wake up, you'll think clearly."

"Do you really think so?" she asked sadly.

"I promise. In fact, I think I'll join you!"

With that he tucked his head under a wing and without further ado, was fast asleep. Amy looked at the other birds and found that they'd all done the same. She decided she might as well join in and stretched herself out in the warm earth of the island clearing.

With one deep sigh she closed her sad eyes and went instantly to sleep.

When she woke in the early afternoon, she found that she was alone in the clearing. She stared out through a gap in the greenery and watched as various humans enjoyed the tranquility of the park. They rowed on the lake, they rode horses, they fished. Some hardy individuals even swam.

Amy could clearly see, even from her seclusion, the sheer enjoyment on the faces of the humans. She suddenly missed the cottage and Cook and her Man! She felt thankful she lived in such a setting and sad not to be there. It was frightening to know where she wanted to be but not have the slightest idea of how to get there.

Amy spent most of the afternoon reflecting on her situation. By evening, she'd managed to make herself very sad, and even as Vo and the other geese returned from their day's efforts and she pretended to feel otherwise, loneliness and homesickness ate away at her.

Vo could tell that she was troubled and tried to ease her sorrow with some lighthearted small talk, but to no avail. He whispered to one of his flock, then took to the air with a determined expression.

Amy tried to join in with the flock as they recounted amusing tales of human encounters, and she even told of her set-to with Cook over the vegetable garden but it only made her more miserable. Finally, feeling completely sorry for herself, she moved off to a spot of ground away from the others and with her head facing away, had a quiet cry.

After a few moments, she heard a loud flapping of wings and turned just in time to see Vo as he landed with great precision. He held a huge slab of beef in his beak. He waddled over to Amy and gently placed the meat at her side.

"I thought that maybe a nice dinner would cheer you up," he said as he turned to go.

"Wait," Amy said as she tried to wipe the tears from her eyes with both paws. "Where'd you get this?"

"It's amazing what people try to cook on those funny little outdoor fires of theirs."

"This was being cooked?" she asked in amazement.

"Not yet, it wasn't," Vo responded with pride. "The poor biped had just brought it outside and made the mistake of putting it down for a moment while he turned his back."

"And you grabbed it?" Amy found the concept quite remarkable.

"We do that a lot. In the summer you can fly overhead and check out what's for dinner. People will try to cook just about anything outdoors as long as it's not raining. We wait until they go inside for something and... voila! We're of course not mad about meat, but it's amazing how much fish they're starting to eat. Or at least trying to," he added with amusement. "Bol over there grabbed an entire salmon earlier this season. "So I'll leave you to feed. You look like you need the time alone. Enjoy it!"

"Vo," Amy said, "thank you. You're sweet"

"Don't be silly! We're all in this world together. If we can't help one another when the need arises, then what's the point?" Vo gave her a nod of encouragement, then waddled off to join the others of his flock.

"What a nice goose!" Amy thought to herself as she bit into her dinner.

nineteen

the next morning Amy was awakened early as the geese prepared themselves for their usual dawn patrols. They would send
out teams to scour the park and to make sure that all was well
within their kingdom. It was a tradition handed down from generation to generation, and Amy was impressed by the organiza-
tion and professionalism with which the task was carried out.

The birds would take off in groups of seven, with one bird in
the lead. Each group would cover one particular section, and
then return to report their findings and to pick up their next
assignment. Amy watched in fascination from her corner of the
clearing. After a short period one of the groups returned, led by
Bol. Instead of reporting in to the command group, he waddled
urgently over to Amy.

"Wasn't one of your group an Afghan?" he asked.

"Yes," Amy responded with curiosity. "But why—"

"Name of Pru?" he continued.

"Why, yes!" she exclaimed. "Where is she?"

"Walking with her mistress by the falls. I picked up her bark
from the air. She's calling for you and the others. I didn't want to
alarm the human, so I came right back to tell you. Want me to
show you where they are?"

"No, thank you, Bol. You've done enough already"

"Thank you, ma'am," he replied with a military tone.

She watched as he returned to his group, who immediately took to the air to complete their sortie. Amy made her way to the shore of the island. She checked that all was clear, then dove into the water. She reached shore next to the boathouse and after a thorough shake, trotted off toward the falls. She wanted desperately to run, but at the same time knew that she mustn't attract any attention to herself.

Amy passed the restaurant and saw a long line of people waiting to select their meal from a brightly lighted display case. What with the harsh neon lights, and the bright metallic packaging of the food itself, Amy was surprised that anyone would be tempted to consume any of it.

She passed by the heavily fenced-in trash bins and smiled at the brief memory that struck her. She reached the sloping path that led to the waterfall and the cave that had sheltered them so recently. Amy looked anxiously for Pru but couldn't see her anywhere. She hoped that she wasn't too late. She had to find her friend to tell her what happened. Then the two of them could start a search for the others.

She checked all around the enclosure, but found no trace of the Afghan. She began to panic. She ran along an adjoining path and still couldn't spot her friend. She should have let Bol lead her from the air as he'd offered.

Amy turned another corner and found herself next to the soft earth of the park's horse trail. A well groomed Arab mix was cantering by, trying to train his nervous rider, when he spotted Amy and came to a sudden halt, almost dismounting his charge.

"Is your name Goldie, by any chance?" he asked.

"Yes," she cried. "That's what the others call me."

"Thought you might be. Her description was spot-on!"

"Whose description?" Amy asked excitedly. "Have you seen Pru?"

"If you're referring to a fine looking redheaded canine, then yes, I am," he replied calmly, ignoring his rider's attempts at moving him on. "She's about a hundred yards down the path just over that rise. I passed her only a few minutes ago. She's anxious to speak with you."

"Thank you. Thank you very much!" Amy shouted over her shoulder as she began to run toward her friend.

"Good luck!" the Arab mix called after her. He glanced up at his irate rider. "Now let's deal with you, shall we?"

Amy covered the distance in seconds, but again saw no signs of Pru. She scanned the park from an excellent position atop the rise but saw no trace of her. She couldn't believe that she'd missed her friend and began running down one path after another hoping to find even the most minute clue.

Finally, out of breath, exhausted and with a heavy heart she made her way back to the boathouse and the island beyond. She passed the waterfall and pond, climbed the sloping path to the restaurant, and walked despondently along the shore of the lake.

"So there you are!" Pru screamed with delight.

Amy looked up and saw her friend as she sat obediently next to her mistress by the same park bench where the two of them had been reunited just the other day.

"I've been looking for you everywhere!" Amy cried out as she dashed over to greet her friend. "I've got to speak with you. Can you break away for a bit?"

"I suppose so," she replied, hesitantly glancing up at her mistress, who appeared completely engrossed by a paperback novel in her hands. "Let's pretend to chase birds. She'll allow that."

"Good idea," Amy nodded. "I'll lead."

With that, Amy suddenly dashed by the bench at full speed, barking frantically as she headed for a flock of pigeons lunching on the grass. Pru tugged urgently at her lead, and with great understanding from her mistress, was released to join in the fun. The two dogs tore after the startled birds.

Once away from her mistress, Pru stopped and turned to Amy with a worried look on her exotic features.

"Where are the others?" she inquired, trying to mask her concern.

"They're gone, Pru! They've been taken!"

Amy could see the color pale under the Afghan's fine coat. She suggested that they sit so she could explain what happened. She in fact thought Pru looked suddenly unsteady on her feet and was afraid the other animal might fall over.

Once seated, Amy told of the events leading up to the capture of their friends. Pru listened intently, occasionally shaking her head in amazement at the antics of the others. As Amy recounted the details of the capture and her subsequent lonely night spent on Sanctuary Island, Pru's eyes welled up with tears.

"...and then... well there you were!" Amy said, finishing the story. She looked into the Afghan's misty eyes and could see not only the sadness that rested there, but the beginnings of guilt.

"Pru, there were too many of them," Amy reassured her. "If you'd been there, you would only have been taken like the others. At least this way you're free, and between us, we can go into the city and track them down!"

"Oh, Goldie, I wish I could," Pru said in a sad and troubled voice, "but I really can't, don't you see?"

"Don't I see what?" Amy tried to conceal her irritation.

"I can't leave home again. It was too much for my mistress. You saw how she looked the other day. Alone, hurt, sad..."

"And what about Rodney and Rex and the others?" Amy snapped. "Don't you think they're feeling just a bit alone and hurt and sad right now?"

"Please don't be angry with me, Goldie. I am what I am. I'm a show dog! All I have are my looks. I'm not brave or smart like you. I'm not fast like Rodney or fierce like Rex or Hans. I'm certainly not cunning like Angel. I'm just a pretty hound who likes to look her best and be groomed by her mistress. I'm no good for anything else. I never have been."

Amy studied the other animal and though angry at her weakness, also felt a stab of pity.

"I'm sorry, Pru," Amy said soothingly. "I didn't mean to suggest you give up your home again. That was unfair of me. I'm just at a loss as to what to do. I don't have a clue as to where to even begin looking for the others... Pru?... Pru?"

Pru was staring up at the sky with a pensive look.

"Pru!"

"Oh, sorry. I was just thinking. You know I really am a silly dog sometimes. I swear if I weren't on a leash half the time, I think I'd..."

"Pru!" Amy interrupted impatiently. "What did you think of?"

"Oh, yes... Sorry," she said blushing. "I do go on, don't I... Well, you said that they were taken by humans in gray uniforms and others in blue uniforms with tall funny hats?"

Amy nodded. "So?"

"The ones in blue sound like policemen. Those are good humans."

Amy nodded. Pru again stared up at the sky.

"Weren't we discussing something important before?" Amy asked.

"Were we?" Pru tried to recall.

"Of course! The others! You started to tell me about policemen and..."

"Oh yes!" Pru interrupted, suddenly remembering. "I think I know where they are!"

"What?" Amy exclaimed in frustration "And you didn't say anything?"

"I'm saying it now," Pru responded calmly. "You know, Goldie, you need to relax. You seem touchy today."

"I'm sorry, Pru. Please go on."

"On our daily walk to the park, we pass a police station!"

"A what?" Amy asked in a forced calm tone.

"That's where policemen live! Anyway, there's a kennel behind the main building, and I think that's where stray dogs are kept before they're sent to the pound."

"What's a stray... and what's a pound? Really, Pru, can't you talk canine? I don't know half these words."

"A stray is a dog that doesn't have a home," Pru began.

"But we do have homes," Amy said.

"Yes, but the policemen don't know that, do they? And the pound is... well the pound is the ultimate bad place."

"Okay... okay... we'll get back to that," Amy said impatiently. "So you think there's this kennel where... how bad a place?"

"You don't want to know. I've heard if you end up in the pound, you're never seen again."

"Oh my!" Amy exclaimed.

Pru gave her a grave nod. "So anyway, there's this kennel which I'm certain is used to hold the strays that are picked up in the park. It takes them a couple of days before the animals are moved to the... pound." Pru had to swallow hard just at the mention of the place. "So I bet you the others are still there."

"Well, let's go. You can show me where it is!" Amy cried.

"I'm not going to leave my mistress, but I'll tell you what. I'll let her know that I've had enough park and I'll lead her down the road with the police station. You just follow us and I'll signal when we're there."

"What if she takes you a different route?" Amy asked worriedly.

"I can usually get her to go my way, but if I can't, you need to find Walton Street."

"How do I do that?" Amy inquired.

"Just ask directions and read the signs."

"You can read, too! I give up!" Amy replied burying her muzzle beneath her front paws.

"I'll go over to my mistress now and let her know that I want to go home. You stay behind us and follow. Not too close. I don't want to upset her."

"Thanks, Pru!"

"I wish I could do more, but I simply can't. I hope you understand."

"I do… really!"

After a brief nose touch, Pru ran off toward the lake and her waiting mistress.

As she had promised, Pru let her biped know that she was ready to leave in what Amy felt was record time. Normally, with humans not being as bright as canines, it took repeated attempts before they caught on to a request. Not in Pru's case. She walked up to her mistress, picked her lead up in her mouth then turned to face the pathway that led back to the city and their home. The female caught on instantly and rose to her feet. She attached the leash and allowed Pru to lead the way.

Amy followed at what she felt was a sensible distance. As they walked past the waterfall, Amy noticed Pru give their old shelter a brief look, and then, as if being driven by the memory of her recently captured friends, she picked up the pace.

After crossing the horse path, they reached the end of the park and the beginning of the city. Amy watched as they crossed the first of what she knew would be many streets and felt a shiver run through her body. She took a moment to look back at the park with its gentle hillocks and sheltering trees and knew somehow that she wouldn't be coming back. She took one last deep breath of the sweet-scented park air, then turned and faced the harshness of the looming city. She swallowed hard then stepped off the grass and onto the cold hard pavement.

twenty

Amy soon found that her biggest problem was not their seeing her but of her making certain she could see them. Pru was maintaining a good pace, and though in the park it had been puppy's play to keep up with them, it was a different thing altogether on the crowded streets. There was a definite method to city walking that Amy hadn't realized existed. When the group had been together and they'd moved through the city, they'd mainly kept to streets where people lived. This was an entirely different game of fetch!

There were bipeds everywhere, moving in every direction at once with, to Amy, little or no order whatsoever. She was amazed to see the humans even run into each other. Sometimes a rapid verbal exchange took place, but for the most part they'd simply collide, readjust their heading, and speed off without any indication that anything had happened at all.

What astonished Amy most were the expressions on the faces of the bipeds. They were clearly all in a rush to get somewhere, and yet they all looked so intensely unhappy. Amy couldn't understand why, if this maniacal rushing and colliding ritual was so distasteful to them all, they didn't just stop or at least slow down. She felt that if they'd all just take the time to perhaps visit the park and, who knows, chase a squirrel or a pigeon, they'd feel a lot better.

She had to dismiss her thoughts because she was having an exceedingly hard time keeping Pru's hindquarters in view. Pru was amazingly good at city walking and was able to dodge and weave with great skill. Even her mistress had the moves down and rarely collided with anyone.

Amy, on the other hand, was having a hard time of it. She had been tripped over, stepped on, kicked, and once almost fallen over. Luckily, she'd seen the shadow and sidestepped the large heavily perfumed female before the biped landed on her.

As she strode to keep up with Pru, something on her left caught her eye. Her jaw dropped open as she looked into the beautifully arranged windows of what she had only recently learned was a place called Harrods. She realized in horror that if she was next to Harrods, then just up ahead had to be... before she could even finish the thought, she saw it. She was about to pass right in front of the biped feeding place that they'd attacked so recently. She felt her mouth go dry, knowing that they were certain to be still looking for the perpetrators of the heinous crime. There was no other choice but to go for it.

Pru and her mistress passed right in front of the place without so much as a glance. Amy readied herself and with every nerve end screaming within her tense frame, she ran past the glass-paned entrance. She waited for the screams and shouts that she knew were imminent, but nothing happened. Nothing at all. She risked a glance over her shoulder and saw that no one even seemed to have noticed her. She returned to the task of following Pru and saw to her disbelief that she was gone!

Amy's panic lasted for only as long as it took her to reach the next corner. Pru and her mistress had turned left off the main street and sensing that Amy might have missed the move, the Afghan had feigned sudden intense interest in a large tabby cat seated on a nearby window ledge. Pru's mistress tried to urge her away from the startled feline, but she stood firm, barking at the cat just long enough for Amy to reach the corner and spot her.

Even from where Amy was, she couldn't miss Pru's expression, as if to say, "Pay attention, silly dog!"

Once they'd left the main street, tracking became much easier for Amy. There were far fewer bipeds to avoid and plenty of stairways on which she could raise herself to get a better view of her two targets. The street they were on was narrow and crammed on either side with one feeding place after another, many of them located down stone stairs in converted basements.

Amy couldn't believe the smells from the many different restaurants, and it was difficult to keep her attention focused on Pru and her biped with so many distractions so close at hand. She tried to close her senses and ignore everything but the Afghan but found it near impossible. Even as she tried to keep her eyes locked ahead of her, she would glance at different restaurants as she smelled one exotic kind of food after another.

"Goldie! Will you keep up!" Pru barked from the end of the street, startling her mistress.

Amy refocused on the task at hand and followed Pru at the prescribed distance down the rest of the street. Though still being assaulted by the sights, sounds and smells of the place, she kept her head forward and simply inhaled the spicy air without letting it distract her.

Pru made a right turn at an intersection and then glanced back to be sure that Amy had seen the turn. She had. The threesome continued their journey for a short distance farther until Pru stopped at a particular lamppost and made a great show of examining it. Her mistress stood patiently by as the Afghan went through the motions of claiming the post as her own. In fact, unknown to her biped, Pru signaled to Amy that they'd arrived.

Amy looked over at her friend and then at the building she was next to. Other than spotting an odd blue lamp hanging in its entrance, Amy saw little difference between that building and many others she'd seen in the city, but as she watched, three blue-uniformed humans stepped out the front door and climbed into a bright red vehicle with a colored dome on its roof.

Amy decided that this must be what Pru had referred to as the police station. She glanced over at the Afghan and saw that she was staring back at Amy with large, sad eyes. Amy couldn't just let her walk away, so with a show of great casualness, she trotted over to Pru and gave her a sniff as if meeting for the first time.

"Are you sure you don't want to stay with me and free the others?" Amy asked in a whisper.

"Stop it, Goldie! You know how I feel. Please don't make it harder than it already is."

Amy nodded as she looked for the last time upon the features of her friend. There was no more to be said and with a final parting lick on Amy's cheek, Pru turned and led her Woman to the end of the block, then turned and walked out of sight and out of Amy's life.

Amy sat where she was for a moment until she realized that a couple of policemen were pointing at her from the front door of the building. That was all she needed, to be grabbed at this point and thrown in a cell.

Pru had told her that the kennels were located at the rear of the building, so her first priority was to find a way to get there. This, it turned out wasn't that simple. The police station was just one building in a row of nearly identical structures all built together without any space between them. Logic told Amy that if there was a front there certainly had to be a back and that she was just going to have to search until she found it.

It proved to be quite an undertaking. She walked the entire length of the street and found no alley or even a gap between the buildings. She rounded the corner and found that the structures on that street were also built tightly together with no access whatsoever to their rear.

Amy sat for a moment and gave the matter some deep thought. She'd walked one length and found no breaks. She'd turned right and done the same. Her mind began to actually hurt as she tried to focus on the problem. Every time she'd get close to figuring it out, the pieces of the puzzle would simply disappear like wood smoke.

Such was her determination to find the back of the police station, she retraced her steps. It was, as it turned out, the best thing she could have done. Amy retraced her steps right back to the front of the police station where she again sat down in complete frustration. As she tried again to piece the puzzle together she heard the distinct sound of another dog's growl. She turned and spotted the Boxer leading Fat Man out of the police station. The Boxer tried to charge Amy but only succeeded in nearly choking himself because of Fat Man's slow reflexes in releasing the leash.

Amy used the extra seconds she'd been afforded to run at full tilt away from the police station back toward the street with the wonderful restaurant smells. After only a few yards, she noticed one of those cobblestone lanes that Angel called a mews leading off the street. Something told Any to make the turn even though she had no idea where the mews led. She managed a quick glance over her shoulder and was relieved to see that Fat Man and Boxer had somehow gotten themselves tangled round a street lamp.

The Boxer was straining to be released to chase Amy, but Fat Man was far more interested in his own release from the leather restraint.

Amy dashed down the mews and found to her delight that it was in fact crossed about halfway down by another mews that led to and opened on to… yes! The back of the police station, attached to which was a long single story annex with high set windows.

She edged round the structure and found that the backside was made up of small meshed enclosures leading from the building. Each one housed a canine.

She came face to face with the oddest looking hound she'd ever seen. He was slightly smaller than she, had short brown hair and was made up, or so it appeared, of nothing but wrinkles. Not the thin narrow lines that appeared on the faces of bipeds when they laughed, cried or simply got older, but huge furrows of flesh that Amy couldn't remember ever having seen before on any living thing.

The strange breed smiled broadly at her, sending a couple of facial folds off to a different location entirely. Amy tried not to stare at the fleshy migration and instead focused on the animal's eyes which she found to her amazement were quite beautiful.

"Would you, perhaps have seen my friends? It's a group of five dogs. A Yorkie, a Rottweiler…"she asked him.

"Are you asking about a group of five?"

"Yes!" Amy responded excitedly. "Have you seen them?"

"Not personally, no, but I've had a lengthy bark with a couple of members of the group. They're isolated inside the barracks here, but that's never stopped a canine from having a tongue wag has it?"

"No, I suppose not," Amy said, warming to the odd-looking animal.

"I spoke with a Yorkie and a Doberman. Fine fellows both of them," he said as he tried to recall something from the back of his mind. "Goldie! You must be Goldie!"

"Amy, actually, but they call me Goldie… yes, that's me. So they really are here, and they're safe," she cried, near to tears. "Oh, please tell me where they are. I must see them."

"Not a chance. They're shut up in the big holding cell inside the building. No windows to the outside… only a skylight on the roof. That's how I've managed to talk with them. Bit of a strain on the old voicebox but you can do it if you really try. It's simply a case of—"

"No!" she interrupted "I've come here to see my friends and I won't settle for long-distance barks. There must be some way to get inside the place. Please think. I need your help."

The other animal looked at Amy with pity, fully understanding her plight. He closed his eyes and repositioned a few more wrinkles as he gave the matter some deep thought.

"There's one way," he said proudly as a thought struck him. "I've only been here a couple of days, but every morning new bipeds show up to look for their lost animals. They're always accompanied by policemen and usually don't stay long, but while they're here, the outer door is left open. You could, if you were daft enough, slip in after them and see your friends."

"Really! Do you honestly think I could?" she asked excitedly.

"Yes, I'm certain you could... it's whether you *should*." His face took on a serious expression requiring the gathering and resorting of a full battalion of wrinkles. "But—once inside the humans will see you. There's nowhere to hide. You'll have to dash in, say hello and dash out and keep your paws crossed that someone doesn't close the door!"

Amy looked back at the other dog with concern mixed with excitement. "I'll just have to be careful, won't I?"

"That you will! Are you certain I can't tempt you with a simple bark chat with them? I'm sure they'd be delighted with that!"

"No, but thank you for caring. My friends and I have been through quite a bit together. I don't think any of them would do any less to see me."

"Well, it's your pelt!" he replied with an encouraging grin. "The door's just down on the side wall, and I wish you all the best!"

"Thank you. Thank you very much... Do you realize I don't even know your name."

"How rude of me," he uttered, clearly embarrassed by his own bad manners. "My name is Rumple."

She gave him a brief nose touch through the wire mesh and then moved off to locate the door. It was right where Rumple had said, and to Amy's relief, directly across from a row of trash bins that made an excellent hiding place.

As it turned out, she didn't have long to wait. She heard the bipeds before seeing them. She could tell that there was a young boy of about seven biped years and his mother, who was attempting with little success to console the child. They were being led by a female policeman, who was trying to act official but was having trouble remaining cold and professional when faced with a small weeping child.

They reached the door, and as Rumple had promised, once they entered, they did indeed leave the door open. Amy took a hard swallow, then dashed across the yard and through the door. The bipeds had only progressed a few paws into the building and were astonished at the sight of a speeding mass of golden brown fur that streaked by them.

Amy didn't even look at the humans as she sped by; there wasn't time. She tore down the narrow corridor past one cell after another as each occupant began barking encouragement for her brave maneuver. At the far end of the building was a large holding pen with a drop cloth hung to ward off prying eyes. Amy covered the distance in milliseconds and without a thought grabbed the cloth in her teeth and pulled it down.

Inside the enclosure, a startled looking recumbent Labrador looked up at Amy as a group of hungry pups nursed hungrily at her exposed teats.

'Oh my!" Amy exclaimed, "I'm so sorry—I thought..."

"Nice one, Goldie!" Rodney said smugly from behind her.

She spun around and saw the entire gang locked up in a smaller but still quite large cell next to the one with the new mother and her pups.

"I can't stay. I just wanted you to know that I'm here and I'll think of some way to get you out," she said as fast as she could. Even as her words poured out, she could hear the sound of biped feet running toward her. She turned and saw the female policeman coming right for her.

"I'll stay close," she cried, "I love you all, but I gotta go!"

She charged right at the oncoming human, which was clearly not what the startled female expected.

As she ran off, Rex called after her, "Be careful, Goldie. Fat Man and Boxer were just here."

"I know!" she shouted back just as she dove under the legs of the female policewoman. The young boy and his mother stared open-mouthed as Amy dashed by them.

Just as she was about to reach the door, Amy heard the young boy scream with delight and yell, "Rumple! You're here! Mummy, look, we've found him! Rumple!... Oh Rumple!"

Amy couldn't help but smile, knowing that the strange-looking animal's recent good deed was being almost immediately rewarded as his lost family rejoiced in his discovery.

twenty one

Amy made her escape cleanly, relieved to find no trace of Fat Man and Boxer as she crept along the mews and then out onto what from Pru's directions she presumed was Walton Street.

She'd seen the others, if only for a fleeting moment and she knew they were safe, yet something was troubling her. Some seed of discontent was trying to take root within her thoughts but she just couldn't seem to grasp what it was. She did know, however, that she'd not had breakfast or lunch and was feeling quite peckish.

She wandered down Walton Street until it curved sharply to the right, then came upon a wonderful vision. A small restaurant was obviously taking delivery of their fresh provisions. It must have been their delivery time, as three vans were parked up on the pavement. One carried fruits and vegetables, another, fish and poultry and the last, and by far the most interesting, meat!

What was astounding was that the biped drivers of the vehicles were all gathered in the restaurant doorway, laughing with exaggerated gusto for the benefit of a poor deformed female biped. She seemed almost normal to Amy, even quite pretty for a human, if it hadn't been for the poor creature's chest. Instead of the usually flat or occasionally slightly rounded area on the front of bipeds, this poor female had been saddled with two enormous mounds that seemed to reach straight out in front of her with their pointy ends trying to leap right out of her scanty top. Amy thought how sweet those young male bipeds were to feel enough charity in their hearts to keep company with the sadly afflicted female.

As she began to creep toward the meat van, the thought that had eluded her earlier suddenly came into clear focus.

Fat Man and Boxer! What were they doing at that police station?

Amy gave that some deep thought and couldn't come close to finding a reasonable answer, so she allowed it to drift away as she turned her attention back to the meat.

She glanced at the drivers and saw that they were still being kind to the female, who seemed to be almost enjoying their charitable attention.

"Poor thing," Amy thought to herself as she watched her toss her long blond hair from one side to the other and laugh toothily at the three males.

Amy reached the meat van unseen and carefully stepped up into its open storage area. She had never seen anything like it. There was so much meat! If only she could take it all, she could feed herself and the others forever!

She couldn't, however, and had to therefore settle on a choice leg of lamb, which though it was heavy, she was able to half-drag, half-carry onto the street.

"Hey! You little thief!" the driver of the van shouted from the restaurant entrance.

Amy froze in her tracks and turned her trembling head to face him. The man was about to step toward her when the deformed female who was laughing at Amy's antics, grabbed his arm and gently calmed him down.

Amy heard the words, "Oh, let the poor animal have it, Burt. Look how hungry she looks."

Whatever the words meant, the male seemed to almost melt under her touch and voice.

"Oh what the 'ell," he said in a gruff but resigned tone. "Get off with ya and enjoy it."

Amy suddenly realized that for some unknown reason she was being allowed to make off with the stolen meat. She slowly edged her way back around the corner of Walton Street, eying the humans every inch of the way, expecting them to change their minds at any instant.

They didn't, and she made it around the corner and out of sight. Still terrified but also elated, Amy hoisted the leg of lamb into a better carrying position between her teeth and ran off in search of a secure environment in which to partake of her booty.

She located a good spot at the bottom of a flight of basement stairs belonging to a residence that appeared to have been vacant for a long time. Amy slid her feast into a small nook under the stone steps, and though it was slightly damp and smelly, she was able to relax and enjoy her meal.

As she ate, she listened intently to the sounds of the city, which never let up for even a second, and then, despite them, she felt her eyes slowly shut as the recent feeding worked to sooth her nerves and warm her belly. She knew that she needed to stay close to the police station and the others, but she had to nap for just a few moments.

twenty two

Even in her sleep she heard it. Even over the cacophony of city sounds she couldn't miss it. Even tucked at the bottom of a basement stairwell with her head buried under her paws she heard her friends. They were calling for help.

Amy's head shot up and she listened. At first she thought that it must have been a dream but she clearly heard them. Something was wrong at the police station.

She climbed the stone steps to the street level. She had a clear view down Walton Street to the station entrance, but could see nothing out of the ordinary. Carried along on the air, however, she heard the pleading cries of help from her imprisoned friends.

Amy broke into a run and passed in front of the station, then turned down the mews. She reached the intersecting mews and heard an engine. An all-too-familiar engine. Then she saw the vehicle to which the sound belonged. The gray van was leaving the kennel area, and Amy could hear the cries from within. The afternoon sun was reflecting off the vehicle's windshield, making it impossible for Amy to see who was inside operating it, but she had a pretty good idea.

She didn't have the slightest clue how to stop the van. It was heading straight for her and she was all that stood between her friends' freedom and the villainous hands of Squat Lady and the others.

Amy felt herself go suddenly calm. A coldness ran through her body, and she knew that she had to stop the rushing gray vehicle, and then sat herself defiantly in its path. As it closed in on her, the sun passed behind a cloud and she could see clearly through the windshield. Fat Man was at the wheel. Next to him, tightly wedged together, were Skull Face and Squat Lady. Amy heard the engine grow louder and suddenly higher in pitch. The van was speeding up.

Amy realized that a dead Retriever wasn't going to be of much help to anyone. She dove off to the side of the mews as the van sped by. She turned just in time to see Squat Lady's pudgy, pig-like features glare out through the side window at her. For the briefest second, Amy's eyes locked with the monstrous female's and Amy realized suddenly that she wasn't looking into the eyes of a normal human at all. These eyes were dark and lifeless almost like those of a fish that she'd seen Cook preparing for her master's supper.

The van reached the end of the mews and turned off onto Walton Street. Amy broke into a run and chased after it. She could hear her friends calling for her from behind the gray metal panels of the van.

Amy reached the street and saw that the vehicle had picked up speed and was already crossing the intersection of Walton Street and the funny road with all the restaurants. She continued running after it, but she already knew that her speed was no match for the power of a human-built engine.

Amy watched as the van rounded a series of curves. As the road straightened out, the vehicle began to accelerate, pulling even further away from her.

As she used every last ounce of strength in her system and ran faster than she'd ever thought possible, she saw something odd happen. First there was a loud squealing of rubber, and Amy saw the van swerve violently off to one side. The gray vehicle then brushed against a lamppost, bounced off it, turned on its side and with a deafening sound of grinding metal, skidded along the pavement until finally it came to rest against another lamppost.

Amy couldn't believe what she was seeing. She wondered what could possibly have occurred until she looked back to where the incident began. There standing on a biped crosswalk, were Pru and her mistress. The Afghan had somehow managed to pull her female onto the crossing in the path of the speeding van, forcing it to avoid hitting the human by whatever means possible.

Pru's mistress was deathly pale, wide-eyed with fright and shaking like a leaf. Pru also looked anxious, but also proud of her brave and seemingly successful ploy.

Amy gave the Afghan a big smile and a nod of thanks but didn't have time to say more. Her immediate concern was for her friends inside the now battered vehicle. Pru tried to force her Woman to move over to the wrecked van, but the female clearly had had quite enough and dragged the straining hound off in the direction of the police station, presumably to report the incident.

Amy approached the smashed vehicle which, though its motor was silent, was now leaking a variety of unpleasantly odoriferous fluids out onto the pavement and street. Steam was also escaping from the thing.

Amy saw that the rear doors of the van had sprung open during the accident, leaving a sizeable gap between them. She climbed over a pool of jet-black liquid and raised her paws to the opening. With only the slightest weight, the left door flew open, slamming against the pavement.

She immediately saw that the occupants of the vehicle had all been dumped unceremoniously to one side of the van's interior and in the case of the canines, creating a large pile of fur, heads and feet.

She saw with relief that the furry mass was moving. Hans was the first to extricate himself from the pile. Then one by one the others untangled themselves and stepped shakily out of the wreck. Amy urged them to hurry, as the humans were busy disentangling themselves at the same time. The Boxer was also trying to sort himself out but was stuck on his back, with the vehicle's spare tire pinning him to the floor. He was struggling madly and was clearly about to hurt himself.

Amy stepped further into the van and raised one side of the tire with her head, allowing the other animal to crawl out from under it. The Boxer got to his feet and shook himself vigorously, then faced Amy with a cold and angry stare.

"What did you do that for?" he asked in a low growl.

"You were stuck and about to hurt yourself."

The Boxer looked over at his humans and saw that they were near to freeing themselves. "You know this doesn't change anything."

"I didn't help you for that reason," Amy responded matter-of-factly. "Go help your bipeds while I help my friends."

"Amy!" Rex called out urgently, "over here, quick!"

Amy turned away from the Boxer and looked over at Rex, who was kneeling next to the still form of Rodney. She moved over to them and anxiously nosed her little friend. His eyes were closed and at first her heart went cold at the thought that he'd left them, but then she realized that he was in fact breathing.

Rex turned to Amy. "He's hurt, Goldie. What are we going to do?"

As if in answer to the question, the humans in the front of the van began moving toward them. Squat Lady had a nasty cut over one eye, which made her already piggish features even uglier. She slid her squat shape along the side of the vehicle as an evil smile began to form on her thin blue lips.

Skull Face also began edging toward them, following Squat Lady so closely that her posterior was only inches from his face. He did not seem to mind.

Fat Man was also on the move as he heaved his sizeable bulk up and through the driver's side window. The dogs all looked anxiously at each other, desperately seeking a solution to their predicament.

"Go!" shouted the Boxer.

"We can't leave our friend," Amy responded gesturing to the small unmoving Terrier at her feet.

"You don't have a choice! Now, get moving before they get all of you!"

"He's right, Goldie," Angel said, gently nudging Amy toward the exit.

Amy looked at the Boxer, then at the humans, then at the others. She took a deep swallow and glanced down at Rodney. "I'm sorry, little friend."

She gave the injured Terrier a final lick and dove out of the van just as Squat Lady was about to grab her. She joined the others as they broke into a fast run but felt no elation at all, only the stinging of her tears and the weight of her heavy heart.

She managed one quick look back at the wrecked vehicle and saw that Fat Man was attaching a lead to the Boxer, presumably to follow their trail. Her final view, however, was one that almost froze her soul. Squat Lady had picked up Rodney and was holding the stricken animal out for Amy to see. The message was clear. Very clear.

twenty three

The five dogs charged across the street and started down a narrow road off to their left. They saw a pair of policemen walking toward them. They turned and saw that Fat Man and Boxer, who was clearly now all business as he strained angrily against the leash, were effectively blocking their other escape route.

The five dogs came to a screeching halt, turning every which way searching for a way past the biped obstacles.

"Harrods!" yelled Lester.

"What?" Amy shouted back.

"Harrods! They'll never find us in there," Lester insisted.

"We're nowhere near Harrods!" Rex said urgently.

"I beg to differ," Lester said with surprising calm. He gestured to a pair of brass-framed doors right next to them. The gilded lettering on the door was becoming familiar to Amy.

"This place must be huge. It's everywhere!" she exclaimed.

The policemen and Fat Man and Boxer were rapidly closing in on them. Five pairs of nervous canine eyes exchanged looks of desperation as the bipeds approached.

"Well?" Lester asked urgently, again gesturing to the double doors.

As if in answer to his urging, the doors suddenly opened as a large female emerged. She seemed determined to get not only her own bulk but also an armful of parcels out of the portal at the same time.

Thinking as one, the five dogs dashed for the door at the same time.

They all dove between her fleshy legs and managed to enter the store, despite the protestations from the hefty human. In the dogs' wake they could clearly hear the angry voices of the policemen as well as the high pitched squealing of the large biped who was now firmly wedged in the doorway.

Amy risked a quick look back and saw with amusement that the police and Fat Man were trying desperately to coax the female into releasing her parcels just long enough to free her from her entrapment. She didn't seem to understand them as she continued screaming and wiggling in place, resulting only in wedging herself still tighter in the door frame.

The dogs dashed through a huge room, filled with items of human male clothing. Bipeds were literally leaping aside as the dogs ran through the store. As they reached the center of the males' clothing area, they were suddenly struck by an all-consuming scent. All five animals came to a halt as their noses began twitching uncontrollably. Their minds couldn't analyze the information that their noses were picking up. It was an odor that went far beyond any normal scent. It had power. It had body and soul. It had weight as it hung on every molecule of air around the dogs. This was not a scent like the ones that appear on wafts of air, pass over you, then dissipate into oblivion. This scent was a solid. It had something to do with food, that they knew, but it wasn't simply one food or even the smell found, say, in a butcher's where many odors were compounded into one odoriferous melee. This scent had layer upon layer of subtleties and varieties that simply baffled the senses of the canines. It was almost too much to bear as their salivary glands began to work. Amy felt herself begin to drool, and though she was terribly embarrassed, was completely unable to stop.

The animals all looked at each other and began to laugh as the vision of their friends standing there drooling, struck home.

"Well, I don't know what it is," Angel stated, "but I certainly am going to find out."

With that, the Spaniel turned toward a marble corridor that led toward the source of the smell. The others glanced at each other, and then, without a word said, followed Angel toward the heart of the huge store.

They didn't have far to go. They passed a row of heavy brass doors that kept chiming, then opening and disgorging a new and different selection of bipeds every few seconds. They had to stop and observe this ritual because it really was baffling. They would have liked to stay longer watching this odd ceremony, but they were beginning to attract attention. Humans were pointing at them as they scurried, alarmed and even scared, as far from the drooling dogs as possible. Amy thought this odd until she looked at her friends with a different eye, seeing them, and herself as the bipeds did. The dogs had been through quite a lot and were for the most part rather ragged-looking. Amy decided that they'd best keep moving; besides, the source of the mystery scent was close.

They stepped into a cavernous chamber, filled with food. It wasn't food of great interest to the dogs; it was more the type the humans seemed to prefer. Cooked, seasoned, decorated, packaged, but still, what a selection! They moved through the place, astounded at how many varieties of food there really were.

"Hey!" Angel cried excitedly, "over here, quickly!" The Spaniel looked stunned and clearly unstable on her four legs as she gestured through a large archway into another massive chamber. The others caught up with her and felt the same sense of awe that had overcome their friend.

"Oh my," Rex stammered.

"I've never seen anything like it," Lester whispered in shock.

"It's… it's…" Hans tried to find words but couldn't.

"Have we died?" Angel asked in a quiet and quite serious tone. "Is this heaven?"

Amy didn't know what to say as she stared open-mouthed into the giant hall spread out before her.

The chamber contained every imaginable form of meat, poultry and fish that the dogs had ever imagined and many that they hadn't as well.

Against one wall was meat. Meat in display cases, on counters and hung in massive slabs from the tiled ceilings. Against another wall was poultry. Everything from the tinniest quail to massive turkeys hanging neatly in a row with heads down and eyes closed.

Then there were fish. Not that the meats and poultry weren't the dogs' favorites, but seeing the fish laid out on a massive bed of ice was enough to impress anybody.

They all felt decidedly weak from both their recent experiences and the awe at the splendors within the hall.

Just as they began focusing on which section to choose from first, their attention was rudely distracted by a team of uniformed bipeds who came charging into the room. It was immediately apparent that the humans were there specifically to deal with them, and judging from their expressions, none too gently either.

With one last soul-wrenching glance into the chamber, the dogs bolted the other way as they tried to ignore the still awe-inspiring odors that followed them out.

They dashed back through the room with the human food, then into another hall, this one filled with strong scents of perfumes and oils and creams that female humans splashed all over themselves to hide their own individual odors.

They made it through this hall even though even more of the uniformed bipeds had joined in the chase. Ahead of them they saw doors. The bipeds were getting close and the canines' options were few. They made for the doors.

As they approached the doors, they saw that still more bipeds were moving in on them from the sides and from stairways that emptied right by them. It was going to be close.

A kind-looking human in a green uniform and top hat stepped forward and ceremoniously opened one of the doors for them even as the other bipeds screamed at him to bar their way.

They ran past him and out into the street, missing a speeding taxi by inches. They made it across and as they looked back, they saw that the bipeds weren't following them. They relaxed slightly until they saw that Fat Man and Boxer were running right for them. They ran as fast as they could, knowing that if they were this close, then Skull Face and Squat Lady were certain to be near as well.

They saw that the corner ahead led to a busy street that they'd have trouble crossing and decided to simply turn and brave the pedestrian traffic. Maybe if they were extremely lucky, they would find their way back to the park.

These thoughts vanished as Squat Lady appeared directly in front of them, blocking their progress.

"Down here!" Lester shouted as he dove down a flight of steps off to his right.

Like Lester, the others had no clue where the steps led but they had no choice. They ran after the Doberman, down a couple of flights of stairs until they reached a large concourse that seemed to lead to yet another set of steps, descending still further into the earth. They had no time to even consider their options. Fat Man and Boxer were right on their heels.

They ran for the stairway, diving under and through strange metallic devices whose only purpose seemed to be to stop any human from reaching the stairs. This struck Amy as exceedingly odd. Presumably the steps had to have been built for bipeds to use, so why stop them? She wasn't able to dwell on this as every conscious thought in her mind evaporated instantly as an icy wave of fear swept over her.

They had reached the steps and looked down a ludicrously steep flight that seemed to go on forever. The worst part was that these steps were moving! All by themselves, they moved in a constant motion, materializing out of the ground. They then formed into stairs and simply carried whatever was upon them to the bottom.

None of the friends had ever seen anything like this before, and though they tried to conceal it, each animal's defense system had taken over. The dogs' ears were laid flat against their heads as the hair along their backs rose. Amy thought of how comical it would have looked if she herself weren't scared beyond belief.

Rex didn't even look at the others. He knew that one of them had to make a move, and he was their leader.

He stepped onto the next stair as it formed in front of him and looked back at the others with a brave smile as he was transported down the moving stairway.

"No way am I getting on that!" Angel announced to no one in particular.

With that she moved away from the others in search of other means of descent.

Amy looked at the tense faces of Hans and Lester, and then, with her eyes firmly shut, stepped onto the metal stairway. It was a peculiar sensation. Especially with eyes closed. There was a definite feeling of motion both horizontal and vertical. She opened her eyes and saw Rex sitting rigidly on the conveyance below her as he neared the end of the ride. She looked up and saw that Lester and Hans were onboard as well, though obviously not enjoying the experience.

She couldn't see Angel anywhere. She barked her name and was rewarded with her voice being amplified and echoed as it reverberated off the tiled walls of the stairwell. Her bark was immediately returned by Angel, who, though invisible to her, sounded close.

"Where are you?" Amy asked.

"Right next to you," came the breathless reply.

"Where? I don't see you."

"You will," Angel said cockily.

Rex had made it to the bottom and was standing at the end of the moving stairs grinning encouragingly at the others as they descended toward him.

"Careful of the last bit," he called up to them. "The steps flatten out again and just vanish. I jumped off a little early. It might be a good idea to do the same."

Suddenly Angel appeared, out of breath but laughing madly. "Looks like I beat you lot, doesn't it," she managed to cry between gasps and laughs, "There's a regular stairway right next to this one. You should have followed me!"

"Oh no!" Rex shouted suddenly as he pointed his muzzle up the moving steps. Fat Man and Boxer were just getting on the top stair. Unlike the others, they didn't simply stand still allowing the stairs to do all the work. They began walking down as well.

"I have an idea," Lester said calmly.

The others all turned to him with urgent expressions.

"These buttons," he said, pointing to a pair of large, important-looking knobs located at the base of the stairs.

"What are they?" Rex asked anxiously.

"I don't know, but it says start on one and stop on the other," Lester responded, "and something about a fine, whatever that is."

"Stop…? It says stop? I think we all know what that means," Hans said in a matter of fact tone. "Humans are always using that word on us."

"It's about time we used it back, then, isn't it!" Lester grinned mischievously as he reached up with his front paws and hit the red button marked stop.

The result was far better than they could have hoped for. The moving stairway stopped moving instantly and with a jolt. Their two enemies were about halfway down the flight when Lester hit the button, and without advance warning, both man and dog sailed forward and began tumbling down the metal steps in a confusion of limbs and curses.

Though wishing they could stay and observe the results of their deed, the dogs realized that the opportunity was better used for their own escape rather than for simple amusement. They turned and dashed down a narrow tiled corridor that loudly echoed their every sound as they galloped along at full speed.

They'd gone only a short distance when they came to a split in the tunnel. On a wall in front of them were two odd tree-like drawings, each with an arrow pointing down a different branch of the corridor.

They all turned to Lester.

"Well?" asked Angel nervously, "what do they say?"

"It looks like names of places," he responded as he tried to read the strange signs "This way says Gre…Green…Pa…Par… Park… then… Pic…Picca…Picca…Piccadilly something."

"Oh for heavens sake!" Angel snapped impatiently. "What does all that nonsense mean? What about the other way. Where does that go?"

"South Ke…Ken…Kennsing…ton and Glo…Glouc…Glouces."

"This is ridiculous. We don't know what any of these places mean. They could be…"

"Angel, let him read. He's trying to help," Amy said in a stern voice. "Lester, go on. Do you see anything that might help us?"

The Doberman kept reading, but the others could now hear the unmistakable sounds of Fat Man and Boxer, moaning loudly somewhere down the corridor and definitely moving toward them.

"As quick as you can, however," Rex added with feigned calmness.

"Sai…Saint…Paul! we can get to a Saint from here!" Lester announced excitedly.

"Is that good?" Hans asked.

"Saints are always good" Lester said assuredly "They are the best of bipeds that even the humans themselves look up to."

"And this… Saint Paul, he can help us?" Rex asked urgently.

"Who said anything about it being a he?" Angel interjected.

"Whatever… he or she," Amy interrupted, "do you really think this St. Paul could help?"

"I think it's worth a try" Lester replied.

"Good enough for me!" announced Rex. "Let's go!"

He began to lead the others, then stopped suddenly.

"Lester!" he called. "Which way?"

"To the right! The sign says to the right" Lester replied as he pointed his muzzle down the appropriate corridor.

"Right," Rex commanded. "Follow me!" He began leading the group down the correct passageway to yet another flight of steps. This time they were stationary and the group descended with ease. They exited into a large cylindrical chamber on the sides of which were posted huge pictures depicting humans performing various acts. In one they drank something. In another, they spoke into hand-held plastic things. They rode horses, drove vehicles… they were strange illustrations. In each one the bipeds looked ecstatic while carrying out the most basic of activities.

What struck Amy was the fact that the stone-like floor only covered half of the ground. The other half was far lower and filthy. It contained three strips of oily metal that ran the entire length of the chamber and then vanished at either end into dark tunnels.

"Stop! You mangy mutts!" Fat Man screamed from behind them.

The dogs burst into a frenzied charge down the slippery floor of the chamber as Fat Man, now limping slightly, and Boxer raced after them.

They covered the distance quickly as they headed for another exit at the far end. As they neared it, they saw with heart-stopping realization that it was shut off with a heavy metal gate. They turned and looked back down the chamber.

Fat Man and Boxer stopped running. They knew they had them cornered. Man and dog shared an evil smile as the pair walked toward the cowering group.

"I can take them!" shouted Hans.

"He's right. Between us we can get them," Lester agreed.

Fat Man reached into his dirty leather jacket and removed a large, nasty-looking knife.

"It's too risky," Rex said with resignation "We've got to find some other way…"

"There is only one other way," Amy interrupted as she leaned over the edge of the flooring and stared down at the filth between the metal strips. She gave the others a resigned nod and then jumped off the edge of the platform.

twenty four

"Amy!" Rex cried in horror.

"Yes?" she responded calmly.

Rex moved to the edge and saw that she was standing between the metal strips smiling back at him.

"I can't believe you did that," he began to scold. "Do you realize…"

"Do you realize that if you don't shut up and get down here with me, I'm going to have to rescue you all over again?" Amy grinned up at the others.

Rex turned and saw that Fat Man and Boxer were closing in fast. "I'll hold them off while you lot get down there with Amy," he instructed.

"Excuse me," Angel said as she looked over the precipice with an expression of disdain. "You're not thinking that I'm going down there, are you?"

"It's your choice, Angel, but I think Fat Man plans to make you into a coat," Amy replied in a calm and almost cheery voice.

Rex moved toward the approaching pair and began to growl viciously as he lowered his body close to the ground ready to pounce should the need arise. He turned back briefly to the others and in a booming voice filled with authority, yelled "Jump!"

Hans and Lester got on either side of Angel and coaxed her over the edge. Because of her size, the drop was substantial for her. She had to ease herself over keeping her backside on the platform for as long as gravity would allow. Complaining all the way, she finally released her hind legs and dropped to the lower level.

"Yech!" she exclaimed. "It's filthy down here."

"I told you," Amy said, smiling at her friend's attempt to not let her dainty feet come in contact with the dirty surface.

Hans and Lester leaped and landed next to Amy with loud grunts as their breath was literally bounced out of their bodies. They all turned to face the platform, waiting for Rex to make his move.

They saw his rear first. He was backing away from his two adversaries keeping them in his sight at all times. His posterior reached the edge and seemed to hang over it for a moment.

"Jump, come on, Rex," Hans called up to him.

The others all joined in the chorus of encouragement until finally, feeling the time was right, Rex spun around and leaped just as Fat Man dove at him. The biped missed by only inches and found himself lying flat on his sizeable stomach with his head leaning out over the precipice. His fleshy features were drawn into any angry mask as he stared down at the five dogs. Not wishing to be left out, the Boxer lowered himself next to the human as he too leaned over the edge and glared at the escapees.

"We'd love to stay," Amy said coyly, "but we have another commitment. I'm so sorry!"

She gave the pair of angry faces a happy grin and then, with tail raised high, proceeded to move toward the nearest tunnel.

The others joined her and keeping close together, entered the dark mouth of the tunnel.

"Do you know where you're going?" Rex whispered in her ear.

"Not a clue!" she whispered back. "My feeling is that Saint Paul's either somewhere down this tunnel or the other one. That gives us an even chance of being right."

Rex nodded his agreement but clearly wasn't happy with the odds.

"I don't believe it." Lester said incredulously. "Look!"

They turned to see what he was referring to and saw that back along their path, in the brightly lit chamber, Fat Man was edging his large rump over the edge of the platform onto the lower ground. As they watched, Boxer leaped down to join him as the two resumed their pursuit of the dogs.

"I'll give him this," Rex said with a note of respect, "he may be a biped, but he sure acts like a bloodhound!"

The others nodded, then began to move faster along the dark interior of the tunnel.

Amy was not happy with the current circumstances. Here they were, deep underground, running inside a pitch-dark tunnel stepping on… well she had no idea what they were stepping on, but would prefer that it remain a mystery. Meanwhile, they were being chased by a pair of despicable characters who appeared intent on causing them great harm. Amy had been taught by her mother and her Man that life gave you back almost exactly what you gave it. She'd never quite understood the part about proportions but she understood and believed fully in the principle.

She knew that if she helped out, say, a young bird who'd fallen from its nest, almost certainly some good occurrence would befall her soon afterwards. The reverse also applied. If she'd say, been greedy and buried her favorite toy so that her Man couldn't find it, odds were that when she attempted to retrieve it, it would either be impossible to find or so grimy and misshapen that even she'd no longer be interested in it.

The basic rule was simple, do good-get good, which was why she couldn't for the life of her understand why she was being forced to flee from a fellow canine and an overfed biped to whom, far from doing harm, she'd only met a few days earlier. She tried to think of what possible infraction of the moral code she could possibly have broken but could see none. She'd been minding her own business lying in front of the cottage, napping contentedly when the bipeds had given her the meat.

"The meat!" she cried out loud.

"What meat?" Angel asked anxiously.

"Nothing… Sorry! I was just thinking."

"Sounds like nice thoughts," Rex commented with amusement.

The meat, of course. She'd had had a proper meal only hours earlier. She hadn't really been hungry at all. She'd been drawn by greed. That was it. This whole thing was a punishment for being greedy!

No! That wasn't it. That simply didn't work. First of all… all right, say she'd been mildly greedy. It had happened before; the appropriate bad reaction would have been a scolding from Cook, a sour stomach or even having to bring up her food in an embarrassing display of overindulgence. Secondly, if she'd been bad, then the reaction would be focused on her alone, not on all those other animals. No, this was something else entirely.

As she trotted along, she started to form a hazy outline of a thought about how maybe bad things could sometimes happen to you even if you didn't deserve them, when her thinking process was interrupted by the sudden halting of the others.

"What is it?" she whispered.

The others stood stock still. She was about to ask the question again when she sensed it. They were not alone. This had nothing to do with their pursuers. This was a sense of being surrounded by something foreign and unpleasant.

Suddenly a pair of small yellow eyes lit up only a couple of paws from them. They were off to the side, halfway up the tunnel wall.

As the nervous dogs edged further along the dark tunnel from the following eyes, another pair lit up, then another then… almost instantly the tunnel was filled with literally hundreds of pairs of small, piercing yellow eyes all staring right at them.

The dogs moved close together as they tried to focus their own eyes on their observers.

"What are they?" Angel whispered in a small frightened voice.

"Rats," Rex stated matter of factly. "Nasty things. I had many a run-in with them on night security."

"What are they?" Amy asked, trying to keep the fear from her voice.

"You've seen mice, right?" Rex said in a controlled and level tone "Well, imagine a mouse the size of a cat with the temperament of a pit bull and you've got a rat!"

"Oh my!" Angel said, moving close to Hans and Lester.

"Stop talking nonsense!" said a whining, high-pitched voice from the gloom. "We're not that bad."

"Yes, you are," Rex said back to the tunnel wall.

"Are not!" replied a chorus of whining, high-pitched voices that surrounded the entire group causing the hair on their backs to rise.

"Excuse me." Amy tried to sound as casual as she could. "If I may interject here, if you're not bad creatures…"

"We're not!" The lead rat announced. "We're simply misunderstood."

"Really!" She continued, "Then why do you hide yourselves down here in this filth and darkness waiting to sneak up on unsuspecting individuals, frightening them half to death?"

"Who's sneaking? We haven't moved an inch. You lot walked up to us, and as for the filth and darkness remark… how would you like it if I turned up at your home without any notice and then criticized your housekeeping?"

Amy tried to think of a good answer but couldn't. The lead rat had a point.

"I apologize for my comment; it was uncalled for," Amy said as she tried to make out even the slightest shape in the blackness of the tunnel wall. "You know it's difficult to carry on a conversation with someone you can't see."

"So?" replied the rat.

"So... I was wondering if we couldn't have some light of some sort."

"We will," he said smugly. "Very soon, in fact."

Even as he said the words, the dogs felt the beginnings of a warm draft of air move over them as they stood squinting in the darkness. They listened carefully for a moment, certain that they'd heard an unusual sound in the distance. All they could hear however was the loud panting of Fat Man as he and the Boxer moved toward them, still some distance sway.

"Are they with you?" the lead rat asked.

"Not really," Amy said to the wall. "Actually, they're trying to catch... look it's bad enough that I can't see you, but I don't even know your name!"

"My what?" the whiny voice snapped back.

"Your name... you know... what they call you!"

"What does who call me?" He asked, clearly confused by her question.

"The other rats!" Amy tried to remain patient. "When they talk to you, they must call you something."

"Why?"

"Because they must! Everybody does!"

"I'm terribly sorry," the rat said, actually sounding quite apologetic, "but I'm not following you at all. When someone speaks to me, they look at me and speak. That's it! What more is there?"

"Names! You have to have names; otherwise you can't identify yourselves."

"What nonsense!" he said with a nasty little whining laugh. "We always know whom we're talking to or about. Why would we want to confuse everything with... what was it you said... names?"

"Look" Amy said with great patience "I don't think you're..."

"It's simple, "Rex interrupted with a definite edge to his voice. "My name is Rex, hers is Amy, though we call her Goldie, that's Angel, Hans and the darker shadow at the end is Lester. That's odd! How come I can see more down here now? I'm certain it was darker a moment ago."

"It's expected. Don't worry," the rat answered calmly. "You might want to lie down, though."

"I beg your pardon?" Rex said in astonishment.

"You don't have to," the rat whined casually. "I mean it's up to you, but I really do suggest you lie down."

As the dogs stared at the tunnel wall, they noticed that the bright eyes of the rats seemed to be fading as their furry outlines became more distinct.

"It's getting brighter!" Hans exclaimed.

"And windier," Angel added as she tried to control the flapping of her long droopy ears.

"We know," said the rat "It's expected!"

"What's expected?" Amy asked urgently, sensing that something bad was about to happen.

"What's about to happen," the rat replied. "But it's expected so it's all right!"

The tunnel was brightening rapidly now. Amy looked back down the way they'd come and saw Fat Man and Boxer silhouetted in the gray light. The biped looked petrified and was trying to drag Boxer backward out of the tunnel.

"This is preposterous!" Hans snapped. "Something is definitely wrong. The wind is stronger. The light is brighter—and listen to that sound! Will you lot please tell us what's going on?" He had to raise his voice slightly to be heard above the grinding, squeaking, metallic groaning sounds that were filling the tunnel.

The dogs could now see the rats clearly in the growing light. There were hundreds of them, perched on wooden supports and cables that ran along the tunnel walls. They were large, just as Rex had said. Maybe not cat size, but certainly as big as rabbits.

They each had long thick tails which hung down behind them making it near impossible to judge which belonged to which rat. As the rats stared down at the anxious dogs, Amy noticed that they were all smiling with their yellow teeth exposed.

The lead rat was a slightly lighter shade than the rest, who all seemed to be a uniform dark gray. He stared at the five dogs with expressionless eyes, and then in a voice that sounded almost bored, again said, "I can't begin to tell you how crucial it is that you lie down."

"Why?" Rex shouted back at him above the increasing din.

Suddenly all the rats, every single one of them, stood up and glared down the tunnel toward the source of the light and sound.

"You know," Amy said nervously shouting at the others, "maybe they're right. Perhaps we should lie down."

"In this mess?" Angel exclaimed in a shrill voice.

"Yes!" Amy yelled back. "And quickly!"

"Why?" Rex looked at her uncertainly.

"I don't know," she said.

Unwillingly, the five dogs stretched out on the dirty ground below the level of the three metal strips. The rats nodded their approval of the canines' new position as the tunnel grew suddenly much brighter and the noise level doubled. Amy raised her head to see what was going on and saw that they were close to a bend in the tunnel and that something was approaching. Even before she could alert the others, a blinding light appeared at the curve.

"Oh my heavens!" she exclaimed as she flattened herself to the floor.

Angel gave her a puzzled look just as the world directly above their heads erupted in a thunderous explosion of sparks and grinding metal. The air was literally sucked from their bodies as the dark entity above them tore by at astonishing speed. The dogs kept their heads pinned to the ground as the thing sent showers of soot over them.

Amy had never been so frightened in her life. She wished only that whatever it was would go away and leave them alone. Even as she tried to cover her ears with her paws to shut out the deafening noise, it ended.

She just had time to raise her head and watch a glowing red light on the thing's rear grow smaller as it sped away. Whatever it was, rounded a corner and vanished from sight. The tunnel was again thrown into total darkness.

As the dogs lay there in shock, trying to recover, they could hear their own frightened panting.

"Is it gone?" Angel was the first to speak. Her voice was little more than a squeak.

"Oh, yes," the lead rat announced matter-of-factly "As expected."

Rex got to his feet and with a look of severe annoyance on his face, approached the tunnel wall. He placed his muzzle only inches from the lead rat's glowing eyes and slowly revealed his savage-looking teeth as he spoke. "Is there anything else… expected that we should know about?" His sarcasm and anger were clear.

"Hard to say, really. What's interesting for us might not be for you," the rat replied.

"Let's just pretend that everything interests us. That way we won't be disappointed."

"All right… Let me think… Oh yes… Well… It's time for us to eat." The lead rat said casually.

"That's hardly of interest!" Rex stated.

"Oh, I don't know," the whiney voice responded. "You may be mildly interested in what we plan to eat."

"Why should we be?" Rex asked with growing impatience.

"Rex!" Amy whispered in the darkness somewhere behind him.

"What?" his voice had an angry edge to it.

"Move away from the wall" she said calmly.

"Why would I want to do that?"

"Just do it!"

"But..."

"Now!" she commanded.

Rex moved back to the group and was about to speak when the dogs heard movement on the tunnel walls. Suddenly thousands of yellow eyes snapped open, all staring at the five dogs.

"I think you'd be interested in knowing what we're planning to eat," The lead rat stated in an excited squeal that sent shivers up the canine's spines.

"Perhaps we should be going," Amy said with feigned calmness.

"No, I don't think so," the rat replied. "Do you?"

The entire tunnel filled with rat voices all replying in unison, "No!"

"Run!" Amy screamed.

The others didn't need prompting. They broke into a mad dash back along the tunnel. They weren't in the least concerned about Fat Man or Boxer. Anything those two could dole out was pretty weak compared to becoming lunch for a thousand rodents.

As they ran at full tilt away from the infested walls, they heard the spine-chilling sound of rat laughter as it echoed down the tunnel after them. They rounded a corner and could see the end of the tunnel before them. The first rays of light began infiltrating the darkness that surrounded them.

They charged by the spot where they last saw Fat Man and Boxer but could see no sign of either of them.

"Do you think that horrible thing got them?" Angel asked with a mixture of horror and disgust.

"Yes," Lester said with complete certainty.

The others turned to face him, curious as to his conviction that their two foes had been taken by the giant metal beast. As they looked at Lester, he bent over and picked up something between his teeth. The others all felt a chill pass through them as they stared at the leash and collar that had until recently belonged to the Boxer.

"It's odd," Angel said dazedly, "but I actually feel slightly sad."

They all quietly nodded.

Amy was the first to speak. "May I suggest that we do our mourning once we're out of this place? I'd prefer to have a little more distance between myself and those rats."

She didn't have to push hard. The mere mention of the yellow-eyed rodents was enough to get the others instantly back on their feet, resuming their mad dash toward the tunnel's end. They covered the distance quickly and had to blink their eyes frantically as they burst out into the brightly lighted chamber from which they'd only just escaped.

Getting down from the platform to the lower ground turned out to have been far easier than getting back up. After a number of unsuccessful and ungainly attempts to reach the upper level, they found a system. Basically they used Hans as a step. Owing to his bulk, he proved perfect for the job. He leaned against the wall below the platform and allowed each animal to leap on his back, one at a time, and then step up.

Various bipeds stood staring at what to them must have been a peculiar sight as the dogs scaled the formidable wall. Even Angel made it, though Amy had to push her rump up onto Hans's back.

Amy was the last to go and tried to put as little weight on her friend's back as possible. Once up the dogs looked down to Hans for him to make his move. He stepped back and jumped at the wall. His front paws just touched the rim of the platform, then he tumbled back to the ground. He made the attempt a few more times but with similar results. He was becoming visibly frustrated, but somehow kept smiling through it all.

They all felt the strange wind at the same moment. Coming from the tunnel, it sent shivers through the five animals. Hans tried the jump again, this time without the smile. Again his front paws brushed the lip of the platform's edge but got no further. The dogs then heard the sound. It was the same as before; metallic and powerful. Amy looked to the mouth of the tunnel and saw that the blackness had been replaced with a gray glow as the beast approached them.

"Hans, you've got to get out of there!" she urged her friend. "You've got to jump like you've never jumped before!"

Hans nodded up at her then took a few careful steps backward. His eyes darted back to the tunnel and the approaching creature. With a deep swallow, he charged the wall.

It was a great jump and he got his paws a good distance up and onto the platform but again, he began to slide backward.

Amy looked into her friend's panicked eyes darting back and forth between the tunnel with its approaching terrors and the faces of the dogs already safe on the platform above.

Suddenly a pair of human arms reached down and grabbed Hans by his front legs and hoisted him up and out of danger. As he was lowered to the safety of the platform, all the animals looked toward the savior of their friend.

Squat Lady stared menacingly back at them as she reached down and took a firm hold of Hans by the scruff of his neck. With her other hand, she produced the dart gun she'd aimed at them only a few days earlier.

At that moment, the beast exploded from the tunnel with a squeal of metal and loud exhalation of its foul breath.

Amy turned to face the beast and was astonished to see a harmless-looking shiny metal conveyance that was partially filled with a broad variety of bipeds who all seemed completely relaxed. All along the length of the thing, doorways suddenly appeared, allowing humans to enter and exit the thing.

She never knew what came over her that day, but Amy suddenly felt possessed by an anger she'd never thought possible for her. Basically she'd just finally had enough.

Squat Lady was leveling her pistol at Rex, to her the most obvious target due to his size and ferocity. Amy used the moment to lunge at the female biped. She drew back her lips to reveal her full array of sharp teeth that she'd been trained never to use on any human. With intense pleasure she sank them into the pistol-wielding arm.

The female screamed as Amy kept her jaws firmly closed around the pudgy flesh. She had to balance herself on her hind legs as the human tried to spin away from her. Hans used the distraction to twist his heavy bulk out of her grasp and leap out of her way. Rex then stepped forward and sank his teeth into the spinning biped's ankle.

The reaction was spectacular. The human shrieked and howled as she tried to free her arm and leg from the two firm sets of teeth.

Just as the other dogs made a move to join in, a loud whistle pierced the air. From the far end of the platform, a dozen or so policemen had appeared. As one of them continued blowing urgently into his whistle, the others ran toward the melee.

Reluctantly, the dogs released their hold on Squat Lady and tried to find some avenue of escape.

"Follow me!" Amy suddenly shouted as she leaped through one of the openings of the metallic conveyance. The others followed instantly.

As the last of them leaped into the silver beast, its doors slid shut behind them as if by magic. Squat Lady lunged after them and managed to poke the end of the dart gun between the closing portals and tried to pry them open. The dogs cowered on the opposite side of the brightly lit interior as the female forced the doors open.

That's when a strange thing happened. A male biped dressed immaculately in a dark suit rose from his seat and went to the doorway. The dogs assumed that he was about to help his kind and began edging away from the activity. To their astonishment, the human grabbed the end of the weapon and pulled it out of Squat Lady's grasp. Then as if that weren't enough, he used the weapon to tap on the female's clutching fingers until they released the sliding doors. As soon as the doors closed, the dogs felt themselves moving and watched in rapt fascination as the irate face of the female and the concerned expressions of the policemen all slid by with ever-increasing speed. Within seconds they were gone from sight as the conveyance entered a tunnel.

That's when the lights went out.

twenty five

In fact, the lights were only out for less than a second but it was long enough to terrify the already frightened canines.

Once the lights flickered back on, Amy had a good opportunity to examine the biped who had saved them. The human moved over to the dogs without the slightest fear. Apparently without thought for his clean and neatly pressed clothing, he dropped to his knees, reaching out a hand which he held politely under Amy's nose so that she could evaluate his scent.

Her mother had been a fine instructor when it came to the sometimes-tricky challenge of categorizing a human's scent. It wasn't easy, especially as most humans seemed to go out of their way to conceal their personal odor whenever possible. Between the soaps, and oils and perfumes it was indeed quite difficult to trace a human's original smell beneath the camouflage.

In this instance however, Amy was able to locate the true scent easily, as the biped used little to conceal his odor other than a mild natural-smelling soap. Beneath that was him. Gentle, patient, calm and without any fear that she could detect.

She lowered her head and allowed the human to stroke her. It felt wonderful, and for a moment, catapulted Amy's memory back to the safe and gentle sensations of the cottage and her

Man's affectionate touch. She looked into the human's eyes and saw the same type of caring and intelligence in them.

"So what's your story, you sad lot?" The human spoke in a gentle tone. "On the run, are you? Well, I have no idea what you've done, but looking at you, I somehow can't believe it's that bad." As he spoke, he continued to stroke her head.

The entire group, biped and all, suddenly lurched forward as the transport applied its brakes and began to slow down. The dogs became instantly wary; even Amy pulled away from the gentle touch of the kind man.

The biped seemed to understand. He rose and grabbed a metal pole for support. He smiled down at the dogs, especially at Amy.

"I have to get off here," he said almost apologetically. "Take care of yourselves."

The conveyance then suddenly burst out of the tunnel and into a chamber that looked just like the platform they'd started from. It even seemed to have the same lights and posters. It was confusing until Angel pointed out that though similar; it was in fact different in subtle ways.

As the transport came to a complete stop and the doors slid open, the dogs nervously stared out, looking for Squat Lady or indeed anyone who meant to do them harm. The nice biped gave each animal a brief but friendly pat, then walked through the doors and onto the platform. The dogs decided that they preferred to stay where they were, having no wish to encounter Squat Lady again so soon.

As they nervously waited for the doors to slide shut, Amy watched the nice human male as he turned from the platform and produced the dart gun from his jacket pocket. Almost ceremoniously he deposited it into a waste bin, then with a brief wave, he turned away and vanished up a flight of stairs. The doors slid shut.

They felt the floor under them jolt as the vehicle began to move again and immediately pick up speed.

Lester was the first to notice that posted above them were drawings and names just like the ones they'd seen back at the first platform. Lester soon managed to actually read the names above the platform at each stop and then locate the same on the drawings. He managed to work out where they were, and amazingly, where they were going. The others were impressed.

He located Saint Paul's name and calculated how many more stops they had to go before actually reaching it. Needless to say, the others didn't much trust his calculations, and as the doors slid open at what Lester insisted was the correct stop, they were stunned as the lettering before them did indeed seem to back up the Doberman's claim.

They stepped out onto the platform. With every nerve ending in their bodies ringing with energy, they waited to be pounced upon at any second.

Nothing happened! Other than a few startled glances from passing bipeds, they seemed to go completely unnoticed.

Rex gathered the group together and in the voice of a leader said to the others. "I think the most important thing at this point is to get back above ground. We need to find a way out."

"How about over there?" Lester suggested smugly as he gestured to a large illuminated sign on which was clearly printed......WAY OUT.

"That should do," Rex admitted, trying to ignore Lester's smirk.

The five animals edged their way along the platform until they reached the sign, which hung above a break in the wall. Rex took a deep breath and stepped through the opening first.

"It's safe!" he whispered back to the group. "Come on, follow me."

He led them up a stairway into an open area, at the base of moving stairs just like the ones they'd battled earlier.

"Not again!" Angel pleaded

"It should actually be a bit easier going up," Amy said encouragingly.

"Why?" Angel pouted.

"I don't know exactly, it just seems it would be, that's all." Amy gave the Spaniel a gentle nuzzle.

"Come on then," Rex said authoritatively. "Let's do it."

He marched over to one of the flights of stairs and jumped onto it. To his surprise, the steps simply lowered him right back to the bottom again. Puzzled but clearly determined, the Doberman turned and again lunged at the steps, this time continuing to run up them as soon as he landed. All he managed to do was stay in almost exactly the same place. As fast as he ran up the stairs they moved down. Finally, flustered, embarrassed, and exhausted, Rex allowed the steps to return him to his starting place once more.

"I don't understand it," he gasped. "I can't seem to make any headway at all!"

"Hello. Oh, hello." Angel's voice rang through the sloping chamber.

The other spun around but couldn't see her.

"Up here, silly dogs." her amused tone said teasingly.

Amy spotted the grinning Spaniel on another of the stairways. This one was definitely moving upward. Angel was almost at the top as she smiled down at the others.

As they watched, her cheery face vanished from view as the stairs carried her to the top of their run and flattened out.

Suddenly they all heard a squeal of pain from above. The dogs mobilized instantly and charged up the moving steps that Angel had used.

Amy was the first to reach the top and found the Spaniel sitting against a wall nursing one of her long ears.

"What happened?" Amy asked gently.

"My ear… it… it… got caught," Angel cried between teary intakes of breath, "I got… to the top… and was… was… laughing so hard… when… when… suddenly the steps… suddenly my ear got caught… caught in the steps."

"Let me see." Amy moved close to the frightened, miserable Spaniel.

The others arrived and stood in a circle around her as Amy examined the damage.

"It's just a little nick Angel," she announced, finding the wounded area.

"Are you sure? It hurts!"

"I'm certain it does but it's not serious. Let me just wash it out for you. All right?"

"All right," Angel replied weakly.

Amy gave the wounded area a good cleaning with her tongue. She even gave the flesh around the wound a gentle chew to get it good and damp.

"There we go," Amy said as she gave the ear one final lick. "Good as new!"

"Thank you," Angel tried to force a smile.

"I hope you learned a lesson today, Angel." Amy's voice became serious.

"A lesson?" The Spaniel was mystified.

"Yes, a lesson. You were showing off."

"You sound like my mother," Angel said as a smile began to form on her still tear-streaked face.

"Maybe that's because you were behaving like a naughty puppy!" Amy answered, trying to suppress her own smile.

The two dogs looked tenderly into each other's eyes, then stepped forward and touched muzzles.

Rex cleared his throat to get everyone's attention. "I think we should keep moving, don't you?"

The others nodded and regrouped into a line as they set off in their pursuit of Saint. Paul.

Rex led them down two more corridors and up one more flight of stairs. Then with no warning they turned one final corner and found themselves on street level back outside, breathing the slightly damp, slightly dirty evening air that hung over the huge city.

"I never thought I'd say this," Hans said as he took a deep breath of the city air, "but doesn't the city look beautiful!"

The others nodded, vowing silently to themselves to never venture below ground again. It was simply too fraught with danger. Maybe it was all right for bipeds, but for canines, no! Even battling city streets was preferable to the underground.

"Which way do we go?" Amy asked no one in particular.

They all glanced in various directions, having not the slightest clue.

"In that case, I suggest that we find a place to hole up for the night," Amy said as she studied her friends' anxious faces as they continued to seek out some hint as to Saint Paul's location.

"What about Saint Paul?" Angel asked, with her large eyes trained on Amy.

"It's getting dark, we don't know where he—or she—is, and besides, it wouldn't be polite to turn up this late unannounced, would it?" Amy looked to each face for acknowledgment. "Besides, I don't know about you lot, but I'm famished. I think we should start thinking about dinner."

The weary dogs began a search for food. They stayed close to the shop fronts and office buildings as they sniffed at each doorway. They noticed almost immediately that the area they were in was different from the others they'd encountered. At first, they couldn't quite put a paw on what it was they found unusual but after covering a few more blocks, Amy stopped the group.

"Humans don't live here!" she stated flatly.

"What do you mean?" Rex asked.

"That's what's so different around here. There are plenty of bipeds, but none of them looks comfortable. The ones we've seen through the windows… did they look relaxed? No! This area seems to be where they come to, I don't know, not relax!"

As they talked, the dogs continued moving down the street, which was growing less crowded with humans by the minute.

"Why would they want to do that?" Angel asked, clearly skeptical of Amy's theory.

"I don't know, but even back at the cottage, my Man would shut himself up in his room and look just like these bipeds.

He'd be serious and would look at pieces of paper and this illuminated box and the black thing you talk into. When he'd reappear much later, his eyes would be dull and his scent would be a little sour."

"Did he stay like that?" Lester inquired with concern.

"Oh no! Usually I was able to get him back to normal with a couple of back rolls and a good lick or two. Sometimes if he was really in a bad way he'd pour himself some foul-smelling brown liquid. I never knew how he could, but he'd drink the stuff and become quite merry and playful."

"I've seen that happen to my masters, too!" Hans said, smiling at the memory. "Only they'd drink a lot of this odd fizzy liquid that smelled a little like bread, and then as you said, they'd get playful and clumsy. They'd sometimes even fall down."

As Amy laughed, trying to imagine her Man ever falling down, except possibly when she let go of Shoe unexpectedly, she noticed that Rex was facing away from the group, looking up at the darkening sky. She stepped in front of him but he turned his head away from her.

"Rex, what's the matter?" she asked gently.

"Nothing. Nothing at all. Just go back to the others and enjoy your memories." His voice had a definite edge of pain to it.

"Rex, look at me," Amy commanded.

The Doberman slowly turned and faced her. She could see immediately that his eyes were moist and his expression strained and sad.

"What is it? Tell me and maybe I can help."

"Thanks, Goldie, but you can't help me. No one can," he said in a whisper so the others wouldn't hear.

"You're sad, I can see that." She nuzzled his neck trying to help relieve his sadness. "Maybe if you talked about it, it would help."

"I can't, Goldie. I don't even think you'd understand. That's part of the sadness."

"Why don't you at least try?" she coaxed.

Rex simply looked up at the sky again as he tried to hold down his rising emotions. Suddenly without any warning he let out a long and soulful howl that made Amy shiver with emotion. The others all turned and made a move to approach the pair, but Amy signaled for them to stay put while she talked with Rex. For a long time, she sat patiently next to him, waiting for him to begin speaking. Rex's eyes were closed but he kept his head high and his muzzle pointed upward.

Angel nuzzled Hans and Lester away from Amy's vigil, then coaxed them to join her in a food hunt while their friends had a chance to be alone.

Rex didn't notice their departure and when he finally lowered his head and opened his sad eyes, he was surprised by their absence. Amy explained that they'd gone off in search of dinner.

"They can't do it alone," he began, "We should help them."

"No! They've gone off just so that we could be alone. You are sad, Rex, and it hurts me inside. You need to let the sad out and happiness in."

"Don't you think I want to? I've tried. Oh, how I've tried." His voice was tight. "You don't have any idea of what I have inside. You think you do, but you don't."

He stared into Amy's deep brown eyes, filled with warmth and concern. With an expression of resignation, he suddenly nudged Amy into a dark doorway belonging to a large office building, shut up securely for the night.

"I don't think you could possibly understand what I feel, but I'll try and explain so you'll let it rest, all right?"

Amy nodded encouragingly back at him. Rex took a couple of deep breaths, then began in a voice almost devoid of feeling.

"One of my few memories of when I was young, was sleeping with my brothers and sisters as my mother watched from her blanket. I remember feeling safe and happy. I remember watching as our door opened and humans entered our room. I saw a strange biped talking to the male that looked after us. The stranger got to his knees and began playing with each of us in turn. Mother was not happy about it and even began growling. Our master had to take her out of the room and shut her away.

"The stranger finally got to me and petted me, tickled me, rolled me over, all things that I enjoyed, yet for some reason I didn't feel any warmth coming from him. It was as if he was simply going through some routine. Anyway, after a few minutes of this, the biped got to his feet and began talking to our human again, and they left the room. I thought no more about it and resumed playing. A little while later as we were all dozing after a rough game of tag, the bipeds came back. Our human reached down, I'll never forget this, lifted me away from my brothers and sisters and handed me to the stranger. I didn't think anything was wrong until the biped placed me in a box with little holes in it and shut the lid. It was so dark. I can remember trying to peer out of the tiny holes and could just see my family for a moment. Then the box rose into the air and moved out of the room."

Rex had to stop for a moment to catch his breath and wipe away a tear.

"I never saw my family again," he sighed, trying to control the emotions that were rising within him.

"It's all right" Amy said gently, moving closer to him "I'm here with you."

He again looked into the night sky before allowing the hurtful memories to surface. Amy sat patiently next to him, knowing that Rex needed to take his time.

"After being taken from my family, I don't remember much until I was quite a bit older. My master treated me reasonably well. I was fed regularly, exercised and taught manners that humans thought appropriate, but in all my puppy time he never played with me. I used to invent little games that I could play by myself, but somehow it just wasn't the same." Rex shook his head." Anyway, when I was in my early adult period I was moved out of the big house and put into a kennel out back. There were ten other dogs, and at first I was overjoyed at the prospect of new friends and playmates, but that excitement didn't last long."

"Why?" Amy asked in a surprised voice.

"These were guard dogs," he continued, "They had no humor, no emotions; they were hard and brutal beasts. I remember wondering why. I found out, though. I most certainly found out." Rex lowered his head and forced a thin smile for Amy, who nodded encouragingly.

"For the next, I don't know exactly, six moon cycles maybe, I was taught to be a guard dog. My master found just about every possible way he could to break my spirit and turn me into as vicious an animal as possible. I learned how to bite and incapacitate bipeds. How to knock a human to the ground in less than a second, how to, well, you get the drift. Eventually he began using me just like the others. We would be sent to protect everything from lavish homes with walled gardens to little junkyards filled with rusted metal and rats."

"How awful!" Amy exclaimed.

"You know, I'd like to make light of it, but I can't. It was awful! I would never know where I'd be placed next. Whether it would be sheltered from the elements or be just an open fenced enclosure where I'd have to keep moving all night long or freeze to death on the ground. After a while all that became an accepted part of my life. What never did though, was the loneliness. Most of the time I could bury my feelings inside and carry on with life relatively well, but other times I'd… I'd hurt inside. I'd hurt badly. It was like a hot ball lodged in my chest throbbing away, making it hard sometimes for me to even think. When you were all talking about your memories with your humans I… I felt so…" Rex trailed off.

"That was stupid of us," Amy stated frankly as she shook her head "We should have known better."

"No! You have every right to remember your good times. I should have become like the other dogs in the kennel and lost all my feelings, but Amy,… I never did. I tried so hard to become a cold and callous dog but I couldn't. I never really learned to hate humans like I was supposed to. Every time I see bipeds, I'm supposed to feel hate toward them, but you know what? I don't. I can't. I want to play with them. I want to be taken for walks and be talked to and have my stomach rubbed and my ears scratched and... I'm so sorry about this," he gasped. "I'm not exactly your stereotypical attack dog, am I?"

"No, you're not, but there's nothing to apologize about. You're simply a sensitive dog who's had a tough life so far, but you know what? Like I said before, I have this feeling that that's all behind you."

"Do you really?" he asked hopefully. When she nodded, Rex gave her a huge toothy smile in appreciation. Amy was about to speak when the other three came trotting round the corner toward them.

"Find anything?" Rex inquired.

"We're not quite sure," Hans replied. "We've found an interesting scent, but we'd feel a little more comfortable if you were with us when we check it out."

"Why?" Rex asked, mildly puzzled.

"You'll see," Angel said with a nervous grin.

Rex glanced at Amy, who seemed as perplexed as he was, then, with a brief shrug of his shoulders followed the others to find out just what they'd come upon. Amy trotted along behind the group, watching Rex, his head held high, resume his position as leader of the team.

After a couple of blocks they reached the area in question. Amy took one look at it and felt a shiver run the length of her spine. The three explorers had found a place where part of the street branched off and ran down a steep incline under a large office complex. Above the sloping entry hung a bright yellow sign with a large letter P on it.

Rex turned to Lester. "What's that mean?"

"I haven't the foggiest idea," he stated flatly.

"What about that over there?" Rex asked, gesturing to a large yellow placard fastened to one wall.

Lester moved over to it and began reading it as best he could.

"P...Pa...Park..."

"There's a park down there?" Angel interrupted.

"Park...Parking! Not a park. Parking!" Lester announced.

"Great! So what does that mean exactly?" Rex asked.

"I haven't a clue," Lester replied calmly. "I know how to find out though!"

"Why should we care what's down there?" Amy pointed out. "I thought we agreed to stay above ground from now on."

"We did, Goldie," Angel said excitedly, "but stand over here and take a deep breath."

Amy gave the Spaniel a look of mild skepticism, then moved closer to the entrance. She closed her eyes, raised her muzzle then took a long, deep breath.

"Chicken?" Amy asked incredulously, "Roasted chicken?"

"That's what we smelled too!" Angel announced excitedly. "Now you see why we should go down and investigate."

"I don't know," Amy said slowly. "We're talking underground again."

"No!" Angel insisted "We're talking roast chicken!"

"Well then," Rex said matter-of-factly, "I think I should lead the way, don't you?"

The others all nodded emphatically.

Rex smiled back at them and led the group down into the dark and unknown territory below.

twenty six

the dogs' nerves were on high alert, making each animal jump or yelp at the slightest sound or movement. It was an odd place. The road-like surface descended for a while, then flattened out for no purpose that any of them could see except to allow biped vehicles to be stationed in neat, diagonal rows. There had to be more to it than that, but the dogs couldn't seem to find out what its true purpose was. They descended two entire levels before they realized that the chicken odor was no longer present.

"Hans, Lester," Rex said, "you two retrace our steps back up toward the entrance and see if you can find where we lost that scent. We'll continue on down and see if we can find out what this place really is."

The two nodded and trotted back up the drive, the sound of their nails on the road surface echoing off the heavy concrete walls.

Rex led the others further down into the place as the three searched for any clue as to its purpose. Every level seemed identical except that as they went deeper, the biped vehicles became scarcer. Those that were to be found seemed to have an abandoned look.

Finally they rounded one last corner and came to a dead end. There were only six vehicles on this level. On the higher levels the walls had all been painted and posted with arrows and signs but these walls were sorely neglected. Amy approached one and noticed that it was covered with a fine sheen of greenish gray moss. She smelled damp and decay on this level, and it made her uncomfortable. It wasn't that the odors were foreign to her; she'd smelled them before on her walks with her master. In those instances, however, the odors had been coming from rocks and trees and seemed natural and appropriate. Down here, the odors had an almost evil quality as they clung to the abandoned surfaces that bipeds had made but forgotten.

Amy allowed a shiver to pass through her. She saw that both Rex and Angel seemed to be having the same reaction. Without a word, the three turned from the dead end and began walking back up the sloping drive.

They had taken only a couple of steps when they heard Hans and Lester barking furiously from somewhere far up inside the structure. The three broke into a run at the urgency in their friends' voices. As they charged up the drive, another sound reached the three pairs of ears, a clanking metallic sound, which for a split second reminded Amy of the terror she'd felt in the rat tunnel earlier that day. This sound, however, didn't have the weight or power of the tunnel beast. This was far lighter in tone. It was like the noise of rattling chains added to the sound that Cook's metal mixing bowls made when they fell to the stone floor of the kitchen.

The two scout dogs sounded even more frantic as the three continued to climb closer to them. They seemed to be yelling something for the benefit of a biped, but Amy couldn't quite make out the words.

"We're almost there!" Rex shouted breathlessly as they rounded one last bend.

The three came to a sudden frantic halt as they saw the reason for Hans's and Lester's outburst.

The entrance through which they'd so recently passed was

now entirely blocked with a secure-looking metal gate! It wasn't solid. It was made of metal links joined together to form an impenetrable barrier that covered every inch of the entrance. Beyond the barrier they could see the frantic figures of Hans and Lester howling forlornly into the night. They were shut out.

Rex approached the barrier cautiously, keeping his eyes firmly fixed on it in case it decided to move or… well, whatever it might do.

"What happened?" he asked through the links to the others.

"We were trying to find the chicken scent when this biped suddenly appeared out of nowhere and chased us out onto the street." Hans glanced quickly over his shoulder before continuing. "We didn't want to make a fuss so we let him have his way, knowing we could sneak back in when he was gone."

"But he went to the wall over there," Lester said, taking over the story telling, "and pushed a button. Before we knew what was happening, this gate thing began coming down out of nowhere."

Hans carried on. "The biped stepped under it as it dropped and kept us away from it. The thing was fast. Before we could get around the human, it reached the ground and stopped. We've given it a good going over, and I've got to be honest, we can't make it budge."

Angel began to cry.

"Angel, what's the matter?" Amy asked soothingly.

"What do you mean, what's the matter?" she howled. "We're trapped. We're never going to get out. We're going to be here forever and I'm scared and I'm cold and… and…"

"And what…? Come on tell us! We're your friends," Amy coaxed.

"And… and… we never found the roast chicken!" her pathetic voice cried.

Rex and Amy turned to each other, both trying their hardest not to laugh at the poor Spaniel's outbreak.

"Oh, we found the chicken," Hans announced peevishly.

"Well, where is it? We're all famished!" Angel exclaimed, her tears suddenly vanishing.

Hans and Lester both tilted their heads to the left of the gated entrance. Rex moved close to the barrier and looked to where they were gesturing. He shook his head in frustration.

Right next door was a small restaurant displaying the image of a bearded biped on a sign above white lettering. Rex couldn't read but knew the sign well. Various night assignments had coupled him with bipeds that would dine from large cardboard buckets of chicken that held the same image.

"It's closed!" Angel announced as she tried to crane her neck against the barred entryway.

"It closed just as we got up here," Hans explained.

"But the scent came from in here," Amy said, somewhat confused.

"It did seem to, didn't it," Rex agreed." It must have been carried in here by a draft."

"So we got shut in here for nothing?" Angel sulked.

"Well…" Amy tried to find the right words, "basically, yes!"

The dogs all stared blankly at one another until Rex suddenly started to laugh. His laugh was so contagious that before long the others had joined in. It was a good release for their emotions, and as their laughter subsided, they all felt better. They were still hungry, but somehow the future didn't seem quite as dismal.

Just as the five settled down to discuss their next move, a human voice shattered the night air.

"Hey, you lot! Get out of there!"

Rex signaled for Amy and Angel to back into the shadows. Hans and Lester tried to squeeze themselves tightly against the outside of the gate, hoping to be unseen by the approaching biped.

"Come on, then!" the voice boomed. "Get out of there, I said."

The towering form of the biped stepped directly in front of the gated entrance. Amy could just make out that the biped was very untidy looking. His clothes were torn and filthy, his hair was matted and uncombed and his face was covered with the hair that most bipeds preferred to scrape off with the aid of a sharp piece of metal. The human was holding a bottle in one hand and a filthy blanket in the other. In addition to his unkempt state, the biped also seemed to be having a great difficulty in standing up straight, constantly swaying from side to side.

Hans and Lester tried to press themselves into the corner between the gate and wall, hoping that would satisfy the biped. Instead, he began mumbling unintelligibly at them and took a step forward.

Maybe because he tried to kick at the dogs while still walking, the biped suddenly cried out in astonishment as he toppled over and fell to the ground. Instead of trying to protect himself during the fall, his hands frantically sought out the bottle. As his body reached the surface of the drive, the bottle slipped through his fingers and landed on the street, shattering into hundreds of bright chards of glass. Amber liquid flowed across the pavement and trickled into the gutter.

The human watched with wide eyes as the last of the fluid vanished from sight. He then lowered his head to his hands and began to cry with loud sobs that wracked his entire body.

Rex and the others eased themselves out of the shadows feeling that this biped was unlikely to do them any great harm. As they approached the gate, they looked over to Hans and Lester, who were also clearly now less afraid of the intruder.

"What should we do?" Angel whispered.

"I don't know," Rex replied "Do you think he's all right? The fall seems to have hurt him."

"I don't think it was the fall," Amy stated as she watched the sad biped weep uncontrollably. "I think it's his life that hurts him."

The others all looked from Amy to the human, then back to Amy, trying to understand her words. She simply smiled gently back at them, knowing that she had just discovered a new side to her personality. She somehow was able to feel some of the pain the poor wretch of a biped held inside himself. The others didn't seem to have the ability, which though puzzling to her, made Amy suddenly feel rather special, as if a barrier had been lifted between her and the human species.

The dogs watched the biped as he continued to sob into his dirt-streaked hands.

"He smells awful!" Angel whispered to no one in particular.

"I don't think he means to," Amy offered.

"Whether he means to or not, he does, and it's foul. I'm going to go down another level," Angel said, flipping her ears back as she turned and walked away.

Amy was about to say something when she noticed Lester moving toward the human. She watched raptly as the Doberman walked up to the biped and positioned himself under his arm. Hans stood, observing for a moment, and then following Lester's lead, moved toward the human.

At first the biped seemed to be absorbed in his sobbing and didn't notice the two dogs, but then slowly raised his head and allowed his hands to descend onto the back of each animal. Amy stood riveted to her spot, fearful that Hans and Lester might be harmed, but instead the biped's large, calloused hands began gently petting each dog.

Hans and Lester both turned their heads slightly to give the others a brief nod which clearly translated to "We're fine, don't worry."

Amy was touched deeply by the unselfishness of her friends' actions. There was clearly no great personal gain expected from their act. They had simply seen the need for a little kindness and sensitivity to be offered and had done just that.

She felt her eyes misting slightly and turned away so as not to embarrass the others. As she looked back into the sloping structure, her eyes caught those of Rex, who was clearly attempting to keep his eyes dry as well. His large brown eyes were quite moist as he too looked away.

Realizing that they'd both been caught in their moment of open emotionalism, they smiled sheepishly at each other.

"Why don't we go down and join Angel," Amy suggested. "She's probably got herself into trouble by now anyway!"

"Do you think they'll be all right?" Rex asked, glancing back at Hans and Lester as they snuggled close to the human.

"I think they'll be just fine," she said smiling.

The two dogs then turned away from the gated entrance and began descending in search of Angel.

They reached the next level down, expecting to find her curled up asleep in some corner or other, but found the area devoid of sleeping Spaniels.

"That's odd," Amy whispered.

"She probably went further down, that's all."

They descended another level but still found no trace of their friend.

"Angel?" Rex called out.

There was no response.

"Angel!" he tried again with more force.

Rex and Amy gave each other a puzzled look, then began walking down to the next level. They were moving slowly now. Something was definitely wrong.

They covered two more levels with no success. This left only the damp and apparently abandoned one they'd encountered earlier.

"Why would she go down there?" Rex whispered.

"Who knows?" Amy replied shaking her head in mild frustration. The two dogs stared at each other for a moment, both preferring not to go down to the next level.

"We're being silly. You know that, don't you?" Rex said as casually as he could. "We've been down there once. It's just a little damp, that's all. There's nothing really frightening. We're just being silly pups!"

"Do you mean that?" Amy asked with a nervous smile.

Rex gave her a wink, which was enough to calm most of her

fears. The two then started for the bottom floor. Amy was about to say how silly she felt having been so scared of going any farther when all of the lights in the place suddenly shut off, plummeting them into total darkness.

They stood there for what seemed like an eternity, trying to accustom their eyes to the darkness. It was simply too dark. Usually there's light of some description even when one's surroundings seem devoid of all light. Not so here! Amy blinked to adapt her vision sufficiently to be able to see her own paws, at least.

"This is ridiculous. I can't see a thing," Rex said in frustration.

"What do you think happened?" Amy asked trying to keep the fear from her voice.

"You sound scared, Goldie. There's no need. The lights were obviously on a timer. I've seen that a lot in my job."

"What's a timer?"

"That's when the humans want something to happen at a particular moment, while they're not there to make it happen. Just like the lights. They wanted them to switch off by themselves while there was no one here. It's quite clever, really."

"I'm sure it is," Amy said trying to sound convinced. "But… why would anyone want something to happen like say, the lights going off, if they weren't around to see it happen anyway?"

Rex said, "The important thing is that you shouldn't let this scare you. The lights went off on purpose and, all right, it is a bit dark but we know where we are."

"Sort of!" Amy said.

"We know there's nothing that can harm us in here, right?"

"Right!"

"So let's keep moving and stay as calm as possible. In fact, stay really close to me and I'll lead you down."

"I couldn't do that!" Amy said, embarrassed. "It's not decent! We don't know each other well enough for that!"

"Goldie, I'm not talking courtship here. For now I'm concerned with getting both of us safely down to the bottom level and locating Angel."

Without another word, Amy moved to touch her shoulder to his, and he began to slowly lead her down the sloping drive.

twenty seven

It wasn't easy. Even with his experience, Rex couldn't see where there was no light. They'd only gone a short distance when she heard him bump into something metallic just in front of him.

"You all right?" she whispered

"Yes, but I may have dented one of their vehicles," he responded in a pained voice.

She tried not to laugh or even smile, as he was certain to feel it through his shoulder. As they continued down the incline even more slowly than before, the smell of the damp and decay began to reach them from the bottom level. Amy tried to ignore it by recalling other, far more pleasant odors. She managed to retrieve a scent memory of Cook preparing a roast chicken in the oven. As she concentrated on the memory, she began to not only smell the cooking bird with its seasoning of rosemary and garlic, but also the smells of the cottage itself, the slight lemon scent of the polish on the wooden floors, the flowers that bloomed directly outside the kitchen windows, even the tangy odor of the burned wood from the fireplace that seemed to hang on the air every-where within the cottage.

Amy was so transported by her memories that she didn't notice when they had reached the bottom of the incline and the drive leveled out. She didn't even notice at first when Rex came to a halt and she ran right into him.

"Whoa! Steady on, girl! Having a daydream, were you?" he asked, amused.

"Actually, yes! I was about to tuck into a fine dinner of roast chicken. Couldn't you have kept going a little while longer?"

"Sorry, Goldie, but we're at the bottom and…" his words suddenly ceased.

"Rex, what is it?" Amy asked feeling the beginnings of icy fingers on her spine.

"Shhh!" His voice was tense "Angel? Are you there?"

There was no reply.

"Angel, I know you're here. Come on, speak up." He tried to make his voice sound as casual as possible but Amy could hear his tension.

They stood silently in the darkness waiting for some sort of response. After what seemed like an eternity, Amy was about to ask again what was wrong when their missing friend finally replied.

"Yes, I'm here." Angel's voice was quiet and definitely that of a scared dog.

"Are you all right?" Rex tried to sound calm.

"Yes, thank you."

"Where are you?" Rex, asked, not sounding interested.

"It doesn't matter," came the strained reply.

"Yes it does. Tell me, where are you?"

There was a long silence.

"You're not alone down here, are you, Angel?" Rex asked casually.

There was another long pause during which Amy was convinced she heard quiet movement all around them.

"Angel," Rex tried again, "I asked if you were alone down here?"

They didn't have long to wait for an answer this time.

The bottom level suddenly lit up, blinding Rex and Amy with brightness.

"No, she's bloody well not alone," said a velvety voice in a superior tone.

It took Amy a long time to be able to open her eyes to the bright lights. Finally, keeping her lids half-open, she peered out and was stunned by the bizarre vision that met her eyes.

Cats! Everywhere she looked there were cats. Some were staring with expressionless eyes at her and Rex, others were slowly moving among the others with eerie fluidity as their lithe bodies twined and intertwined.

In the center of the teaming mass of fur was Angel.

She was terrified. She was standing bolt upright surrounded by purring and pushing felines who, though formidable, did not seem in the least threatening. In fact, Angel did not seem to be in any danger at all unless she was damaged by over-affection. As each cat passed Angel's rigid body, he or she would press against Angel and with sensual deliberateness, rub against her. While clearly pleasurable for the cats, Angel seemed to withdraw further into herself with each caress.

One cat was approaching them. Slowly, deliberately, fearlessly, one cat had broken from the melee and was now walking toward them with as much nonchalance as one would expect from a house cat approaching a saucer of milk.

While Rex and Amy looked on cautiously, the animal circled the pair a number of times as his eyes passed over them almost clinically. He wasn't a big cat. In fact, as street cats go, he was quite small. His coat showed his obviously questionable lineage. His back was patterned randomly with black and white shapes that dissolved seamlessly into grey stripes as they wrapped under his belly. His head was entirely black, except for one ear which was stark white. His tail was almost the exact reverse, being almost entirely white but with a black tip. Three of his legs were black while one was grey striped with a white sock.

Though not a classically beautiful cat by any means, he was certainly a striking figure.

He finally finished his examination of the dogs and moved closer to look each one over. Amy almost gasped at the sheer beauty of the creature's eyes. They were green, but of a shade she'd only once encountered before. It was the color of the ocean after a storm as the first shaft of sunlight hits the water.

"So," the cat said calmly as it sat directly in front of them, "you're expecting our help?"

"No," Rex responded, slightly surprised by the question.

"Then why are you here?" the cat countered.

"It's a long story," Amy began.

"But you do want our help?" the cat interrupted.

"Actually... no!" Amy replied with mild amusement.

"You must have intended to ask us for something," the cat explained, "or you wouldn't be here."

"To be quite honest," Rex joined in, "we're not entirely sure where here even is, so you'll have to take our word for it that we didn't come here to ask for anything from you."

"You're joking!" the cat replied in amazement.

"Not in the least," said Amy

"No, we're not," added Rex.

"How frightfully odd." The puzzled feline began to lick his left front paw. "So if you don't know where you are, you therefore presumably haven't a clue who I am or indeed, who we are?"

"Exactly!" Amy responded happily.

"Most odd! Most odd indeed." The cat began to clean its other paw. His eyes, however, never left the two dogs. He gave the matter some deep thought until he suddenly lowered his paw and began to laugh.

At first it was just a lighthearted little titter, but it grew rapidly into an out-and-out guffaw of incredible proportions.

Amy and Rex stared at the laughing creature in complete puzzlement.

The cat turned to the other felines and announced, "They don't know who we are!"

Laughter then erupted from every corner of the level. It jumped from one group of cats to another, then back again. Angel had the sense to use their mirth to slip out from between the yowling animals and move closer to Rex and Amy.

"What is going on down here?" Rex whispered to the Spaniel.

"You tell me! I was checking around a few levels farther up when a couple of big tomcats grabbed me and led me down here."

The lead cat finally stopped laughing, and after wiping a tear away with one paw, he again focused on the three dogs.

"You've heard of *Los Gatos de la Noche*?" he asked, expecting some sign of recognition.

Amy and Angel shook their heads in unison. It wasn't until Amy noticed that Rex not only seemed to have heard of *Los Gatos de la Noche*, but was suddenly pale and shaky, that she realized something serious had just taken place.

"Perhaps you should take a moment to acquaint your friends with the G.N.," the cat said, smiling at Rex.

Rex turned to Amy and Angel, and after a deep breath began. "The *Gatos* are famous. Legend has it that during the time of the Dark Years in Spain and other adjoining countries a few cats got together and…"

"Sorry to interrupt" Angel interrupted "But what were the Dark Years… and where or what is Spain?"

They turned and faced the Spaniel in amazement. Even Amy was stunned at this hole in her friend's knowledge, especially as she had come to believe that Angel was a well-informed pup.

"May I?" Rex asked the lead cat almost humbly.

"Please," the cat replied with a wave of his paw.

"Spain is a far away country across a great expanse of water and the dark years, well…, where do I begin?" He thought a minute and began. "The Dark Years, or Middle Ages as humans refer to them, was a time long ago when the bipeds began condemning cats as symbols of paganism and agents of Satan."

Both Angel and Amy looked confused. Rex leaned over and whispered, "I'll explain some of those words later." This brought relieved nods from both dogs.

"Cats were hunted and slaughtered sometimes even in front of audiences," Rex continued "In some instances, they were actually tied to wooden stakes and burned alive."

Amy let out an inadvertent moan, then looked down in embarrassment.

Rex smiled understandingly at her. "Needless to say, those were horrific times for felines. Within a matter of a few generations, the cat population was nearly eliminated. At that point, in a village in Spain, a small band of cats decided to show their claws and do something about it. They formed a secret society whose members were willing to avenge their fallen brethren and fight the biped oppression, returning felines to their rightful position as noble and beneficial beasts. This society was called '*Los Gatos de la Noche*' or 'The Cats of the Night.'"

Rex looked at the cat to see if he approved of his rendition of the tale. The green eyes stared calmly back at him without a trace of emotion. Rex began to feel uncomfortable and glanced over at Amy for moral support.

"Close enough!" the cat said finally. "Actually we're not so much into the... what did you call it, 'fighting biped oppression' any more. We're now more into... how shall I put it... more refined pursuits!"

"Like what?" Angel asked innocently.

The cat took a step toward her and suddenly rubbed his head against her chin. "Such innocence. How refreshing! I'm talking about crime, my long-eared friend. Crime! More specifically, crimes of the night."

"Oh," Angel murmured, subtly trying to back away from the still-pushing feline. "Then this must be your... hideout?"

"Hideout! What a lovely term. It has a nice ring to it... Hide... out. Yes you could I suppose, call this, our... hide out. Wait!"

The cat suddenly jumped back, causing the three dogs to edge closer together.

"I haven't introduced myself, have I?" he said apologetically. "It's astonishing how one's manners seem to simply vanish when dealing with the scum of the earth." He glanced back at the other cats behind him, who smiled at their leader.

"Allow me to introduce myself. My name is Byxorician Ovintle Blyltrix."

"You're joking!" Amy said before she could stop herself. "I do apologize. That was rude of me. It's just that that's a most unusual name."

"Do you really think so?" Byxorician Ovintle Blyltrix asked with mild interest.

"Don't you?" Amy found herself replying.

"Actually, no, but if it makes it easier for you, everyone here calls me BOB," he said with a grin.

"In that case... Bob, allow me to introduce myself and my friends. That's Rex. He's our leader."

"Charmed." Bob held out his paw which Rex touched with his own.

"Angel you know, of course."

"Delighted." Again the paw was offered. Angel was clearly slightly dubious about the whole thing but gave the proffered limb a brief touch with her paw.

"And I am Amy."

"Simply enchanted," Bob purred as he presented the paw for the last time.

Once the introductions were complete, a silence fell over the group as each tried to think of something to say.

"So," Bob said as he began to lick his own belly with long careful strokes, "now that you know who we are, you must be bursting with questions. I will allow you one, as you are our guests."

"How'd you get the lights to work on those cars?" Angel blurted out without conferring with the others.

Rex and Amy both shot her a disapproving glance which she stoically ignored, keeping her eyes on Bob.

"I offered you the answer to a question that could have uncovered any of the most cherished secrets held by the *Gatos* but instead you want to know how we control a light! How simple-minded! I like it! Well, my long-eared friend, it's simple. The bipeds leave these vehicles here for varying lengths of time to be safely looked after and maintained. The ones down here on our level have been here by far the longest, yet they are still washed weekly but, more important to us, they have their batteries charged regularly as well. All we do is send one of our Biped-Hand Dexterity Specialists into each car and turn the lights on. It's simple."

"Biped-Hand Dexterity Specialists?" Amy repeated questioningly.

"Oh yes! In our business it's no longer possible to simply rely on feline instincts and abilities to carry out our work. We now use cats with specialized training in basic electronics, security systems, computers, you name it!"

"What exactly do you do that requires that sort of knowledge?" Amy inquired with keen interest.

"You'd really like to know?" Bob asked casually as he moved his grooming efforts to his tail section.

"Yes, please," Amy replied.

"What a shame then that your friend... Angel, isn't it, used up your one question. Oh well, life can be hard sometimes."

"Please, Bob, we'd love to know more." Amy pleaded.

Bob stopped his washing and stood facing the three dogs. "Let me make one thing clear. The reason the G.N. has survived and, in fact, thrived, is due not simply to our devotion to the cause and our talents, but because of our codes and rules. They were set down long ago, but no cat today ever breaks any of them. Part of the code is that whatever we say, we mean. It sounds mind-numbingly simple, but it is, I believe, one of the strongest attributes of our society. We always know exactly where we stand with anyone. It's what makes us so unified and efficient. That's the main reason human beings are always in such a mess. They always will be as long as no biped can trust anything another one has to say. I personally would have thought that by now they would have learned this, but I am obviously giving them far more credit than they deserve."

"But what's that got to…" Amy began.

"What's that got to do with my only answering one of your questions?"

Amy nodded.

"Very simple. I promised you the answer to one question! I meant one question. It's what I said, it's what I meant, and it's what I did. See how simple it is!"

"But I didn't know," Angel mumbled sadly.

"You should always know the rules before entering someone else's domain. It's common sense," he replied matter-of-factly.

"Now look here, Bob," Rex said using his most serious tone "We didn't know you were even down here. We were searching for chicken when we got shut in this place. Then Angel went missing and we had to come down here to find her, so you see, it's not as if we were prepared for this encounter. We simply didn't know any of this would happen."

"Do you realize how silly that story makes you sound? You blindly stumble into a place you know nothing about purely because of a good smell! Then, you allow yourselves to be trapped with, if I'm not mistaken, half your team still up top, shut on the other side of the gate! Let me be blunt. Stop thinking with your noses! You have brains. Use them. I watch dogs every day sticking their noses in places I don't even wish to talk about. I mean, really! I've seen you lot begin a romantic encounter after no more than a sniff at another dog's backside. Stop acting like such animals. You have eyes and ears and brains. Use them. Think before you leap, for a change."

The three dogs all hung their heads in embarrassment.

"There's no need to get down on yourselves," Bob added to try to cheer them up. "Most of it's in your genes and you can't help it. I know that. All I'm saying is give your brain a chance occasionally. All right?"

The three dogs nodded their heads. Amy was the first to look up into the smiling face that was observing their every reaction.

"Enough of my lecturing! You lot haven't told me of your quest!"

"Our quest?" Angel replied blankly.

"You obviously have a quest, otherwise you wouldn't all be together stuck here in the middle of the city, would you?"

"Well…?" Angel began.

"In case you think that anyone's going to mistake you for a pack of street dogs, forget it," Bob said with amusement. "I've never seen a bunch of hounds with so much man sense about them. It does show, you know!"

"I didn't realize," Amy said with surprise. "What do you mean, it shows."

"Simple, your poise, your speech, your coats, your figures, everything about you points to lives that have been governed by humans."

Rex nodded slowly as if accepting the cat's words without any great problem.

Angel, on the other, hand seemed quite upset at Bob's observation. "I think that's very rude," she began. "Here we are, guests in your… your… whatever this place is, and you're calling us…"

"I'm not calling you anything." Bob interrupted gently "There's nothing wrong with it at all. In fact, if anything, it's a plus."

"But you said…" Angel whined.

"I said you don't look like street dogs! That's good! Street dogs usually look underfed, fight-scarred, nervous and dirty. You're getting close in the dirt department, but apart from that, there's no comparison."

The three dogs checked each other out from their new perspective as non-street dogs.

"So someone tell me about your quest!" Bob persisted.

"It's not a quest, exactly," Rex began

"It's more of a…." Amy tried to find the right words "A…."

"Oh for heaven sake, you two!" Angel interrupted "It's perfectly simple. We were all dognapped by the same gang of bipeds and imprisoned together in a horrible place near a river which is where we met. We were trying to get out of London when one of the group got caught by the gang who is now holding him at the same place they held us. Clear enough?"

"And you're going back to try to rescue him, are you?" Bob asked with interest.

"Of course," Rex replied.

"Do you have a plan?" Bob asked.

"Not really," Amy said, slightly embarrassed.

"Well, where exactly is this place they're holding him?"

"We're not sure," Rex also looked a little subdued.

"So let me see if I've got this straight," Bob said. "You're on your way to rescue your friend, but you don't know where he is or what you'll do when you find him. Is that about it?"

"Not exactly," Amy said defensively "We're actually on our way to meet Saint Paul. He'll help us find Rodney. That's our friend's name, by the way."

"Very nice," Bob said clearly uninterested. "What's this about Saint Paul and his helping you nonsense?"

"It's not nonsense," Angel declared. "Everyone knows that saints are good humans and are always there to help bipeds or animals."

Bob looked to each face, trying not to burst into laughter. "You lot are too much, you really are! I don't know how you've stayed in one piece so far, but it's time you realized that it's not a game out there. The streets are tough and mean and are ready to swallow up a group of wide-eyed, pampered innocents like you in nothing flat!"

Bob noticed Rex shaking his head slowly from side to side, clearly not accepting his words of warning.

"You think you're a tough one, do you?" Bob asked him coldly. "Been around, have you?"

"Actually, yes," Rex answered forcefully. "I'm not a house dog. I'm a guard dog. I can take care of myself."

"Really!" Bob said casually as he gestured to one of the tomcats standing behind him.

"Yes. Really," Rex countered as he watched the tom slowly approach him from the side. He tensed, knowing that the large cat obviously was there to show him a thing or two about street smarts and toughness. He knew he was ready for any move the cat would try as he shifted his weight onto his haunches ready to spring up and out-maneuver his adversary.

The next thing he knew, something had hit him from the other side. One moment he was readying himself for an attack from the approaching tom, the next he was on his back with legs splayed as another tom that he hadn't even seen, held a paw full of razor sharp nails against the pink flesh of his exposed belly. He dared not move as the cat clearly had the upper hand and could all too easily mortally wound him even before he could have shaken him off his stomach.

"Thank you, Claude," Bob said matter-of-factly to the tom, who then dismounted Rex and with a brief bow turned and rejoined the other cats.

Rex got to his feet and after a shake to rid himself of the dirt and dust from the floor, turned to Bob with a growing smile on his muzzle.

"Point well taken," he said with complete sincerity.

Bob simply nodded. He then turned to Amy and Angel, who seemed stunned by the demonstration. Their eyes were wide open, as were their mouths. Bob could see that they were breathing fast and panting.

"Please accept my apologies, ladies," he said sweetly, "but I felt a demonstration in this case was worth more than a thousand words."

Rex grinned broadly for their benefit.

"It's all right. I'm fine. He had a point to make and he made it! He's right. We're obviously not particularly well suited for street life."

"But such violence!" Amy said, her voice still trembling slightly.

"If I get Bob's meaning, that was nothing compare with the violence we could expect to find outside," Rex stated matter-of-factly.

"So," Bob said as if nothing had happened, "let's outline a couple of things you may find helpful in your quest. By the way, yours is a quest. And a noble one, too!"

The three dogs felt a sudden moment of pride as they realized that the cat was right.

"First," continued Bob "Saint Paul is not a human. St. Paul's is a cathedral!"

"A what?" Amy asked.

"A cathedral!" Angel replied as she shook her head. "I knew that! It's like a big church. Oh, how silly of me! Of course! St. Paul's Cathedral. Completed in the year 1711 by Christopher Wren as a symbol of…"

"Thank you, Angel," Amy interrupted gently. "We get the point."

"I don't," said Rex. "How's this cathedral thing going to help us?"

The others all turned and stared at Rex in astonishment.

"I don't think this is funny at all," Amy said seriously. "What do we do about Rodney now? Who's going to help us?"

There was a long silence as one by one, the three dogs looked at Bob.

"Oh no! Don't even think about it," he said swishing his tail rapidly from side to side. "The G.N. doesn't do mercenary work. I'll give you some advice, but that's it."

Amy pleaded. "Rodney is an animal like you and me who's been imprisoned wrongly by the same type of bipeds that forced the creation of your society in the first place."

"Maybe, but…" Bob tried to counter.

"Maybe nothing!" Amy continued firmly. "What happened to all that stuff about *Los Gatos de la Noche* fighting for their oppressed brethren? What about vengeance against tyrannical humans? What about…?"

"Stop! Enough!" Bob said rising to his feet. "I told you, we don't do that anymore. We can't afford the luxury of softhearted ideals getting in the way of our primary interests."

"And those are?" Amy was beginning to sound peeved.

Bob stared long and hard at each canine face before replying. Finally, he said defensively, "Profit!"

"Profit?" Amy cried "What happened to the…"

"Amy!" Rex interrupted sternly. "This is none of our business."

"But…" she tried again.

"Amy!" Rex again stopped her and then turned to Bob. "I'm sorry. Goldie here is passionate about her views of right and wrong. Sometimes she insists on voicing them at inappropriate moments like this."

"There's no need to apologize. I only wish we could help," Bob said, slightly defensive.

"You could if you really wanted to!" Angel piped in.

Everyone turned and stared at her in amazement.

"Well, he could!" she stated with timid force.

Bob checked each face again as he began to carefully wash the underside of one paw. This went on for a while as the three dogs nervously looked on. Finally the washing stopped.

"You three are rude!" Bob announced.

"What?" the three stammered in unison.

"Yes, very rude indeed! You come into my home and then, without so much as a by your leave, you start lecturing, not only to me but to the entire society of the *Los Gatos de la Noche*, on how we should run our lives. That is what I call rude! I would like to ask that if you plan to remain here any longer…"

"Like we have a choice!" Amy mumbled under her breath.

Bob continued, glaring at Amy "…and that you will from this point on begin acting like guests."

Amy was about to respond, but Rex bit her gently on the rump.

With a furious look she swallowed her words and stared angrily down at the ground. Rex looked at Angel, who was also focusing on the floor. With a slight smile on his muzzle, he then dropped his eyes to join the others.

Finally, the three dogs slowly lifted their eyes and saw that Bob was smiling quite genuinely toward them.

"Would I be correct in assuming," he said with light amusement in his voice, "that a little supper would do down quite well about now?"

"Food?" Angel shrieked, forgetting all else as her tongue began lolling out the side of her mouth. giving her an imbecilic look.

"Yes, my dear, food. Sustenance, nourishment, feed, call it what you like! This is Wednesday, and Andre usually prepares something quite exceptional on Wednesdays. Shall we see what he's put together this evening?"

The three canine heads nodded in unison as each dog began to fantasize on his or her own vision of Andre's feast. Bob stretched himself into a standing position and then, with a flip of his tail spun around and began walking away from them.

"I suggest you follow me," Bob said without looking back. "We don't deliver!"

The dogs obediently got to their feet and followed the cat past the biped vehicles and through the sea of feline figures, which parted noiselessly to allow their leader to pass through.

Bob led the dogs to the farthest wall of the lowest level and with pride and a sweep of one paw, gestured for them to behold the Wednesday night buffet. Against one wall and laid out on a flat protruding section of concrete, was the cats' feast.

There could be little doubt for whom this meal was intended. Andre, it seemed, had done an outstanding job to cater to a feline's every whim. The spread began at one end of the banquet table with a selection of tiny sparrows each artistically arranged on its own cabbage leaf; next were what Amy had first thought were raisins, until on examination proved them to be flies, thousands of them. The display continued with delicacy upon delicacy until it culminated with Andre's *piece de resistance*. At first, the dogs couldn't even begin to guess what they were looking at—small round balls, each with a stick-like protuberance that stuck straight up out of each. It wasn't until they observed one cat bite into one that they realized they were roasted field mice!

"Help yourselves," Bob encouraged. "There's plenty. Andre always overdoes it!"

The three dogs looked the length of the banquet and then forlornly back at Bob without saying a word.

"I thought you were hungry?"

The three shook their heads sadly. They were of course famished, but not enough to eat any of the bizarre assortment currently spread before them.

"It's not the food, is it?" Bob asked with concern.

"No, of course not," Amy answered politely.

"Good. Good. I'd hate to think you didn't approve of our little buffet."

The three dogs offered him their best smiles.

"You know, I just thought of something," Bob said as if to himself.

He turned and trotted off toward one of the biped vehicles. He crawled under the front of it and could be heard scratching at something. They all then heard something drop to the ground. Bob reappeared backing himself out from under the car dragging a large brown paper bag. He managed to pull the hefty bundle over to the three dogs and left it at their feet.

"I know you can't wait to dive into our fine feast, but just in case our meal might be a little too refined for your palates...." he said with a slight smile.

With that he turned away and joined a couple of comrades already in line for the buffet. Amy looked to Rex, wondering what exactly was expected of them, when Angel acted on their behalf. She bent her muzzle to the large brown bag and grabbed the bottom of it and lifted. The contents spilled out onto the ground, revealing piece after piece of still warm, succulently prepared roast chicken. Even Angel simply stood and stared at the dream meal that had been produced for their enjoyment.

Amy looked up and sought Bob out among the myriad of feline banqueters. She spotted him almost immediately, in the midst of a group of tough looking tomcats, clearly telling them some sort of story. The toms hung on every word as they stared in rapt fascination at their noble leader. As if sensing her look, Bob glanced over toward her. She mouthed the words "thank you" to which she was rewarded with an amused wink from Bob before he turned back to his story telling.

The three dogs settled to the ground and began their long overdue meal. At one point Amy suddenly remembered Hans and Lester shut out in the night somewhere overhead. A passing Siamese assured her, however, that they'd been recently checked on and were fine. They'd been taken some dinner earlier in the evening and were fast asleep, still nestled up against the unkempt biped.

Once fully sated, Amy found it difficult to keep her own eyes open, but knew it would be terribly rude to simply eat and then nap when in someone else's home. She turned to the others to begin some conversation but found that both were already fast asleep, Rex in a dignified curl with his head resting on his own hindquarter and Angel in an unladylike pose, flat on her back with her legs splayed out. Her tongue dangled out of the side of her mouth and her small but bulging belly rose and settled rhythmically in sleep.

Amy looked over to the cats and saw to her astonishment that they were gone. Not all of them, but certainly most. As she watched, she saw the few remaining felines cleaning up the last traces of their buffet. Then, one by one, they walked to a particularly dark corner of the level and simply vanished into the wall. As she continued to observe the parting felines, the light of the vehicles suddenly clicked off one at a time. Finally the last pair of lights was extinguished.

She felt her eyes growing heavier by the second as she heard the sounds of the last few cats depart to begin their night's endeavors as decreed by membership in *Los Gatos de la Noche*.

As Amy closed her eyes, she heard Bob's voice only inches from her ear.

"Don't stir, my tired friend," he whispered almost dreamily. "Now you need to sleep. Tomorrow your adventure continues and I wish you and your friends every possible success. Remember, the *Gatos* will always be with you."

Amy then felt the gentlest of licks on her muzzle. Feeling a new sense of warmth and security, she allowed sleep to pull her down into its bosom.

twenty eight

Amy woke before the others and realized that she was able to see. She raised her head and saw that light was coming from above from a series of long tubular devices that also exuded an annoying high pitched buzzing sound.

Suddenly something tapped her on her shoulder. She yelped and leaped up in surprise. She spun around and involuntarily began to growl at whatever had touched her.

She only saw the briefest glimpse of a full and colorful tail whisking out of sight under one of the biped vehicles. Amy walked slowly over to the vehicle and cautiously bent her head to peer under it. Cowering in the darkness was a cat. A very nervous and frightened cat. Even in the gloom, Amy could see that it was a unusual-looking animal. She had long hair, which gave an immediate impression of bulk, but on closer inspection, Amy could see that the animal, under her heavy coat, was actually quite petite. Amy couldn't make out much more because of the shadows, and for a few moments simply looked back into a pair of rapidly blinking olive eyes that were nervously trained on her.

"I'm sorry if I startled you," Amy said in as gentle a voice as possible. "But you see, you actually gave me quite a start as well."

There was a long silence then a tiny timid voice wafted out from under the vehicle.

"I'm terribly sorry... I... I... didn't mean to frighten you... I... I... simply wanted to introduce myself."

Amy smiled back at the animal, waiting for the introduction. None came. In fact, the cat didn't utter another word. Finally Amy felt it necessary to break the silence.

"You mentioned something about introducing yourself," Amy prodded softly.

"Oh yes. I... I did, didn't I? Thank you for reminding me."

Again there was silence.

"Well?" Amy tried to keep the impatience from her voice.

"I'm working on it," the cat replied nervously. "It's not easy, you know."

"Yes, it is. Look, I'll begin, shall I? My name is Amy. What's yours?"

Again, no reply. Amy waited and waited and was finally about to give up n the whole encounter when the timid voice responded.

"My name's Ryphoryl Ynextril Eytludnur."

Amy shook her head at the complexity of yet another cat name.

"I presume they call you Rye?" Amy inquired hopefully.

"No," came the answer.

"Well, what then?"

"I... I... told you. Ryphoryl Ynextril Eytludnur."

"Oh" Amy said somewhat embarrassed "I'm afraid that your name is simply too much for me to cope with! If you have no objection, I will call you Rye."

"If you must," Rye replied dejectedly.

"And you'll have to come out from under this vehicle if you wish to carry on a conversation with me."

"All right," Rye again replied.

Amy waited for the cat to appear, but after a good few moments realized that Rye hadn't budged.

"I'm waiting," Amy announced.

"I'm… I'm… working on it," Rye replied nervously. "It's not easy, you know!"

"Why do you keep saying that?" Amy asked crossly. " It's perfectly easy. Now come out from there."

"I will." Rye sounded quite distressed. "Just give me a moment."

"I'm not going to hurt you, you know," Amy said comfortingly.

"Okay," came the unconvinced reply.

Amy again waited for the animal to appear. Finally to her delight and surprise, Rye's head came into view.

"Well, hello!" Amy said cheerfully to the just visible face.

"I can't," Rye squeaked and shot back under the vehicle. "I'm sorry. I thought I could, but I can't."

"What's wrong with you?" Amy asked feeling pity for the obviously disturbed creature.

"I'm… I'm…" Rye tried to speak.

"You're… sick?" Amy offered.

"N..No. I'm… I'm…"

"Shy?" Amy tried again.

"N..No.. I'm… I'm… a…"

"Oh come on. Spit it out!" Amy was again becoming impatient with the cat.

"I'm a scaredy cat!" Rye blurted out.

"A what?"

"A scaredy cat! I can't help it. It's what I am."

"Well, there's nothing to be afraid of out here, so please come out from under that thing so I can at least see you."

"Why?"

"So I can talk to you."

"You… You're talking now!" the voice said hopefully.

"That's enough!" Amy snapped, her good nature wearing thin. "You come out here this minute or I'll simply have to crawl under there after you!"

"You wouldn't!" Rye said with weak defiance.

"I most certainly would!" Amy stated firmly.

Amy heard some movement under the vehicle, and then, with agonizing slowness, Rye slid out. With her eyes darting about fearfully, Rye got to her feet and faced Amy.

The first thing that struck Amy was Rye's beauty. Her coat was gorgeously long, full and resplendent as it gleamed under the lights. It was multicolored with patches of white, black and orange that covered not only her coat, but her face as well.

The second thing that struck Amy was that Rye couldn't seem to sit still. Not for a second. As Amy tried to comfort the terrified cat with a glowing smile and happy pant, the poor feline seemed unable to control any part of her body. She'd sit for a second trying to be still, then suddenly begin frantically licking a paw or leg, only to stop abruptly and begin scratching at her shoulder or her ear. What made it worse was that Amy could tell these actions were a side effect of her almost debilitating fear.

Amy tried to ignore the licking and scratching, but found that the longer she stared at the animal, the more she herself began to itch as if catching the cat's affliction.

Finally Rye's nervous movements began to abate slightly, and Amy felt she could converse without sending the cat into a frenzy of some sort.

"You know, Rye, you have the most beautiful coat."

"Thank you," Rye replied with a tremble to her voice.

"I hope you don't mind my calling you Rye, but those names of yours really are complicated."

"Do you think so?" Rye asked quite sincerely.

"Yes, I do. They're so long and so… different."

"I think that's the whole point," Rye said meekly.

"The point of what?" Amy inquired with real interest.

"The point of having a name!" Rye said with timid conviction "With cats, every name is different. Just as every cat is different. I mean what's the point of being born a completely unique creature and then carrying a name that's been used hundreds or even thousands of times before? We feel that every single cat will always have their own name, fresh and new for them to keep as their own. That's why they are a little long and complicated. It's not that easy to make up new names after hundreds of generations have gone before."

"I see," said Amy with a mixture of surprise and interest.

A silence ensued as Amy waited for Rye to speak further, but no words came.

"Rye?" she asked casually.

"Y...Yes?"

"Did you want something?" Amy inquired.

"No, why?" Rye replied nervously.

"Well you did wake me up for some purpose, unless I'm quite mistaken."

"Oh. Oh... Yes. I forgot. I'm sorry. I get so scared sometimes, I can't think straight."

"That must be terrible," Amy offered sincerely.

"It is. It is," Rye said, nodding her head emphatically.

Amy waited for Rye's reason for waking her. Again no words were forthcoming. She finally cleared her throat noisily as a hint to the trembling cat. Rye simply stared back at her with a terrified and completely blank gaze.

"Oh, yes!" she suddenly cried, remembering what she had to say. "I am your guide!"

"My what?" Amy asked suspiciously.

"Your guide! I was chosen to stay behind and help lead you on your quest."

"Pardon my bluntness, Rye, and please don't be offended because I'm sure you mean well, but... Aren't you just a tad edgy to act as our guide?"

"No... Not really. My scared disposition has no effect on my tracking ability whatsoever."

"So what have we here?" Rex boomed playfully as he suddenly appeared behind them.

Rye's beautiful coat instantly enlarged to double its size just fractions of a second before she dove back under the biped vehicle with a shriek.

"What was that?" Rex asked, clearly startled by Rye's frantic departure.

"That was our guide," Amy responded straight-faced.

"I see," Rex said as he lowered his head to peer under the vehicle. "Sorry to have startled you... Uh..."

"Rye! We're calling her Rye. Her cat name is was too complicated," Amy said matter-of-factly.

"Rye... you can come out. It's quite safe," Rex coaxed.

It took quite a while, but eventually after enormous patience, they managed to convince Rye that none of her nine lives were in jeopardy. Once out from under the vehicle, she gave herself a thorough wash with fast darting motions that made Rex and Amy fidgety. They tried to interrupt the cleaning process a couple of times to ask a question or two but were utterly ignored.

Rye finished with one last convulsive lick of her left shoulder, and then with a deep sigh, sat and faced the two dogs.

"So... where am I taking you exactly?" she asked shyly.

"I thought you were supposed to guide us!" Rex said stiffly. "I mean isn't that the point..."

"I think Rye needs some idea of where to guide us to?" Amy interrupted gently. "Am I correct?"

Rye was staring intently down at the ground next to her feet. Amy assumed the cat was deep in thought until she suddenly began pawing at something small that was moving across the road-like surface. She managed to ensnare whatever it was in one claw, which she then raised to eye level for examination.

"Rye?" Amy said with gentle annoyance.

"Mm?" Rye murmured to herself, her attention focused on her paw.

"Rye!" Amy snapped angrily, causing both Rye and Rex to jump.

"What did you do that for? "Rye whimpered as tears began to form in her eyes. "You yelled at me!"

"If you're going to guide us, you are going to have to pay attention," Amy scolded. "And besides, that was hardly a yell."

"I was only grooming!" Rye replied with moist eyes downcast.

"Well, I'm sorry if I frightened you," Amy said softly. "Are you all right?"

"Yes," came the sullen reply.

"And you won't go dashing off at the first thing that startles you?" Rex added.

"No." Rye raised her eyes to the two dogs. "I was chosen to guide you, and that's what I'll do!"

"Good," said Rex.

"Yes, good for you, Rye!" Amy said sweetly. "Once we get going, I'm sure you'll be fine."

"Do you really?" Rye asked hopefully.

"Absolutely!" Amy replied.

At that moment Angel let out a loud howl in her sleep for no apparent reason. Rex and Amy smiled over at their sleeping friend then turned back to Rye. She was gone. Well, not completely, the tip of her multi colored tail was just visible as it flicked from side to side back under the biped vehicle.

"As I said," Amy grinned over at Rex, "...once we get going!"

It took a while to coax Rye out from under the vehicle for the third time. Once out, however, she seemed intent on trying to relax and help formulate some sort of plan to find where Rodney was being held prisoner. The first phase was to join up with Lester and Hans, which turned out to be easy. Even as Rye volunteered (to everyone's surprise) to sneak up to the top level and check on the two dogs, they came striding down the sloping drive, both looking none the worse for wear.

Amy introduced them to Rye and highlighted the previous night's encounter with the G.N. They were suitably impressed and eager to start off on what they all now termed their "Quest."

The dogs took turns describing to Rye every detail they could recall about the place in which they'd all been imprisoned. Rye tried to connect their details to any area she knew but with no success. The problem was that the dogs' descriptions of the run-down dilapidated buildings could quite easily fit miles of Dockland territory.

"There must have been something unusual," Rye urged.

"No, there wasn't," Rex insisted. "There was simply row after row of old brick buildings. There was nothing different about any of them."

"We're forgetting. There must have been something out of the ordinary," Amy said as she racked her brain trying to remember anything that would help. "We're just not thinking hard enough."

The dogs all strained themselves trying to sort through the thin memories they all held of their escape.

"Wait," Angel suddenly squealed. "I know... the... the... oh, come on! What was it called... you know... the thing... the..."

Her face began to turn red with exertion. The others looked on in silent hope, as she grew more and more crimson. "The anchor thing!" she finally blurted out joyously. "The big anchor, remember?!"

The others all did.

"Very good, Angel!" Amy cried. "The anchor, of course!"

"The anchor!" sighed Lester.

"The big anchor! How silly of us," Hans said, shaking his head.

"That's a landmark, all right!" Rex stated.

The five dogs turned happily to face Rye.

"What's an anchor?" she asked timidly.

The dogs looked at one another with a mixture of disbelief and frustration.

"Oh come on, you must know!" Lester stated with conviction. "I think bipeds must use them to keep their water vehicles in one place."

"Big hook like things," Angel added.

"On the end of lengths of chain," Amy contributed.

The dogs all stopped their descriptions to see if anything was sinking in with Rye.

"Oh, *those*," she said.

"So you do know what we mean?" Rex asked hopefully.

"Of course. I may be scared, but I'm not stupid."

"So what do you call them?" Lester asked.

"What?" Rye replied.

"Anchors!" the dogs yelled in unison.

That only caused Rye to visibly shrink in front of them, and as she took a step backward toward the vehicle, Amy rushed to her side, full of apologies.

"We're awfully sorry. We quite forgot how sensitive you are. We only wanted to know what the cat word for anchor was."

"There isn't one."

"But there must be," Lester insisted.

"No, there mustn't!" Rye countered with surprising strength. "Cats don't bother with things like that. There's enough to do without wasting our time needlessly."

"So what do you call something if you need to discuss it and there's no word for it," Angel asked with interest.

"If there's no word for it, it obviously isn't worth discussing now, is it?"

The dogs all glanced at one another, and by some silent signal between them, decided to venture no further into cat logic.

"All right," Rex said as patiently as he could, "But have you even seen the… anchor… that we're referring to? It's a huge thing on a stone base."

"Of course"

"And you can take us there?"

"Certainly!" Rye answered matter-of-factly "I'm your guide!"

"When can we leave?" Amy asked.

At that moment the animals heard the sounds of a biped approaching the lower lever. The human was whistling discordantly to himself, and by the sound of it, was dragging a squeaky wheeled object along with him.

"I would suggest right now," Rye said urgently. Her earlier calmness began ebbing away right in front of them. Her tail re-inflated and her twitching resumed.

"Is, is, Ev…Everyone ready?" she stammered.

They all nodded.

Rye took a deep breath and dashed to the darkest corner of the level. Just before she vanished in the shadows, she looked back to the dogs that hadn't budged an inch.

"C…Come… Come on then… Hurry!"

They all looked to Rex to see if he was willing to hand over their safety to the neurotic feline or would rather stay and take a stand against the rapidly approaching biped. With one formal nod of his head, the dogs dashed off after Rye's retreating tail. Rex and Amy were the last to step into the dark corner and took a moment to look at each other before doing so. Rex gave her a warm hearted push with his fine muzzle then followed her into the blackness ahead.

twenty nine

At first the dogs could see nothing at all in the darkness that surrounded them and simply followed by sound.

Finally, after what seemed an eternity, they stepped down into a long, narrow cavern. Rye explained that it was a branch of the city's sewage system canals that only transported water run-off, not actual… well you know. She led them through one cavern after another as the canals branched and re-branched forming an arterial network far from the eyes of the bipeds above ground.

As the dogs followed Rye along a narrow raised walkway next to the fast flowing water, they all took extra care with their footing, as a fall into the rushing torrent would end in disaster. They finally reached the staggering sight they had seen before, from above, the huge and mighty Thames. The cavern they were in simply stopped at the retaining wall of the river. The dogs stared out through the circular opening that would have been the continuation of the cavern had it in fact continued. As their vision adjusted to daylight, the five dogs and the cat looked out upon a bright, sunny and bustling day that awaited them, if they could find a way out of the cavern.

After a pause, Rye pointed out a narrow stone walkway on the cavern wall and a stairway, at the top of which was a circular metal disk. She asked Hans, whose head and neck were the largest, to push upward with all his might to dislodge the obstruction. His push sent the metal disk rolling off along the street, much to the consternation of some passing pedestrians.

Rye stuck her head up through the hole and pronounced their escape route clear. The exit placed the dogs smack in the center of a busy sidewalk which paralleled the river. Instructed by Rye, who was indeed proving herself to be a skilled guide after all, the animals dashed up and out into the bright sunlit day, making directly for a large row of neatly manicured bushes only a few feet from the opening.

From their vantage point in the bushes, the dogs could see that they were next to an odd-looking structure that ran right up to a bridge that spanned the river. The bridge was not however anything like the one they'd crossed only a few days earlier. Even with their limited memories of the crossing itself, they knew that this bridge was different.

First of all, on either end of its span were what looked like tall narrow houses, each with decorative windows and blue roofs.

The second thing was that the bridge, for that was what it must have been, didn't quite reach all the way across the river. It almost did, but in the center the roadway opened in the middle, rising in the air at an angle and leaving an empty space between the two sides. They looked on as a large water vehicle passed between the two raised roadway sections hooting loudly as it went.

They shifted their attention finally when they heard Angel let out a single long-winded whine.

"What's the matter?" Amy asked with concern.

"That!" she said pointing with her muzzle toward the large and ancient structure situated at the start of the bridge.

"What about it?" Rex asked.

"T...Tow...Tower...Tower...Of...L...Lon...Lond...don. Tower of London," Lester read from a banner that hung from one wall of the place.

"Exactly!" Angel whispered. "The Tower of London! Do you know what used to go on in there?"

The dogs and cat all shook their heads.

Angel's voice was low and clearly filled with fear. "That's where the biped rulers used to chop off the heads of other bipeds. Sometimes even those of their mates."

"So why are you so upset?" Rex asked bluntly.

"They cut off their heads!" Angel exclaimed.

"Did they ever cut off any dog's heads?" Rex asked.

"Well… No!" Angel replied, sounding surprised.

"Then I hardly think they'll start with us!"

He continued smartly, "Rye, what's the next move?"

"We have to cross that bridge," Rye said.

"Hardly!" Amy mumbled more to herself than for anyone else's benefit.

"It's easy. I'll show you." Rye said calmly.

The dogs all turned back to face the incomplete bridge and were dumbstruck. The roadway was no longer separated in the center. The bridge was fully intact. As they watched in amazement, biped vehicles moved across it as if nothing had happened.

"But…" Rex tried to voice his confusion.

"That's Tower Bridge," Rye stated. "The bipeds built it quite cleverly. The middle bit rises and lets the bigger water vessels go under it."

"It's called a drawbridge," Angel added. "In fact, Tower Bridge is one of the oldest examples of its kind. It was built in the eleventh century for the purpose of…"

"Thank you, Angel" Amy interrupted gently." But I think we should be going while the going's good, don't you?"

She turned to Rye for her opinion, but there was no Rye to be seen.

"Oh! Oh!" Hans cried, pointing at Rye, who was chasing a leaf. Not a big or particularly special one. Just a leaf. She seemed oblivious to the passing bipeds who stopped and watched her antics with open amusement. The gentle breeze was strong enough to keep the leaf just ahead of Rye's pounces, and with each gust, the leaf and Rye moved farther away from the dogs and the bridge.

They tried to call after her, but she either didn't hear or chose to ignore them. Rex took a deep breath, then without a word of warning, dashed out from the safety of the bushes and ran at full gallop along the riverside pavement.

He covered the distance quickly and didn't even pause to alert Rye of his intentions. With as much care as he could muster, he grabbed the distracted feline by the scruff of the neck and hoisted her into the air. He made certain that he didn't pierce her skin with his sharp teeth, which wasn't easy, especially once she began to squirm and wriggle in his grasp.

Rex carried the furious cat all the way back to their temporary hideout before putting her down on the ground. It took a moment before they could understand a word she was saying, as all she could do was spit and hiss until she finally began to calm down.

"How. How…How dare you!" she finally cried indignantly. "I was hunting! You never stop a cat when he or she's hunting!"

"You were chasing a leaf!" Amy said sternly.

"Maybe to you it looked like a leaf, but to me it was a dangerous and worthy adversary!"

"But how were we…" Amy tried to continue.

"And I almost had him!!" Rye shrieked with annoyance.

"I'm quite certain that we all feel rotten for interrupting your hunt," Lester said in a sincere tone, "but you must remember that we are all counting on you to get us across that river and to the anchor place. Don't forget, one of our friends is in extreme danger and in need of our help."

Rye stared down, embarrassed, at her front paws. At first the dogs thought she was still angry until they saw a tear run off her cheek.

"I'm sorry," Rye said in a trembling little voice. "I can't help chasing things. I'm a cat. It's what we do. Haven't you lot ever suddenly felt some deeper emotion that compelled you to… I don't know… go chasing after birds or something? Even when you know it's not appropriate?"

The dogs all shared a guilty look between them.

"Now that you mention it," Amy said with a growing smile, "we may have done just that!"

There was a moment of silence before all of them suddenly burst out laughing. Even Rex, who tried to remain serious and leader-like finally let go and howled with the others.

Laughed out, teary-eyed and exhausted by their own hilarity, the group was near collapse and would undoubtedly have done just that had not Rye announced that it was time to cross the river. This statement alone seemed to rally the dogs back to their prior serious and determined frames of mind.

Rye checked outside the bushes to make sure their path was clear and then led the group at a fast pace along the river walk toward the bridge.

"The important thing," she explained while running, "is speed. When we reach the bridge, there'll be a lot of humans and a lot of vehicles. Just stay close to me and keep moving. Remember whatever happens… keep moving."

They ran past the formidable exterior of the Tower of London and reached a flight of wide stone stairs leading to the approach road for the bridge. Rye led them down the steps and then turned sharply to the right, keeping them on a sidewalk which paralleled the busy roadway.

The group picked up the pace at Rye's signal and veritably flew along the sidewalk, which, as Rye had promised, was crowded with bipeds. They were met with shrieks and yells of both amusement and anger as they forced the humans to jump out of their way.

After covering about a quarter of the bridge's span, a series of loud bells began to ring, followed by a loud claxon sound that made the dogs' ears hurt.

"Uh oh!" cried Rye from the front of the pack.

"What is it?" Rex called to her.

"Nothing! Just run. That's all!" came the near-winded reply.

Just ahead a pair of ornate gates began descending from either side of the roadway, blocking all the biped vehicles from moving across the bridge.

Amy knew that something was clearly amiss, but she followed Rye's lead even as her stomach turned, alerting her to some as yet unseen danger.

They ran right under the gates (even Rex and Lester, who had to duck their heads) and continued along the bridge, which was now empty of both bipeds and vehicles.

Suddenly it began to rise up in front of them. At first Amy thought she was simply seeing things, but she quickly realized that the roadway was indeed rising right in front of her. Every instinct told her to stop and go back, but she remembered Rye's emphatic instructions to "Keep moving!"

The problem was that it was difficult to keep up the pace as the incline increased. Amy could feel her heart pounding madly within her chest as she used every ounce of strength to maintain her speed up the roadway. The good thing was that she could see the end of the rise just up ahead. Obviously the road evened out or even proceeded down from that point on. She somehow found another bit of strength and hurled herself the last few yards up the even steeper slope.

Before she knew what was happening, she was in midair, high above the rushing waters of the Thames. She was about to let out a howl of fear when she saw beneath her a sharply descending roadway replacing the lethal chasm that had been there only milliseconds before.

Amy could see Rye and Lester, who had been in front of her, trying to keep their balance on the steep downward slope of the road. She desperately wanted to turn her head to be sure that the others made it across safely, but knew that such a maneuver could easily make her to loose her footing and tumble the rest of the way down to the flat part of the bridge still ahead.

Luckily, they all made the jump safely. Even Angel, who managed to turn herself around in midair as she clawed the empty space in an attempt to retrace her steps, landed on the other side and slid half the way down the slope facing the wrong way.

Once on the flat roadway again, they dove under another set of gates and rushed through a large group of bipeds who were madly applauding something. It wasn't until they reached the end of the bridge and veered off its approach road, that the group finally slowed down and allowed themselves to get their breathing and heartbeats back to normal.

"What happened back there?" Angel asked in a dazed voice.

"Look for yourselves," Rye said shakily.

They all turned and saw that the bridge was again broken in the center, with both halves pointing straight up to the sky. A large water vehicle with smoke pouring from it was slowly passing between the raised road sections as it moved under the bridge.

Amy could only murmur, "Wow!"

thirty

Once the shock of the bridge experience began to wear off, it was replaced with anger at Rye for jeopardizing their safety without so much as a word of warning.

Surprisingly, Rye let each dog vent his or her fury without any show of emotion, not even her usual flinching or twitching that they'd come to expect. When they were finished with their verbal reprimanding, Rye looked each dog straight in the eye and began to smile.

"All better now?" she said in a voice suited to dealing with small puppies. "As your guide, my responsibility is to get you from point A to point B in one piece. Now… are any of you hurt?"

The dogs grudgingly shook their heads.

"Did we get across the river?"

They nodded half-heartedly.

"Well then, stop acting like a bunch of spoiled babies and be happy for the successes, instead of whining over bad things that might have happened!"

The dogs turned to face each other and talk over Rye's statement with the exception of Amy, who kept one eye on their feline guide. She watched Rye, who believing herself to be unobserved, slid behind the cans and out of sight.

Amy waited till her friends were well into their conversation before she carefully backed herself unnoticed from the group and moved over to Rye's hiding place. She could hear the cat before she saw her. Rye was crying. As Amy got closer she could hear the distraught feline as she sobbed to herself behind the metal obstacles.

Amy stood on the other side of the barrier, allowing Rye a few more moments of privacy. After what she considered was a suitable period Amy stepped around the end bin and saw Rye, huddled into a tight ball as she continued to sob almost uncontrollably.

"Are you all right?" Amy asked gently.

"Go away!" Rye answered between sniffly intakes of breath.

"No, I don't think I will. At least not until I know what's upsetting you."

"Don't you know? Can't you guess?" Rye voiced with weepy surprise.

"Is it because the others got cross with you?"

"Hardly, though I think I would have preferred a slightly warmer show of gratitude."

"Well what then?" Amy asked with concern.

"Do you have any idea what it took for a scaredy cat like me to lead you lot across a river like that?"

"Were you scared?"

"Yes!"

"Mind-numbingly terrified?"

"Yes, Yes, Yes!" she blurted out "All of those and more. You have no idea what it's like."

Rye began crying again, this time quietly into her crossed front paws.

Amy stood and watched her for a moment then said, "No, I don't, you're right. But I'll tell you what I do know. And that's that it takes a special creature that feels fear the way you do and yet can manage to overcome the feelings when it's time to ensure the safety of others. I think you are a very special cat, Ryphoryl

Ynextril Eytludnur, and I for one am honored that you chose to be our guide."

Amy turned and left Rye to digest what she'd just said. Rejoining the other dogs, she entered into their discussion of which way each felt they should go to get them to the anchor. Amy found it amusing that no dog shared the same directional judgment. She was about to add her two kibbles worth when Rye interrupted the discussion. No one had noticed her approach.

"I suggest we continue on," she said with calm assurance "We've still got a ways to go."

"I don't suppose we could stop somewhere and find something to eat on the way could we?" Angel asked in near pathetic whine.

"Why?" Rye answered, "Didn't you eat yesterday?"

Rye glanced over at Amy and gave her the briefest of winks. Amy felt a moment of real joy at seeing the usually troubled feline appear not only in control of her fears but even displaying a touch of humor as well.

Rye took her place at the head of the group and led them off at a brisk pace. Angel was not satisfied with the cat's glib response to her serious question regarding food and after walking only a short distance came to an abrupt halt.

"I'm not taking another step until I hear something about when we're going to eat." Angel pouted.

Rye froze in her tracks and then turned slowly to face back along the line. She eyed each dog long and hard without a trace of any emotion showing on her face. She then focused on Angel and began to smile. Not a happy smile. Not even an amused smile. This smile was cold and soulless.

Angel took a deep swallow as she watched Rye walk toward her with slow deliberate steps. The cat came to within inches of the Spaniel, holding her face directly in front of Angel's.

"So you're hungry, are you?" she asked flatly.

"Yes, I am," Angel replied trying to sound unaffected by the cat's frigid glare.

"Well, you know what? So am I. And I'll wager you Amy is as well. And Rex and the others, but the strange thing is that I don't see any of them acting like a loud spoiled human child!"

"I am not..." Angel protested.

"Oh yes you are, and do you know what makes your whining all the more unbearable at this moment?"

Angel stared defiantly back at her.

"It's that you are willing to hold up the entire group, which, may I remind you, is in the midst of a quest to rescue one of your own. A dog that I understand jeopardized his own safety to rescue you. And for what purpose do you wish to delay this expedition...? Well...?"

"Never mind," came Angel's weak reply as she cast her eyes down at her paws.

"That's better," Rye stated as she strode back along the line and resumed her position at the head of the group. "Is everyone ready?"

They marched on for most of the day with only a few brief stops for water or toilet needs. The sun finally sank out of sight behind a row of old warehouses, and the temperature dropped drastically.

Amy felt a chill run through her and was having great difficulty in not thinking about food. She was hungry but was determined not to be the one to raise the subject of eating. She also tried to ignore the aching in her muscles and blisters on the pads of her paws. Though she didn't want to admit it, she was becoming concerned as to just how much further she could walk without the benefit of food or rest.

She glanced at the other dogs and saw that they were all in similar shape. Each animal had his or her head low to the ground with eyes focusing only a few paws ahead. They all were tired.

Rye gave the signal to stop, which they all did without complaint. They didn't even form into their usual circle, just lying where they were in line.

"How long are we breaking for?" Rex asked their guide in as casually as he could.

"What do you mean?" Rye asked him, clearly puzzled.

"I just want to get an idea how long this stop is going to last," he tried to explain.

"As long as you like." The cat replied still confused by Rex's queries. "Unless you want to go somewhere else."

"Well, of course we do," Amy said, wanting to make sure that Rye didn't get any notion that they didn't want to proceed. "We're all just a little tired and wanted some time for a quick nap."

"Take as long as you like." Rye was starting to sound really agitated and confused.

"But we have to reach the anchor by dark," Angel stated flatly.

"I give up!" Rye dashed back past the exhausted dogs and jumped up onto a large stone block. She began to climb up what looked at first to be a large black tree limb.

Amy watched the cat climb and felt a memory stirring deep inside her. She continued to watch Rye, knowing that she was meant to recognize something in the cat's actions.

"You lot are too much!" Rye yelled down at them from the top of the black tree-like structure.

Amy got painfully to her feet and walked to the other side of the thing. When she was alongside it at a different angle, she began to laugh, quietly at first, then with all her remaining strength.

Rye observed Amy from her perch high above the ground and could only shake her head at the dog's actions.

"Well, finally!" she called down to her.

"What's wrong, Goldie?" Rex asked as he walked over to her.

She gestured through her laughter for the Doberman to examine more carefully what Rye was seated on. He turned and then he too began to smile.

"Well, I'll be!" he exclaimed joyously.

The two dogs stood side by side and admired the huge black anchor for a few moments before sharing the news with the others. Rye climbed gingerly down and approached the dogs with pride.

"Well done, Rye," Amy said sincerely.

"Yes, well done," Rex added.

"It was nothing," the cat replied smugly, as she began washing her tail.

"Now if we could just find something to eat, we'd have it made," Rex said more to himself than to anyone else.

"That's easy," Rye stated simply. "All that's been taken care of."

With that, she jumped to her paws and set off along the metal fencing that surrounded the anchor square. Without being asked, Rex and Amy followed closely behind. The cat came to a halt by a gate located at the entrance to the square.

Rye turned her back to it and began pacing away from it, counting out loud.

"One...two...three...four..." she counted.

When she got to ten, she stopped and turned ninety degrees to her left, pacing ten more steps in that direction. Again she stopped and made a course change, this time proceeding only six paces.

She had reached a pile of rusted metal piping, which had clearly been discarded long ago. She stepped into one of the larger pipes and vanished from sight. After a few moments, Amy felt the beginnings of concern, but then saw Rye's rear end as it reappeared at the pipe's opening. She was dragging something heavy out from inside the thing.

Amy and Rex went over to help her and almost immediately picked up the scent of food. Fresh food. Fresh meat food!

"Here let me," Rex said as he stepped in and picked up the large plastic bag by the handles.

"What is it?" Amy asked excitedly. "It smells like meat!"

"You'll just have to wait and see, won't you?" Rye replied smugly.

"But...but how did it...? What is it...?" Amy tried ask.

"Don't underestimate the G.N. We are well organized." Rye stated proudly "When you told Bob where you needed to get to, he not only assigned me as your guide but he sent out a team to arrange for some food to be waiting for you."

"Amazing," Rex mumbled, his mouth full of plastic bag straps.

"Not really. It's just how we operate."

"Well, I for one am greatly impressed," Amy announced.

"Me too," Rex mumbled.

As they approached the other dogs, Amy noticed that they were all looking excitedly in their direction.

"Where have you been?" Angel shouted enthusiastically at them. Her face then was transformed as she spotted the bag hanging from Rex's muzzle.

"What's that?" she cried "I smell... I smell... meat!!"

Rex made them all step back as he emptied the bag to the ground. As always, Angel's nose was accurate. There in front of them were five of the largest, most perfect-looking sirloin steaks that any of them had ever seen.

They were all about to tuck in when Amy spotted something.

"Rye, where's yours?"

"It's time I was off. My dinner's waiting back at the H.Q."

"But..." Amy started to object.

"Shhh! I've done what I was supposed to and that's all I'm permitted to do. G.N. code again! Anyway, you know your way from here."

"You'll remember everything I said?" Amy asked.

"Yes ma'am. I certainly will," Rye stated formally.

"You did an excellent job," Amy said as she took a step toward the cat. She lowered her head and whispered into one of Rye's orange and black ears.

"And I don't think you're a scaredy cat at all."

Rye stepped away and brushed away a tear, which she pretended was merely a displaced whisker.

"Good luck, Amy. Good luck all of you. It has been an extreme pleasure."

Everyone bid her fond farewell as she turned tail and ran off, vanishing into the shadows.

Amy immediately felt the loss of the little cat deep in her chest. She also, however, felt the hunger in her belly. She looked over to the others who seemed to be waiting for some signal to start eating. She looked to Rex, who as leader, took the initiative and sank his teeth into the tender red flesh.

The others did not need to be coaxed to follow suit.

thirty one

after finding shelter in an abandoned, unlocked warehouse, they slept long and hard, and the next morning, discussed tactics to force their way into the prison building. They fantasized about of how each would deal with Squat Lady or Skull Face, and they all agreed that it was a shame that Fat Man and Boxer wouldn't be around because that would have been a great fight.

As the morning stretched into early afternoon, the five were no closer to a formal plan of any kind. It became apparent that not only did they not know quite what to do, but also that they were a little hesitant about tackling the vicious humans in the first place.

In the middle of a particularly weak plan suggested by Hans, a scratching at the warehouse door interrupted the group. Rex got to his paws and went to one of the many soot-streaked windows to see who could be trying to gain access to their current lair.

"What the..." he said in astonishment at the sight that confronted him. "Everyone come over here and look at this."

The others all joined him at the window and followed his gaze. They were equally shocked. Lined up outside the warehouse door were dogs. Dozens of them. They stood in single file waiting patiently for entrance into the warehouse. Rex moved over to the doorway and pushed aside the piece of brick they'd used to wedge the warped wood in place.

As the door swung open on its rusty hinges, the five dogs looked out at the lengthy canine line, wondering what they wanted. The dog nearest the door, presumably the one who'd scratched for their attention, explained their presence.

"We're here to volunteer for the mission," the burly Wolfhound stated.

"The what?" Rex exclaimed.

"The mission!" the Wolfhound reiterated. "The word's out that you lot are planning on going after the dog prison."

"Yes...Yes that's right. But..." Rex stammered.

"Then you'll need volunteers, and by the looks of things," he cast his eyes along the ever lengthening collection of canines, "you're going to have quite a few of those!"

"But how..." Amy tried to ask.

"Anyway..." continued the Wolfhound, ignoring her completely, "my name's O'Neil, and my specialty is taking down the larger adversaries. I've done work in Croyden, Clapham and Chelsea. I'm fit and I'm ready!"

With that O'Neil marched right past the five dogs and proceeded to the back of the warehouse. Rex gave his friends a confused shrug and greeted the next applicant.

"My name's Curtis," said a thin but fit-looking Lab mix. "And I do walls. Natural balancer, I am!"

"Good...Good..." Rex said appreciatively. "Welcome!"

The Lab mix nodded and made his way into the warehouse.

The process took most of the afternoon, but by sundown they had amassed an impressive group of canine volunteers, all tough, well seasoned and ready to storm the prison.

After formulating a precise battle plan, the dogs went off in search of food. Rex offered any who wanted it a place in the warehouse to sleep, but they all preferred to find their own shelter. They agreed on a sun-up rendezvous for the start of the mission.

O'Neil was the last dog out the door and as he was about to go off into the approaching night, Rex said to him, "You mentioned when you got here that word was out about our mission, but you never told us what that meant exactly? How did you hear about us?"

O'Neil gave the Doberman a crusty grin, then lowered his huge head to Rex's ear. "Let's just say a little kitty told me." And with that he raised a paw to his nose in a gesture of "Say no more" and trotted off into the night.

Just as he was about to vanish into the deepening shadows, he turned and called back across the deserted square, "Oh, and another thing. I was told to tell you that your supper'll be in the same place as last night!" He then stepped into the darkness and vanished from sight.

"Did he say supper... like in food?" Angel squealed joyously from somewhere within the warehouse.

Indeed he did, and for the second night in a row, the dogs ate a hearty, satisfying dinner. Instead of steaks, the G.N. had left them an astonishing quantity of incredibly tender and tasty lamb chops. For the first time in any of the dogs' limited memory, they ate until they could actually eat no more. Even Angel with her seemingly bottomless belly, finally gave up with a couple of meaty chops untouched in front of her.

Little was said among the animals that night as each thought his or her own private thoughts. They knew that what lay before them at dawn the next day was far more than a game or a chase. The next day was going to bring real danger, and though unspoken, each dog knew that some of them might not survive.

As Amy stretched to try to relieve some of the pressure she felt from her overfilled stomach, she tried to imagine what death actually was. Her mother had told her that it was like a long sleep from which you didn't wake. That explanation had always satisfied her until now, but she couldn't seem to put the sleep part together with death through injury. Did one simply fall asleep when hurt badly enough? How badly, exactly, did one have to be hurt to fall into that kind of sleep? Could regular sleep become that sort of sleep? Who decided when a hurt became a sleep?

She decided to ask Rex, who was certain to know more on the subject than she did, but found him to be fast asleep, flat on his back with paws twitching up into the air. Not a dignified image, but he did seem content, at least in his dreams.

She lowered her muzzle to her front paws and let out a long sigh, which she hadn't even realized she'd been holding inside. She closed her eyes, knowing she had to get some sleep before the big battle in the morning.

The volunteers began filing into the warehouse before dawn. They looked rested and ready for battle. Some did morning stretches. Others practiced paw to paw techniques, while others played in one corner with a tennis ball that one of them had brought along. There was a sense of tension in the air, both exhilarating and slightly frightening.

Amy looked over the assembled crowd and wondered who among them would be hurt and who, if any could even be…

"Impressive, isn't it?" Rex said excitedly as he trotted up alongside her.

"It certainly is! I almost feel sorry for those nasty bipeds. They're certainly going to be surprised when they see this lot!"

"Amy!" Rex said in a mock serious tone. "You feel sorry for them?"

"I said almost," she replied with a wink.

The two stood for a moment longer, watching as the final preparations for battle were completed. O'Neil then climbed up on an upturned crate and barked for some quiet.

The volunteers settled down and all turned to face the Wolfhound.

"Gentle dogs, we are here today joined together as one fighting unit for the task of freeing our captive canine friends. I would like to remind each of you that what you are about to do is dangerous. Some of you may be hurt, some may not even return, but the fact is that you—each of you—is about to not just free your imprisoned brothers, but will be striking a mighty blow against the tyrannical hand of bad bipeds. So, let's move out. And remember; keep your heads high and your teeth bared."

He looked down at the surging mass of eager dogs and then raised his head high into the air and let out a chilling howl. A dog in the crowd joined him, and then others did the same. Soon the entire assemblage had their heads in the air, howling for all they were worth.

Even Amy let out a brief howl then looked at the others with embarrassment.

"Sorry," she said blushing. "I got carried away."

"Amy," Rex said suddenly, "there's something I've been wanting to say to you…"

"I know Rex… I feel the same" she said interrupting.

"So, you'll stay?" he said relieved.

"What?"

"I wanted to ask you and Angel if you'd stay back here at the warehouse where it's safe."

"I thought when you said you had something to say…" Amy tried to speak.

"Look, we've got plenty of animals for the attack. I just don't want you hurt."

"If you think for one moment that I've come this far to sit like a good little bitch waiting here for you, while you go out and rescue Rodney, then you have another think coming!"

"But…" Rex tried to say.

"No buts!! We're going with you. Right, Angel?" She turned to the Spaniel, who was staring back at her with an expression of disbelief.

"Of course," she said sarcastically. "Why would anyone want to stay here where it's warm and safe when we could be out there risking our coats! Thanks, Amy."

"You're welcome," Amy said.

"Hounds Ho!" came the command as everyone began filing out of the warehouse.

Amy just had time to give Angel a good luck nod before being swept outside by the crowd in readiness for the attack. It was all she could do to stay close to Rex among the troop of canines. Once they were all outside, the dogs broke into two groups. One was led by O'Neil, the other by a rugged looking German Shepherd.

With hardly a word being spoken, the group split up, leaving the anchor square from either end. Amy, Rex and Angel were in O'Neil's group and left the square by the river end. Hans and Lester were in the Shepherd's group. There was a strained silence in the ranks as the dogs marched toward their objective.

Amy was surprised that the volunteer dogs knew exactly where the prison was. It seemed that the place had a reputation not only among former inmates, but among most of London's street animals as well. She managed to glean from a few snippets of conversation within the ranks that the place had been in operation for many years and that it was about time that someone rallied the dogs into attacking the place.

As the assault group moved along the shadows provided by a row of abandoned storefronts, Amy began to recognize bits and pieces of the neighborhood. It wasn't clear, and her memories were a little foggy but certain things definitely rang a bell for her. A doorway here, a cracked window there. She tried as hard as she could to put the memories into some semblance of order so she could gauge just how close they actually were to the prison. While she was still trying to sort out her memories, the group rounded a corner and there it was!

Amy had no trouble recognizing the place. As soon as she spotted it, she felt an icy shiver run the length of her back. She heard a low growling from somewhere close by and realized it was coming from her.

They were at the back of the prison close to the rear yard door through which they'd escaped, thanks to Rodney and his knowledge of doors. The team assembled directly across from the corner they'd hidden behind when they'd spotted Pru on that fateful day so long ago.

O'Neil carefully checked all about them and then gave the sign for the fighting force to cross the street and form around the actual "Pru" corner. Rex gave Amy and Angel a knowing smile, as it was clear that each of them had clear memories of their escape.

They kept their positions until O'Neil saw the Shepherd and his group reach the far corner on the other side of the prison's main entrance.

The tension was thick. Amy could hear her own stomach rumbling with nerves and noticed that she wasn't alone. The harder she listened, the more rumbling stomachs she could hear. She smiled to herself, knowing that even these proud and brave fighting dogs suffered from the same fears and nerves that she did.

O'Neil checked the front entrance again then signaled the Shepherd at the far corner.

The attack was beginning.

Both groups moved out from their cover and began edging along the wall in single file. The two columns converged on the entry door located halfway along the wall.

Amy felt an almost uncontainable pride deep within her as she watched her new friends in action. They were so professional, so brave, so utterly...

Both lines froze. The front spotters had seen something and given the warning tail wag.

Amy tried to follow the other dogs' line of sight but could only see a deserted building with cracked windows and... there was something moving on its roof. She had to squint to make out exactly what it was but finally recognized it was a squirrel.

She knew that couldn't be the reason for the entire squad to be frozen in place, but as she watched the slow, oblivious movement of the squirrel, she realized that every pair of canine eyes were riveted on the little creature.

With one last spring across the space between two weathered brick walls, the squirrel vanished from sight. The dogs refocused their attention on the prison entrance and again began to edge toward the front door.

They were only a few feet from their target when Amy caught a flash of movement out of the corner of her eye. She looked around just in time to see the squirrel reappear and leap from one of the old buildings onto the branch of an adjacent tree. She prayed that she alone had noticed the reappearance of the creature and casually returned her gaze to the others.

Every single dog was staring wide-eyed and was panting at the squirrel.

Amy couldn't believe what she was witnessing. What had happened to the training, the dedication, the...

Her thoughts were rudely interrupted as the poor witless squirrel trotted down the side of the tree then jumped onto the ground.

The volunteers went crazy with maniacal cries of "Get it!" or "It's mine!" or in most cases, simply the word "Squirrel!" The dogs literally tripped over each other to break ranks and give chase to the now fully aware and very nervous squirrel.

Amy, Rex, Angel, Hans and Lester suddenly found themselves alone only a few feet from the prison entrance, watching as the last of the brave troops rounded the far corner and vanished from sight in hot pursuit of one small, and to Amy, inconsequential rodent.

She turned to her friends, glad that they'd at least not given in to their hunt-lust emotions. She was astonished to see the three males shaking and drooling as they tried desperately to control their urge to dash off after the others.

"Rex, stop it!" she commanded in as quiet a voice as she could. After all, they were close to the prison doors. "Hans? Lester?"

"We're trying!" Rex managed to say between firmly clenched teeth.

"Well, try harder. We're too close to fail now!"

"I know," came the strained reply.

Amy looked over at her four comrades, three of whom were battling their primal urges to chase a squirrel, and wondered what could possibly go wrong next.

She didn't have to wait long to find out.

thirty two

Just as Amy was about to suggest a calm retreat to regroup and
re-plan now that the assault force was down to just the five of
them, the prison door swung open and Squat Lady stepped out.

"What's all the din out here?" she bellowed, causing far more
noise than before she appeared.

Amy looked at the others to see if they all were thinking
along the same line as she was. She felt a surge of satisfaction as
each dog gave her a brief nod.

Rex was the first to move. He launched his muscular frame
straight at the startled biped who tried to step back into the
entrance. She might have made it if Angel, in a surprise show of
bravery, hadn't dashed forward and sunk her teeth into Squat
Lady's bulging ankles.

The biped let out a blood-curdling scream and was about to
reach down to grab Angel when Rex hit her full force, knocking
her backward through the open doorway. Such was the force of
Rex's assault that Angel was still in the same position, except
instead of an ankle clenched between her teeth, she was now
clasping one of Squat Lady's black lace-up boots.

Hans and Lester vaulted over the Spaniel and were the first
inside the prison proper. They ran up on either side of the
downed biped but found her to be groaning and dazed and

thereby of no immediate concern. Hans even took a moment to give the hideous creature a lick of compassion. The two dogs then separated and went to either side of the entry hall, each covering one of the two doors that led from it.

With a look of reluctance, Angel dropped the now well-chewed boot, and together with Amy, stepped into the building. Once inside, the five dogs were uncertain as to how to proceed. Their choice of action, however, was determined for them when Skull Face walked casually into the entry, completely unaware of the situation.

He took one look at the five snarling dogs, then at the unconscious figure on the floor and did the one thing that none of them was prepared for. He laughed. It wasn't a pleasant laugh either. It was more like a cross between a horse's whinny and a squirrel's chatter, but it was a laugh. The dogs were so amazed at the biped's reaction that they made the mistake of hesitating. Not for long, but long enough for Skull Face to grab a club from a rack on the wall next to him.

He slammed the wooden weapon hard against the wall, sending an earsplitting crack echoing within the cramped space of the entry hall. It hurt everyone's ears and made the point that he was not only now armed but also clearly willing to use the weapon if necessary.

"So then, you scruffy mutts," he said in the reedy nasal voice they remembered from their earlier stay in the building, "what do you think you're doing here?"

He took a step toward the dogs with the club held at his side and ready for use.

"Wait a minute, I know you, don't I?" he said pointing the club directly toward Angel.

"You, too," he gestured at Amy "You're some of the bunch that scarpered out of here! Well, well, nice to have you back!"

He stepped toward the open entry door and kicked it shut. At least that was his plan. The door swung to within inches of its jamb then stopped and slowly swung back open.

"What the…" Skull Face exclaimed.

He kicked the door again but with the same results. He kept his eyes on the five dogs and stepped out through the doorway to find out why it wouldn't shut. He no sooner passed through the entrance when a flurry of orange, black and white fur dropped onto his head and began yowling as it kicked, scratched, bit and clawed the unsuspecting biped.

The dogs heard the familiar voice of Rye yell, "Shut the door! Now!"

Rex leapt forward and putting all his weight against the heavy wooden door, slammed it shut.

Amy spotted an old-fashioned sliding bolt lock similar to the one she was used to defeating in the cottage. She stepped over, and nudging Rex aside, maneuvered the bolt into place.

"Nice one, Goldie" Rex said, impressed.

She grinned smugly back at him just as one of the interior doors flew open. There, standing before them, was Fat Man. His face was bruised in a few places and appeared burned in a few others, but he was alive. Alive, and at the moment, furious.

As he stepped into the entry hall, Rex and Hans both dropped low to the ground and began growling with menacing intensity. Fat Man reached cautiously into his pocket and produced an odd looking black object. Suddenly the object sprouted a thin metal blade that momentarily caught a shaft of light, causing it to glint in the biped's hand.

Amy found herself suddenly in midair, launching herself directly at the human. He raised his weapon to counter her move but Amy wasn't going for his body. She shot between his legs and through the open doorway. She heard the biped yell out with a mixture of fury and surprise, which then changed to vicious obscenities aimed toward the others who had clearly used Amy's distraction to move a step or two closer to their prey.

Amy found herself in her old cellblock. The door through which she'd dived led down a couple of worn and sagging wooden steps to the smelly, cold stone passageway floor. She turned back to make certain she was not being pursued, only to see the heavy door swing hard on its squeaky hinges and slam shut, separating her from the others.

She felt the icy tendrils of fear creep along her body and fought to keep herself focused on the job at hand. She began walking slowly down the passageway checking each enclosure as she came to it.

She didn't recognize most of the dogs. Many seemed like newcomers and for a moment, she had a vivid flash of recall of her first day in this cold and heartless place. She could suddenly remember clearly the fear she'd felt and the pain… Strangely, she could almost still feel the hurt.

With difficulty she forced herself to shake off these memories as she continued along the gloomy passageway. She raised her head and saw the door to the exercise yard. It was closed as she'd expected it would be.

Some of the inmates were starting to notice her arrival and began barking excitedly. Others, especially the newcomers, greeted Amy with mad enthusiasm, throwing themselves at the rusty mesh barriers and asking all sorts of hopeful questions.

Amy managed to calm them down with guarantees of their impending rescue. The newcomers accepted her word with complete faith, whereas the others, those who'd spent serious time in the place, some as much as a month, gave her words little credence and remained calmly unimpressed.

It melted her heart to see one scared dog face after another, pressed up against the barriers gazing at her with desperate hope. She found time to give every single one an encouraging word or nod. She was, however, beginning to feel concerned about not finding Rodney. She'd never considered for a moment that perhaps he wouldn't be here. That perhaps he'd been too seriously injured to justify the bipeds' returning him here. What if he'd been so badly hurt that they'd…they'd…

"Goldie?" came a familiar, though weak, voice. "Goldie, is that you?"

She looked anxiously down the passageway hoping to see the small Terrier, but instead, only saw cell after cell with each occupant pressed up against the wire mesh.

"Rodney, where are you?" she called excitedly.

"I'm not exactly sure, but you sound close." Again, Amy heard the weakness in his voice.

She ran down the remaining length of the passageway. She reached the far door but still couldn't see him. She was about to retrace her steps when Rodney's little voice came at her from only a few paws away.

Amy turned and looked into the nearest enclosure. As before, she thought it was empty, until to her surprise, she saw movement at the back of the cell. There, blanketed in shadow, was Rodney. He looked terribly small from her perspective and Amy felt an almost overwhelming urge to hold and comfort her dear friend.

"Hello, Goldie," he said warmly. "I'd get up and greet you properly but... well I'm not doing too well. Actually. I'm a little weak."

"Don't you move! I'll come in," she replied confidently without a clue as to how she would do this.

She took a step back and examined the metal-framed gate with a careful and critical eye. She was by no means an expert on the subject but had by instinct alone managed to foil many door latches back at the cottage. Sadly, her limited memory couldn't recall the specifics of how she managed it in the past, only that she somehow had.

She tried a variety of pushes and nose lifts and even one hard head butt, all to no avail.

"Goldie, if you..." Rodney tried to speak

"You just stay quiet and rest," she ordered. "I'll work this out."

She continued with every door maneuver she could think of but the thing just wouldn't budge.

"Goldie?" Rodney said gently.

"Yes, what?" She answered with growing frustration.

"I think you'll find you just need to pull it, not push it. It's not locked."

She closed her eyes for a moment in frustration and embarrassment, and then pulled open the gate and stepped gingerly into the cell. She approached Rodney, wanting desperately to know what was wrong with him.

As she stepped closer, she was finally able to see the Terrier through the gloom and was shocked by what she saw. His usually shiny coat was matted and dull, and he had clearly lost weight. His eyes still had a small trace of their normal sparkle, but nothing like their usual radiance.

She leant her head down and gave him a couple of gentle licks, hoping to reassure him.

"It's my leg, Goldie," he stated matter-of-factly. "I think I broke it when the vehicle tipped over."

"Haven't the bipeds seen to it?" she asked with growing anger.

"No, they tossed me in here as soon as we got back and just left me."

"Do you mean they haven't even fed or watered you?" she asked incredulously.

The tiny Terrier shook his head.

"Oh, Goldie!" he suddenly cried. "I've been so scared. I thought I'd never see you again, and I was certain I was going to die here."

"Well, that's just nonsense. I'm here now with the others, and you are leaving with us."

"You came back here for me?" he asked in amazement.

"No. I missed the fine food and company. Of course it was for you, silly! Now I suggest we get you out of here and have that leg seen to."

"If you insist," he said forcing a brave little smile, "but I can't walk."

"But I can," Amy said as she gently took him by the scruff of the neck and easily lifted him into the air.

"Comfortable?" she mumbled.

"Fine, thank you," he said hesitantly.

Amy was about to leave the cell when a large shadow fell across both of them. Amy felt pure terror for the first time in her life.

"So…" said the all too familiar voice. "Isn't this a pretty picture!"

Amy gently placed Rodney back onto the stone floor so as to free her jaws for what was coming. She had only once used her teeth against a biped, Squat Lady, in any serious way, and the thought of now having to do so again filled her with dread.

Squat Lady stepped into the cell, and as Amy turned to face her she saw that the female was holding the everpresent club, not in a state of readiness, but in an almost casual manner at her side. This sight, instead of relaxing Amy, made her feel even more fearful, knowing that it could only mean that the biped had something far worse in store for them.

Careful to not put any weight on his bad leg, Rodney got shakily to his feet. Unseen by Amy, he took a tentative step forward and began growling in as menacing a fashion as his tiny damaged frame could muster.

"You get behind me, Goldie," he said gallantly. "I'll protect you from this… this… monster!"

Amy was touched. She saw Squat Lady suddenly step aside, and then the Boxer appeared. As the dogs looked on in dread, he stepped confidently into the cell and positioned himself next to the human.

"You!" Amy exclaimed in shock. "But I thought you'd… you'd…"

"You thought I'd gotten what I deserved back in the tunnel?"

She nodded at him in stunned silence. It wasn't just seeing him here, alive, that she found so amazing. It was his voice as well. It was the first time she could recall hearing it do more than snap single word commands and she was astonished to find it was not the voice of a common canine criminal, but rich in timbre, unquestionably belonging to a dog of intelligence and breeding.

Squat Lady grabbed hold of the gate and violently slammed it shut with herself and the three dogs inside. She lowered the metal horseshoe-shaped fastener into place, then turned and with a scowl fixed to her already hideous features, glared at the trapped animals. She reached into her dirty charcoal-colored sweater and retrieved a small box from which she shook out a white tubular object. She placed the thing between her puffy lips and then, with the aid of another object she retrieved from her pocket, set the tube alight.

Amy could smell the odor of burning leaves and felt the smoke as it began to sting her eyes. She watched in fearful fascination as the biped inhaled a large cloud of the smoke, then after a moment's pause, blew it back out into the air.

Squat Lady continued to look down at Amy and Rodney and began to smile in a grotesque display of yellow teeth and pale gums. She suddenly turned to the Boxer and her face took on a cold and lethal expression.

"Kill!" she commanded. "Kill them both!"

She pointed a pudgy finger directly at the pair to emphasize her point. The Boxer looked at her, then at Amy and Rodney but didn't move.

"I said kill them, you stupid beast. Now do it!" Her voice was now raised and angry.

As if to enforce her command she began to raise the club from her side.

"Kill them now, I say!" she shrieked.

The Boxer took a step toward Amy and Rodney and began to bare his teeth. As the two huddled closer together, they watched in horrified fascination as the Boxer prepared to strike. His muscles began to swell and ripple as he lowered his hindquarters readying himself to spring into attack position.

"I'm not scared of you," Amy cried defiantly at the Boxer.

"Neither am I," Rodney weakly concurred.

"I've noticed," the Boxer replied with a gleam in his eye.

He then sprang into the air.

thirty three

Amy and Rodney had never seen anything like it.

The Boxer did indeed launch himself into the air, but only after he'd suddenly spun his muscular body around so that he was facing Squat Lady. She had no time even to scream before he hit her full force in the chest. She fell backward and hit her head with a loud crack against the brick wall. Her eyes rolled back into her head as she slid to the floor. The Boxer ran to her side ready to pursue the attack if needed, but after a quick inspection, announced, "She's out cold!"

The other two looked on in open-mouthed astonishment. The Boxer stepped over the prostrate figure of Squat Lady and approached them with a warm smile.

"You stay back," Rodney said defiantly.

"Perhaps I should introduce myself," the other said with calm self-assurance "My name's Sergeant Bonzo."

"Sergeant?" Amy said with surprise.

"Yes Ma'am. Scotland Yard Canine Squad. I'm a Police Dog."

"What!" Rodney exclaimed "But you were... I saw you... we thought you were..."

"One of them?" Sergeant Bonzo offered.

"Well... actually... yes!" Rodney admitted.

"That was the whole point. I was here undercover. We've had our eyes on this group for a while now. Nasty bunch."

"But you let them take me away," Rodney exclaimed angrily. "They could have used me like the others and…and…"

"Actually, they wouldn't have gotten far," he replied calmly. "We were covering all the exits from the country, and your description was well circulated before you'd been gone more than a couple of minutes. In fact, if you hadn't escaped from the posh couple, we would have nabbed the lot of them days ago."

"Well, perhaps you should have let us in on it," Rodney said. "We could have helped!"

"Yes and no," Bonzo explained "The fact is, I wasn't the only one working for them. You see…"

"Wait a minute," Amy interrupted. "Are you saying that while you pretended to be working with the bipeds, there was another dog who really was?"

"Yes, only he wasn't a Police Dog, he really was a bad'un."

"Well, what happened to him? Where did he go?" Amy asked anxiously.

"Didn't it ever surprise you how we were able to keep locating you no matter where you seemed to go?" Bonzo asked gently.

Amy and Rodney glanced at each other then turned to Bonzo and nodded in unison.

"Come with me," he said gently.

Bonzo walked to the gate and pushed it open. He led Amy and the limping Rodney down the passageway until they reached a particular enclosure. He gestured with a flick of his muzzle for them to look inside.

All they could see was a dog standing in the shadows facing away from them. Amy turned to Bonzo with a puzzled look.

"That's him," Bonzo stated.

She peered through the mesh but couldn't see who it was until the dog moved into the light and turned to face her.

"Hans? " she exclaimed "Not you! There's been a mistake!"

She turned to Bonzo and was about to speak when Hans stepped to the barrier.

"Yes Goldie... Me!" he said coldly "You bunch were so stupid. I tell you one story about a farm and a bunch of loving bipeds and you fall for the whole thing. What a bunch of dumb dogs!"

"Why you big..." Rodney growled through the mesh "I oughta..."

"You oughta what, you little..." Hans sneered back.

"Enough!" Bonzo snapped "I trapped him in here earlier. He's not going anywhere."

Amy turned to Hans and shook her head slowly from side to side. "How could you? We were your friends."

"I don't have any friends. I don't need them. They only get in the way," he answered coldly. "I do what I do, for myself. I'm the only dog I trust and that's the way I like it, so why don't you take your happy helpful self outta here and leave me alone."

Bonzo nudged Amy away from the mesh barrier and led her from Hans's enclosure. She was clearly upset and shocked by the Rothweiler's words.

"Don't let him upset you. He's not worth it," Bonzo said grimly.

Rodney limped slowly behind, growling to himself about what he'd like to do to the likes of Hans. Angel, Rex and Lester appeared at the end of the passageway and seeing the others, began to smile until they spotted the Boxer. They began to tense until Amy trotted over to them and calmed them down with explanations.

Bonzo took the dogs to a window leading off the entry hall. It was jammed open and looked out over a back alley filled with discarded trash and junk.

"Is this how we're getting out?" Rex asked with concern.

"No, this is how I demonstrate the Canine Corp's Communication Grid," Bonzo replied proudly.

He stepped to the window and leaned his head out. He then let out a series of howls and barks for a few moments and then stopped and listened.

Almost immediately another dog could be heard somewhere in the distance repeating his signals. As the others listened, yet another dog picked up the call and transmitted the signal still farther.

"The lads at the yard will get the word in just a few minutes," Bonzo stated.

"Then what?" Lester asked.

"Can we eat?" Angel inquired.

"Then they'll lead the biped squad out here and we'll close this case," he responded.

"We kind of messed things up for you, didn't we?" Amy said apologetically.

"Not really. We have enough on these monsters to lock them up for a long time." Bonzo gestured to the two unconscious figures of Fat Man and Skull Face.

"What will happen to us?" Amy asked anxiously.

Bonzo turned and looked into her gentle features, then to those of the other dogs and smiled warmly. "I think you lot have had enough excitement to last you a lifetime or two. I think we need to get you back to your homes, don't you?"

Amy felt tears of joy suddenly well up in her eyes as she realized that the nightmare was nearly over. She looked across at the dogs that until a few days ago had meant nothing to her but now were her closest, most treasured friends. As her eyes rested on Rex, she could see the pain in his face and she realized that he had no home to return to. He had only the hard and lonely existence that had become his world. He looked over at her and tried to mask his feelings with a huge grin, but she knew it was only for her benefit.

The dogs all went quiet as they heard the return message arrive from Scotland Yard. Bonzo smiled as he listened then turned to the others.

"They're on their way."

It wasn't long before the animals heard approaching sirens. By the time the policemen arrived, Sergeant Bonzo had cleaned up Amy and the others and lined them up according to size. When the front door flew open, he gave the order and the five dogs stood to attention. First through the door were the biped policemen, who scattered in various directions to secure the premises. Then in walked Captain Sulty, a Labrador.

He was clearly in charge. Tall, proud and professional, the captain eyed the goings on with a careful eye as he evaluated the crime scene. He was older than the others though fitter than officers half his age. His gray muzzle simply added to his look of elegant strength. The Labrador spotted Sergeant Bonzo and stepped over to him pulling a biped on a leash after him.

"Sergeant!" he snapped "What have we here?"

"Sir!" Bonzo saluted. "These are the famous dogs we've been tracking throughout London. They came back to rescue the others and helped capture the bipeds."

Amy snuck a look over at Rex who caught her glance and simply shrugged. As she faced forward again, Sergeant Bonzo gave her a brief wink and a grin which still didn't explain what he was up to.

"Well then…" The captain said proudly, "It would appear that we have some true heroes amongst us, wouldn't it?"

"Yes, sir," the Sergeant replied. "It most certainly would."

"Well done, Sergeant," the captain said as he raised a paw in salute.

He turned and joined the biped officers as they continued with their work.

"I'd better join them," Sergeant Bonzo announced to the others.

"Thank you, Sergeant," Amy said tenderly as she leaned forward and gave his muzzle one brief lick.

"Now steady on there, girl!" he blustered in embarrassment. "I'm on duty, you know."

The others all laughed. Even Bonzo had to give in to the comedy of the moment and suddenly found himself rolling on his back laughing boisterously.

"Sergeant!" came the commanding voice of the captain from somewhere in the building.

Sergeant Bonzo leaped to his feet and cleaned himself off with great urgency.

"Yes, sir," he replied when he was suitably neatened.

"Come and give us the breakdown of this lot," the captain commanded. "We're in the cell block."

"Yes, sir!" Bonzo answered.

"What about us?" Rex asked.

"Stay here. Some bipeds will be here shortly to pick up all the prisoners."

"What about going home?" Angel asked pathetically. "You said we could go home now!"

"And you can," the Boxer answered gently. "But first we've got to get you out of here and sort out where your homes are."

"That sounds a bit complicated," Amy said, trying to hide the concern she was starting to feel.

"Actually, it's quite simple," he explained "We've got all the reports of kidnapped dogs at headquarters. All we have to do is notify your masters that you've been found and you're home in time for supper!"

"Now you're talking," Angel said with relief.

"Sergeant! " The captain's voice echoed through the premises.

"I'd best be off," the Boxer announced nervously.

"Well again… Thank you." Amy nodded at him.

The others all offered their thanks as he turned and disappeared through the door to the cellblock.

The dogs all looked at each other expecting someone to say something, but they all remained quiet as their thoughts took them back over the last few days and what they'd been through.

By the time the white-coated bipeds arrived to take them away, they were all fast asleep.

thirty four

they were transported in large gray vehicles filled with individual metal enclosures. The ride lasted a long time. Finally, the vehicles came to a stop and the rear doors were opened. Different bipeds were there to greet them.

"Oh my!" Lester suddenly shouted. "We're in for it now!"

"Why?" What's the matter" Rex and the others asked anxiously.

"Look!" Lester gestured to a large sign in front of the building they were to be loaded into.

"What does it say?" Amy asked urgently.

"Pound. It says we're at the dog pound!"

His words sent such a wave of panic through the enclosures that it took the bipeds forever to unload the animals and get them one by one into the building.

Finally every dog was placed in their own enclosure, not much bigger than the ones back at the prison place. The bipeds in attendance, however, were nice and spent a great deal of time with each animal, calming and grooming them as best they could.

After they'd left, the dogs were alone and began calling through their gates to locate their friends and find where each had been placed.

Amy found that she was in a section filled with complete strangers. She called down the line and was informed that the rest of her group were in an entirely different wing.

Even when a kind and smiling-faced biped brought her a bowl of chopped beef, she couldn't help feeling almost unbearable pain at being separated from the others. She tried to eat a little, but was so anxious she couldn't even manage that.

She lay in her enclosure trying to visualize each member of the group, hoping that by keeping their memory alive in her mind, she'd feel some comfort inside. As she was thinking of Angel and her devious and gluttonous ways, a smiling biped returned to her enclosure and let herself in.

"Hello there, pretty girl" the biped said affectionately. "Sorry we had to put you in here, but the wing with the others was full until just a few minutes ago. Would you like to come and be with your friends?"

Amy of course didn't have a clue what exactly was being said, only that the words were kind and filled with caring. She looked up into the friendly eyes of the biped and gave her one polite bark.

"Good for you!" the biped replied.

Amy was then led from the enclosure and out of the wing. They walked through various holding areas then through one final door and into another section filled with dogs. Amy couldn't grasp why she was being moved until she heard Angel's unmistakable voice cry out.

"Goldie! It's Goldie!"

At that point she heard the others each in a different enclosure dotted along the passageway, and each delighted to have her back.

The one voice that she'd missed the most came from the far end of the row. Rex sounded not only happy but highly relieved to have Amy back close at paw.

"You had me worried there, Goldie," he said with feigned casualness.

Amy was led about halfway down the passageway and placed in an enclosure only two down from Lester.

"Where's Rodney?" she asked through the gate.

"We thought he was with you," Lester replied.

"I hope he's all right," Amy said more to herself than to anyone else.

There was a moment of silence as each animal tried to find
words to say.

Angel was the first to speak up "What did you think about
the beef?"

The others had to laugh.

The dogs spent the rest of the day introducing themselves to
the other inhabitants of the wing. Each dog, one by one, introduced himself and then gave a brief account of how they'd been
captured. The session went well into the night and as the last
dog told his story, the rest began to settle down for sleep. The
wing fell silent for a moment.

"Good night, Angel," Amy whispered.

"Good night, Goldie," she answered.

"Good night, Lester," Amy continued.

"Good night, Goldie," he responded.

Amy hesitated for a moment before continuing. She felt her
heart soften at the thought of him.

"Good night, Rex."

"Good night, Goldie."

She closed her eyes and allowed a tear to roll down her muzzle as she accepted the joyous realization that she had a true life
companion.

The entire wing was awakened at the crack of dawn as a
young biped wheeled a food cart down the passageway and dis-
tributed a bowl to each resident. The biped was wearing round
black pads over his ears and singing loudly and discordantly at
the top of his voice.

The bowl turned out to be filled with a tasty kibble mix that
Amy devoured without any trace of manners or breeding whatsoever. She felt slightly embarrassed when she realized how
revolting her display must have appeared to the others but upon

raising her head to check their reactions, found that all of them had done the same thing. They were all looking guiltily out of their enclosures expecting a reprimand from some quarter or another.

After a period of grooming, the passageway doors were opened on either end and to the dogs' huge delight, bipeds began funneling into the wing, each with an expression of urgent anxiety. Almost immediately, one group of humans, a male, a female and a small child, began squealing excitedly. They were joined in their excitement by one of the dogs. They were apparently his masters. The dog was released and left with the bipeds, as they hugged and nuzzled each other with complete abandon and disregard for biped-canine protocol. It wasn't long before another family was reunited with as much, if not more, joy.

One by one, each dog was claimed. At one point Amy distinctly heard Angel scream with delight as her mistress located her. She was only able to call out the briefest of farewells to the others before being whisked away.

It was that simple. After all they'd been through together, in one brief second she was gone. Amy found it disconcerting to realize that the Spaniel was on her way home and that she would almost certainly never see her again.

A short while later Lester's human arrived. Their reunion was a little more formal than some of the others but still as touching. There was none of the screaming and yelping, but as his gate was opened, Lester stepped out and walked soundlessly into his master's waiting arms. The two simply stayed holding each other for a long time, and then, again without a word, they separated and walked side by side out of the building.

By the end of the morning, there were few dogs left in the wing. There was little talk as the tension rose with each passing minute. Amy began to feel concern about her situation. Where was her master or Cook? Maybe they weren't coming for her. Maybe they didn't care that she'd gone? Maybe they'd found life easier without her. Maybe…

"Amy? Amy! Amy, where are you?" She suddenly heard her Man calling from the far end of the passageway.

"Here! I'm here!" she called out breathlessly. She could hear him break into a run and then suddenly he was there. Standing right in front of her separated by the thin wire mesh of the gate. Her Man! He'd come for her! He almost tore open the gate. Amy tried to think of the proper greeting but found herself leaping into his arms. Oh, the joy she felt! She licked him and nuzzled him, smelling and tasting him over and over again.

"My poor girl," he whispered. "What did they do to you? Cook called me in America, and I flew right back. I've been so worried. Oh, my sweet girl!"

He hugged her still closer.

Finally exhausted by their emotions, they rose to their feet and Amy allowed him to place her collar... yes her collar, around her neck and then attach the lead. He walked her out of the enclosure and toward the exit.

They'd gone only a few paws when Amy remembered something. She stopped and turned back.

"What's the matter, girl?" her Man asked. "It's all right. I'm just going to take you home."

Amy pulled at the lead, knowing that she was breaking all the rules, but she had one more thing to do. She continued tugging her master, pulling until he gave up and followed her back along the passageway.

thirty five

Amy opened her eyes slowly and watched as the mother duck escorted her young into the pond. She couldn't be certain, but the ducklings looked larger than she remembered them. After the last one slid into the water, the mother took her position in front and led the group in single file across the open water.

Amy rolled onto her back and glanced up at the billowy clouds as they sailed rapidly by overhead. A shaft of sunlight freed itself from the heavens and warmed her belly as it moved across her.

She stretched her legs to their fullest and then rolled over and stood up. Amy glanced over toward the Grangers' property, hoping to see the hunters, but then remembered that they were in competition at that moment up in the city.

She took a moment to glance about her and feel the happiness of being back home in a place and with humans she loved. She looked at the cottage and then at the gently rolling hills of the Downs. She was home!

Amy wandered over to the entrance and stepped inside the cottage. She took a moment to breathe in the tangy smoke smell and then went toward the kitchen. Before she'd gone more than a couple of paws, she heard a commotion coming from just around the next corner. She trotted over and cautiously peered in the direction of the disturbance.

"Why you mangy, good for nothing…" Cook's words were playful as she scolded Rex as the two fought over a tea towel. Rex seemed to have the upper hand and was actually pulling Cook along the polished kitchen floor. Amazingly, Cook seemed to be thoroughly enjoying every minute of it. Without notice, she suddenly let go of her end and Rex went rolling backward, muzzle over rear end!

Cook laughed herself into a fit and had to hold herself steady with one hand on the counter top.

Amy looked on with a pretence of distaste as she scowled at both of them. They pretended not to notice, but then both suddenly took off after her in an unexpected game of chase.

As the three tore through the sitting room, her Man called for their immediate attention. He had in his hand a paper with gold edging and fine squiggles on it.

"You're not going to believe this," he said excitedly to the others.

"What?" Cook squealed breathlessly.

Cook read the paper, then looked at the dogs with open-mouthed astonishment.

Amy and Rex didn't know what was going on exactly, only that their Man and Cook both seemed suddenly pleased about something. Amy hoped this might mean Cook would let them have some of the bread she knew was being baked at that moment in the hot oven.

epilogue

there wasn't a cloud in the sky or even a hint of wind as they were led out onto the forecourt of Buckingham Palace. Amy and Rex had dimly recognized the place the moment they'd arrived. At first they'd been a little nervous, but everyone else seemed happy and relaxed, so they decided everything must be all right.

Amy glanced over at the ornate fencing that enclosed the parade ground, and for a moment, vividly recalled when they'd sneaked through that fence to evade the gray van. She was surprised to see that today the area beyond the fencing was crowded with bipeds all pointing toward them.

As they reached the center of the forecourt, Amy spotted Angel and Lester. They were fully groomed and standing next to their formally dressed masters. After some brief catching up of what had happened to them all since their rescue, they heard a murmur rising through the crowd. The dogs all turned and looked toward the portico through which they'd escaped capture with the help of the two Corgis and saw to their joy a small Yorkshire Terrier being carried toward them.

Rodney spotted the others, then wriggling like a maniac, had to be placed on the ground. He limped toward them, his head up and his left hind leg held securely in a white plaster cast.

When Rodney reached the others and greetings were exchanged, a silence fell across the entire area. As breaths were held, the main doorway to the palace opened, and an elegantly attired biped made her way toward the group. Behind her were the two Corgis, William and Mary, and behind them, to the delight of the dogs, were Captain Sulty and Sergeant Bonzo. There were also numerous bipeds in attendance.

They moved to a spot directly in the center of the forecourt facing the others. The elegant female stood in front of the group and began to speak into an odd metal thing that seemed to take her voice and make it not only louder, but make it come from many different directions at once.

Amy didn't know what she was saying, only that it appeared to be directed mainly at her and the other dogs. After a while the biped ceased talking and stepped back alongside the police dogs and their bipeds.

Captain Sulty's biped then stepped forward and spoke a few words, at which point Angel's master walked forward with her in tow. They stopped in front of the elegant female and were each given a small metal thing attached to a piece of colorful ribbon. The two bowed, then walked back to rejoin the others.

After another couple of words from the captain's biped, it was Rodney's turn. Lester was next. Then it was time for Amy and Rex. She suddenly felt slightly nervous but couldn't for the life of her think why.

Her Man and Cook led the two dogs into position in front of the female. As Amy looked into her face, she suddenly remembered her. She'd been the one sitting drinking from a dainty cup that day the Corgis had led them through the palace. In a flash, Amy's simple mind put the pieces together and realized who the elegant biped in fact was.

As the Queen of England placed the ribbon around their necks, Amy felt her chest swell with almost impossible pride and joy. She gave the Queen a happy pant, then gracefully stepped back with her Man and rejoined the others.

The crowd surrounding the forecourt began to applaud and cheer. At first, Amy was puzzled as to what exactly they were cheering about, but then, as she looked down the line of dogs, she knew that each of them, Angel, Lester, Rodney, Rex and she herself were the ones being honored that day.

She glanced over at the elaborate fencing and the crowd beyond and noticed that among the throng of humans were many familiar faces from the animal world. She spotted a pair of cats as they dashed from shadow to shadow. They stopped for a brief moment and gave Amy the unmistakable G.N. salute; then just as she was about to wave back, Bob and Rye vanished into the crowd, completely unnoticed by almost anyone.

She then caught sight of Pru, beautifully groomed and attracting a fair amount of attention on her own.

"You should be in here with us," Amy called to her.

"No, I shouldn't," Pru replied through the fencing.

Amy knew that Pru meant just that. She didn't want the adventure or the ceremony. She was happy simply being beautiful.

As Amy continued to scan the onlookers, she saw still more faces she recognized. She saw the kind biped from the underground train. She saw some of the policemen from the park. She even spotted Rumple, the kindly dog from the police kennel. He lifted a paw in a wave and Amy noticed his entire coat begin gathering at his shoulder.

She was about to turn away from the fencing when she spotted something else. At the far end of the forecourt where the crowd was much thinner, she spotted an angry-looking biped chastising his dog as they walked away. She couldn't be certain but the dog looked from a distance to be a Rottweiler. Somehow she knew who it was. She silently wished that Hans would someday find happiness somewhere in his life.

As she faced back toward the gathered dignitaries, she realized just how much help so many strangers had given the dogs without asking for anything in return. She knew that there was a lot of bad in the world. She'd certainly seen some of it during her adventure, but she'd found that there was also a lot of good out there as well.

She smiled to herself as she realized again what she'd been through and how much she'd learned. For one thing, the world was far bigger and more exciting than she'd ever begun to imagine, and she'd only seen a fraction of it. She began wondering if she'd ever get to see any more it when the crowd began murmuring and pointing excitedly to the sky above. Amy raised her head and saw immediately the reason for their interest.

Flying toward them at low altitude was a squadron of geese. In perfect formation the birds flew by in salute to their canine friends. In the lead position, Vo led his fellow fliers at roof level over the forecourt, then tipped his wings and smiled down at the dogs as he led the others in a gentle banking turn back toward the park and their sheltered island.

Amy looked at the faces of her friends once more, and, as had become almost habit recently, found herself focusing on Rex's hard, strong features. She felt her heart beat faster at the mere sight of him but also at the joyful realization that their life together was only just beginning. Sensing her gaze, Rex turned and looked back into her eyes. His face broke into a huge and amiable grin as he nodded his fine head back at her, acknowledging and returning her own sentiments.

Amy couldn't have been happier.

author biography

Chris Coppel was born in California but his family soon moved to Europe, living in Spain, France, Switzerland, but mainly, England. He has written numerous screenplays, but FAR FROM BURDEN DELL is his first novel. He currently teaches advanced screenwriting at U.C.L.A.

Chris is also an accomplished drummer and guitarist. He currently lives in Los Angeles with his wife Clare and their very own scaredy-cat, Samantha.

If you'd like to write to Chris, his e-mail address is *amyathome@ aol.com*.

DISCARD

DISCARD